What Readers Say About *Guilty As Zin*

A fast moving plot with twists and turns and crisp dialogue. You care about the characters, and the cliffhanger climax blew me away.

——————— L.F., businessman, Nice, France

Guilty As Zin is a page-turner. I can see this as the first in a series starring the vineyard Columbo."

——————— T.M., journalist, New York, N.Y.

"I love Gene Ventura! What a guy—a smart, sensitive private eye who's a gourmet cook, an opera buff, and a consummate baseball fan. The beautiful love story is an added bonus.

——————— C.H., CPA/Mediator and new grandmother, Houston, Texas

"I've read hundreds of mysteries. Some authors write good plots, others create characters you care about. Chuck Toubin shows he can do both, and I enjoyed the subtle use of humor.

——————— S.F., boutique owner, Austin, Texas

"I found Guilty As Zin fascinating. The story is a thriller, and I got an education about the wine business."

——————— G.F., attorney, Chapeda Park, Colorado

"Guilty As Zin is terrific! I found it entertaining from start to finish. Gene Ventura rocks.

——————— H.S., art gallery owner, Houston, Texas

"Lots of action and great food, what more can a reader ask. I can't wait to try the recipes mentioned. I couldn't decide whether to finish the book first or go to the kitchen. This is a fresh, original work."

——————— L.F., food editor, Galveston, Texas

Guilty As Zin

Chuck Toubin

Publishing Visions

Guilty As Zin

Copyright © 2002 by C. Toubin Company, Inc.
Cover art Copyright © 2002 by Stanley Gilbert.

Grateful acknowledgment is made for permission to re-print portions of HOWL, by Allen Ginsberg. Reprinted by permission of City Lights Publishing.

Library of Congress Control Number: 2001119217

This is a work of fiction. All the characters and events por-trayed in this book are either products of the author's imagi-nation or are used fictitiously.

ISBN 0-9708669-6-8

Published by

Publishing Visions
3107 White Rock Drive
Austin, Texas 78757

www.guiltyaszin.com

First edition: February 2002

Printed in the United States of America

For

Mary, who tugs at my heartstrings.

Acknowledgements

My deepest thanks to:

Authors Jan Grape, and Marty and Annette Meyers for guidance and encouragement.

Syd Fisher, Stan Gilbert, Michael Morgan, and John Watts for their valuable assistance or contributions.

Mary Mast Toubin, most of all, for her skill, involvement, and love—making the writing of this book an experience I will always treasure.

Guilty As Zin

PROLOGUE

"I HATE TO LEAVE," Warren said.

I know."

Maybe we can get away for a business trip."

That's not enough," she said.

Spending secret hours with Carol had demanded a change in his orderly routine, but Warren couldn't stay away from her. The last four months with her had jump-started him out of a period of malaise and boredom.

They stood in Carol's kitchen. Only the soft light leading from the hallway illuminated them as Warren fastened the top button of his shirt and knotted his tie. Carol helped him on with his suit coat and, as he turned, he pulled her close for one final caress of her naked thigh. He buried his face in her lemon-scented hair and felt the tingle of excitement once again.

What was it about her, he wondered, but not for the first time. Was it her exuberance? Her imaginative lovemaking? The sex was intoxicating but that wasn't the whole picture. He could talk to her about anything. She understood his work and the stress he was under. Carol appreciated the creativity he used to solve complex civil engineering problems; most people didn't. His wife, Fran, certainly didn't. He and Fran spoke to each other but did they listen anymore?

1

Carol patted his cheek, rose up on her toes, and lifted her face close to his for a last kiss. Warren tasted the sweetness.

"It's the best we can do for now," he said. "Let's go to the environmental conference in LA next month. I'll make the arrangements."

Carol smiled up at him feeling a glow of warmth. She cherished his thoughtful caring.

He saw her smile as he pulled the baggy black sweatpants and the XXL black sweatshirt over his standard gray suit and regimental red tie.

"A whole week together would be marvelous! You won't bring this silly outfit, will you?" Carol teased.

"OK," he said, "it's settled. We'll go."

He placed the black New York Yankees cap on his head and pulled the brim forward over his eyes. No one who knew the fastidious Warren Roberts would ever have imagined him dressed in sweats.

When he first started seeing Carol, Warren carefully planned his exit from her house to make it as safe as possible. He always left at dusk and walked the one long block down the dark alley behind her house on Terrace Street. Then he walked south two blocks in the quiet residential neighborhood to Imola Avenue. He would wait in the deep shadows for the traffic to clear and scurry across Imola to his car. He always hid the old BMW at the delivery dock behind Grapes of Wrath, a local wine bar. No one made deliveries at night.

As he walked, he thought about Carol and where it all would end. Leave Fran? Marry Carol? He knew his father-in-law's temper and how much damage Jack Phillips could do to him.

Warren Roberts pushed aside thoughts of his wife and his girlfriend. He worried more about the damned research study he had agreed to do for that lady county supervisor. At first, he had thought this important study would enhance his reputation in the community and he'd been flattered she'd picked him for the job. Then he found that the magnitude of the pressure to influence his conclusion was over whelming.

When he reached his car, he would always strip off his sweats, cap, and Nikes and place them in the backpack that he then stashed behind the spare tire in the trunk. They would stay there until his next visit to Carol's. Then he'd drive home in time for dinner with his wife, Fran.

Only this evening, a glitch interrupted his routine. Dusk had already turned into darkness, and Pegasus and his friends were just making their entrance in the clear Northern California sky. As Warren sneaked down the alley behind Carol's house, he recognized the gait of a familiar figure walking towards him.

"What are you doing here……..?"

He hesitated before he could finish the question. He saw the glint of a shiny object being raised toward him. He heard a small pop, not unlike the sound of a Chinese firecracker, and felt something like a bee sting under his chin at the top of his neck. He put his index finger into the tiny hole, and his mouth opened in surprise. He called out but made no sound. The bullet had lacerated his carotid artery. His right arm reflexively reached out to swat the gun away as the blood spurted from his neck. Another pop, and this bullet exited, shattering the atlas vertebra and severing the spinal cord.

Warren Roberts reeled, spun around, and jerked knocking over a plastic garbage container in the alley and spilling its contents. He collapsed in a heap. His life forces oozed a scarlet stain against the cold dark asphalt, mixing with the eggshells, banana peels, and coffee grounds from the toppled garbage can.

The killer moved closer to Warren's supine body and, with the gun six inches from the victim's groin, fired a third bullet and a fourth and a fifth. Most likely, Warren Roberts never heard those last three telling shots.

CHAPTER 1

IT WAS ONE OF THOSE TWEENER DAYS WE GET IN Napa
Valley in February, not yet spring, with a chilly breeze coming
off the Pacific. The yellow flowers of the mustard plants already blossomed between the rows of vines.

The winter sun burned off the thick morning fog covering
the rows of grapevines below the house. Rachel and I sat on the
redwood porch at the front of the house waiting for the air to
clear. She wanted to show me the new trellis she had designed
for me to install before spring, when the dormant plants begin
to grow. We both shivered as a gust of wind blew in from the
north.

Rachel put on her glasses, leaned forward, and peered down
Howell Mountain Road.

"Who do you know that drives a shiny, new, green
Mercedes?" she asked.

"Damned if I know. Why do you ask?"

"Because there's one barreling up your road, throwing up a
white cloud of dust."

The driver parked his car by the house and jumped out. It was
Franklin Reed. I almost didn't recognize him. I last saw him some
twenty years ago. I heard that, after practicing criminal law in

Oakland, Franklin had returned to Napa to join a small local firm. So many of us return to Napa after exploring the world outside. Something calls us back to this magic green valley nestled between the Vaca and the Mayacamas mountains.

Rachel and I walked down the steps to greet him. Franklin now weighed about thirty pounds more than when we played basketball together at Napa High. He still sported a full head of reddish brown hair but now with flecks of gray on the sides. At six foot one, he stood just a shade taller than I. His gray beard completed the new image. Franklin wore a tan tweed sport coat and an open collar, sky-blue, button-down shirt and Roman sandals with no socks—the standard Napa upper crust leisure uniform.

"Franklin, I'd like you to meet my friend Rachel Bernard."

They shook hands, but Franklin had no time for pleasantries. He started talking even before we reached the house.

"Hey, Gene, Franklin said, 'I heard you were back in town. We'll have to catch up one day soon, but today I'm here to talk business."

"Then let me sell you some terrific grapes. They ripen in the fall, but I can take your order now," I said.

"Oh, not that kind of business. I need your help, not your grapes. Someone killed Fran Roberts' husband two nights ago, and the police suspect Fran for his murder. Her dad hired me to defend her in case they charge her."

"That's terrible. I'm sorry to hear that, but how can I help?" I asked.

"Jack Phillips, Fran's dad, wants to clear Fran as soon as possible to avoid further scandal. He wants me to find the real killer. He doesn't believe the police will pursue other options since they're certain Fran did it. I need an investigator. You qualify and you might want to help since you knew Fran so well back in high school."

"Gosh, Franklin, I haven't seen Fran since high school graduation. I came home to run the farm. I thought that some-day I might do some security consulting on the side because most wineries are so vulnerable to theft. But the grapes take all of my time now. I don't see how I could do both jobs and do them well. Besides, I don't even have a P.I. license."

"That's not a problem. I called Sacramento and got you a 120-day temporary permit because of your police background," Franklin said.

"What happened to Fran's husband?" I asked.

"Someone shot Warren Roberts twice in the neck and pumped three bullets into his crotch."

"Ouch," Rachel said.

"Yeah, the killer used a .25 caliber just like the Walther automatic registered to Roberts."

"Why do the police believe she would kill him?" I asked.

"Because of the gun, and they think she had a motive be-cause it's no secret that she and Warren weren't getting along; they were seen fighting in public. And she also has no solid alibi; she says she was waiting at home alone for dinner with Warren."

"What about the gun?"

"Fran says it's missing."

"That does look bad for her,' I said, 'but why me?"

"You worked homicide for San Francisco PD for years and you made lieutenant. You'd be right for the job. Besides, my other private eye options in the valley leave much to be de-sired. Fran's dad gave me an unlimited budget, and I can pay you top dollar. I know you can use the money," Reed said.

Hairs rose on the back of my neck.

"I'm not sure I know what you mean," I lied.

"One of my partners represented your dad's creditors. I know the vineyard was in bad financial shape before your dad died.

Take the case and you can help Fran and earn some needed money at the same time," Reed said.

"That's nobody's business. I hope you're not spreading that money story around."

Franklin looked down and nodded.

"I'll think about working with you and let you know in a day or two. I want to talk to the police and see what they have before I decide to take the case."

"That's fine. See John Lawrence right away. He's the detective assigned to the investigation. Nice meeting you, Rachel," Franklin said as he hurried back to his car.

We watched the Mercedes get smaller as it descended Howell Mountain Road. I turned to Rachel, and I brushed my hand against her arm.

I needed Rachel's help to show me how to grow better grapes from these old Zinfandel vines. Over the past year, our relationship had developed from grower/consultant to something much more personal. We now saw only each other. The emotion felt so strange. My wife, Alexandra, and our unborn child were killed four years ago. And I didn't know if I could ever risk that kind of love again.

"He's right about the money. The vineyard deteriorated during Pop's illness that last year. I borrowed against my police pension to bring the mortgage current, but the bank now wants their old loan paid off, and we need working capital and some equipment to bring the crop in."

"You'll have a good crop this year. I know you can pay all the bills when you sell the grapes."

I shook my head.

"But the harvest isn't until the fall, six long months away. I sure could use Franklin Reed's fat fee. The only way I can take Fran's case and still watch over the farm is if I can get Buddy to share the investigation with me."

I went into the house and called Buddy Bennett to discuss Franklin Reed's proposal. I invited him to come for lunch tomorrow after I talked to the police detective and knew more about the case. What hard evidence did they have against Fran?

CHAPTER 2

THE MODERN NAPA CITY ADMINISTRATION building looked out of place in an otherwise picturesque downtown dating back to the 1880's. The post-modern style with all that glass just didn't fit. I liked the old city hall on Napa Street a lot better. I entered the police department from the entrance on First Street and turned left.

"My name is Gene Ventura. I'd like to see Detective Lawrence," I said to the beefy sergeant sitting behind the front desk. Seems like all desk sergeants are beefy.

The sergeant called Lawrence on the intercom, and the detective came out of the squad room to meet me.

John Lawrence stood well over six feet and must have weighed a rock solid 250. He looked like he could still play linebacker except for the gray sideburns and stubble and the wrinkled forehead. The ends of the collar of his white short-sleeve shirt barely came together. He wore a spotted tie that looked as if cut from one of Jackson Pollack's "drip" paintings—drops of orange, yellow, and chartreuse overlaid with Pollacks' typical black lines. The Windsor knot drooped down to his second button. And he wore brown polyester pants. This guy was not going to make it in Gentlemen's Quarterly Magazine.

They had designed the squad room as a large bullpen with two long rows of gray steel desks. Metal frames covered with what looked like gray tweed carpet for soundproofing separated each cubicle from the next. Most police departments seem to be hooked on the idea of an institutional gray workplace. You wonder what they have against a little color?

The scene was like what you might see in any squad room. About half the desks remained vacant since they do most of their police work outside the office. Five or six people typed reports on word processors—no more clackity typewriters—and two men and a woman stood by the coffeepot shooting the bull as we walked by. The coffee smelled old and strong, and I got a whiff of stale cigarette smoke. Some things never change.

I introduced myself to Lawrence as we walked back to his desk

"Yeah, I heard the big shot city detective had come back to Napa," Lawrence said by way of a cold greeting.

I ignored the snide remark. "After Pop died last year, I came back to work the farm."

"What to you want from me?" Lawrence growled.

"Fran Roberts is an old friend, and I want to see if I can help her. What can you tell me about her husband's murder?"

"Mrs. Roberts is in deep shit, I can tell you that. Otherwise, I don't have to tell you nuthin'."

Before he dismissed me, his phone rang, and I saw a deep frown cross his face as he listened to the voice on the other end. He hung up.

"Chief Mike Edwards just called. He said he saw you in the building. Said you're an old friend and that I'm supposed to cooperate with you. Guess you have pull with our new boss."

"Mike Edwards? I didn't know he had been hired as the new chief. Mike and I went to San Jose State together," I said.

Detective Lawrence's expression indicated he didn't seem too happy about his new boss. I wondered if he had been passed over in favor of Mike for the job or if he just resented an outsider being brought in to take over.

"Chief wants you to stop by before you leave. He offices upstairs. Go past the dispatcher. So what do you want to know about Fran Roberts?" He thawed just slightly.

"Tell me about the crime scene."

"Not much to tell. Three nights ago, February second, a perp shot Warren Roberts twice in the neck and three times in the crotch at close range with a little .25 caliber popgun. The neck wounds killed him, severed the carotid artery and the spinal cord, and he bled to death. The shots in the balls were just to make her point. Real messy, blood all over the place."

"Did you find the weapon?"

"Not yet, but you can bet your ass we'll find out it was the same gun the Roberts kept at home."

"Why do you suspect his wife?" I asked.

"The angle of the neck shots for one thing. Since the bullets entered at an upward angle, it's clear the killer was shorter. We also believe he knew the killer since the neck shots were at close range. Plus we have information," Lawrence replied as if he knew a secret.

"I expect lots of people are shorter than the victim. Where was the body found?"

"In an alley behind Terrace Street. One of the neighbors found him about eight o'clock when taking out the garbage."

"What was he doing way over there?"

"We don't know yet. We're canvassing the neighborhood. We found his car a few blocks away parked behind Grapes of Wrath. He wore black sweat pants and a black sweatshirt over his dress suit. Even had on black sneakers and a black baseball cap. Strange outfit. We found his watch and wallet were still in his backpack along with his dress shoes, so we know it wasn't a robbery," Lawrence said.

Didn't seem like much of a mystery to me. Warren Roberts didn't belong there and didn't want to be recognized.

I thanked the detective and walked upstairs to say hello to Mike Edwards. I entered the open door to Mike's office and climbed over several cardboard boxes waiting to be unpacked. He gave me a bear hug as a greeting.

"It all happened so fast. I was going to call you this week, Gene, but the moving has been such a hassle. A headhunter found me and recommended me for this job. Your mayor came to Philadelphia to check me out. Mayor Francis asked me to keep my candidacy confidential for political reasons. He then came back to Napa to line up the council votes before anyone could organize opposition," Mike said.

"I'm excited you and Sally have moved here, but I thought you had it made with the department in Philly."

"I wasn't looking for a new job, but a chance to run my own show and get away from the cold winters was too tempting to pass up. Maybe I needed a change. I joined the Philadelphia PD right out of college and climbed the ranks. A captain's slot came up last year, but I didn't make it. The mayor made me a good offer, so here I am." He flashed a broad grin.

I started helping Mike unpack boxes. Mike Edwards and I went to college together. We kept each other out of trouble enough so that both of us finished our degrees in criminal justice. I first met Mike at baseball tryouts. Mike had a scholarship; I didn't. Mike made the team; I didn't. But we became friends and found we had the same major and a lot in common, so we roomed together two semesters our sophomore year.

Mike's a handsome black man, a real black man with skin as dark as espresso. Mike tossed an empty box aside.

"What's it been—three or four years since we came to San

Francisco for Alexandra's memorial service?" Mike asked.

"It'll be four years in May," I said, clinching my fist.

I last saw Mike and his wife at that time. It meant a lot to me for them to come. I had just gotten out of the hospital and felt pretty damn low. A lot of people attended from the city and the department, but Mike and Sally and Pop and my brother, Robert, were the most important ones there. Mike took a week off, and he and Sally stayed to cheer me up.

We stopped unpacking boxes about five-thirty, and Mike pulled a couple of Rolling Rocks out from the small refrigerator in the corner of his office. He handed me the green bottle, and we raised a silent toast.

"See, I brought a piece of Pennsylvania with me for happy hour. Has your shoulder gotten any better?" Mike asked.

"Yes. I've got a beautiful scar, an artificial shoulder, and a steel pin where my arm was broken. I don't have the range of movement in my left arm I once did but I've learned to adjust. Hurts some in cold, damp weather, though."

"The son-of-a-bitch with the shotgun aimed at me, but Alex got the brunt of the blast. She had leaned forward to get something out of the glove compartment. Some of the pellets tore up my left arm and shoulder, but it damn near blew away her entire left side."

The recollection sent a cold, sharp pain through my left shoulder.

"I remember you telling me about the drive-by. They caught the shooter, but did you ever find out who hired him?" Mike asked.

"Yeah, it was, as we figured, Judith Ludlow. He gave her up for a reduced sentence— twenty-five years at Chico without parole. I wish it had been life at hard labor. The shooter was much better with a shotgun than he was at covering his tracks. God, I wish it were the other way around! A witness identified the stolen car he used. His prints were all over the car," I said.

"Who is Judith Ludlow?"

The cold beer tasted fine. I took another swallow.

"Ludlow came from an old-line, Knob Hill banking family. While she was getting her MBA at Stanford, she discovered the tremendous profit potential of coke, over two thousand percent. She came back home and created a corporation to control the sale of coke in Northern California."

"Bringing Management 101 to the dope business," Mike commented.

We looked at the door when a light knock interrupted our conversation. Mike went to the door and opened it. Detective John Lawrence took a step or two into the office.

"Sorry, Chief. I didn't know you were still in a meeting. I'll come back later," Lawrence said.

"That's fine, John," Mike said. Lawrence left and closed the door behind him.

I wondered how long the detective had stood outside the door. I thought he was eavesdropping. No doubt he wanted to be included and invited in.

We both sat in the two comfortable brown leather chairs facing Mike's desk, and I continued telling him about Judith Ludlow.

"Doesn't sound like she used muscle to keep everyone in line," Mike said.

"Not at first as she was young and naïve. She soon learned she had to hire thugs to keep the pushers from killing each other over territories—we figured one or two attached to barbells rest at bottom of the Bay."

"Bet being compelled to use force shocked her."

"Yeah. Didn't fit her image. She hid behind the façade of an investment firm. She was society and a major contributor and fundraiser for the local Democratic Party."

"Why did she want to kill you?" Mike asked.

"She blamed me for bringing down her operation because I headed the task force investigating cocaine distribution in the Bay area. I symbolized her downfall because I was the one who got the publicity after eighteen months of tough police work."

"How did you finally catch her?"

"Pure luck. We got a break after months of dead ends and a dozen cops working with me. Her CPA picked up a beautiful policewoman we had planted at an opera fundraiser. He served on the opera board, and we knew he'd be there. She seduced him, got him on videotape. Oldest trick in the book—he didn't think his wife and family would understand. Delivered the records to us and became a witness. DA gave him probation for naming all the players, including Judith Ludlow."

"So how did that lead to the shooting?" Mike asked.

"All hell broke loose when she was indicted. The Examiner had a field day, front-page news. The story stayed on local TV for several days. The media interviewed her country club friends and family. They all turned their backs on her. She was embarrassed, and boy was she mad! Her lawyer got her out of jail on a million-dollar bond. She decided to get even with somebody, and I got picked. She hired the killer."

"Where is Judith Ludlow now?" Mike asked.

"She's the prison librarian at Atterbury. Friends keep me informed. She hired Melvin Belli's old firm, and they got her a deal. She got forty years—only forty years for murder and seventy counts of conspiracy to sell dope. Go figure.. I would love to watch her executed. I almost hit her at her trial. After the verdict, she came up to me and, with sarcasm in her voice, asked if catching her had been worth it since it resulted in the deaths of Alex and my unborn son."

I squirmed in Mike's leather chair.

"I couldn't bring myself to respond. All I could think of

when I was in the hospital was killing Judith Ludlow. I hated that name. I stayed awake many nights devising all sorts of schemes of slow torture and agonizing death for that sociopath."

"So you left the department when Pop died?" Mike asked.

"It was time to go, anyway. They gave me a medal and a desk job after rehab. The job was shitty, and the city wasn't the same with Alex gone. I just lost enthusiasm, so I took my retirement and disability pension and came home. Now I'm growing Zinfandel grapes."

"What did you talk to Lawrence about?" Mike asked.

"Fran Roberts' lawyer has asked me to help him defend her as his investigator. She's a suspect in her husband's murder. I may take the case if I can get Buddy Bennett, the former sheriff, to help me. Fran's an old friend from high school. I don't believe she's capable of murder," I told him.

"I'll look into the Roberts case, Gene. By the way, Sally and I want to have you over one day next week. I'll check with Sally and call you."

We shook hands, and I left the way I came in. John Lawrence just happened to be standing by the door as I came down the stairs. I caught the scent of his heavy, cheap cologne. He grinned at me and winked. Was he making a pass or did he know something I didn't?

CHAPTER 3

"ARE YOU GOING TO DO IT?" RACHEL ASKED.
A sudden breeze came from the west. I smelled salt in the air.
"Do what?"
"Take Franklin Reed's offer."
The next day had dawned. The fog lifted, and we walked over
to the area by the first row of grapevines where Rachel had built
the trellis model. Rays of golden sunshine showed through the
clouds, illuminating the dormant Zinfandel vines. For then, in early
February, the plants looked like neat rows of four-foot tall, black,
gnarled trunks with leafless branches reaching for the sky. Nature
had hidden the promise of wonders yet to come.
"But is it something you want to do?"
"Yeah, I wouldn't mind. I'm a little rusty but I think I can
do it. I haven't worked a case in what, five years.
"With my tongue planted firmly in my cheek, I asked, "Did
Walter Middy draw the blueprints for this thing?"
"It does look somewhat strange, Gene, but, if we can
have each grapevine grow vertically up a trellis, you
should get even better grapes. They would grow more
uniformly and ripen earlier," Rachel replied.
She had built the contraption of wooden posts strung to-

17

gether with galvanized wire in a complex pattern. It stood about seven feet high. I plucked one of the taut wires.

"I've seen your books; I know you could use the money. Reed's anxious. I bet he'll pay a good size retainer," Rachel said.

"The farm comes first. If Buddy will work with me on the case and I can still look after things here, maybe I'll give it a try. Using trellises is new to me. Have you seen it work elsewhere?" I asked.

"Sure, trellises like these are not all that new. This design allows each individual cluster of grapes to receive more sunlight and better air circulation. Without a trellis, leaves and other cluster tend to overshadow some of the grapes."

"You think the results will justify the expense?"

"You bet. You should see a significant increase in the quality of your grapes."

"OK; if you're that confident. Let's give it a try."

"I can help you around here if you take the case. Now is a slow time at the wineries, so I have more free time. I can help Ernesto and his crew put up the trellises. It might work out if you can wrap up the case before I get busier in the spring," she said.

I put my arms around her waist. Even dressed for work, Rachel looked like what my generation called a knockout. Although she wore loose-fitting clothes, I had a hard time concentrating on the task at hand. She wore faded jeans covering brown Wellington half boots, a blue chambray work shirt, and a tan windbreaker. Her shiny dark brown hair almost reached her shoulders in a series of soft waves. A faint shower of freckles highlighted her oval face, and her hazel eyes sparkled with green flecks.

When I moved back to Napa from San Francisco to take over the vineyard last year after Pop died, I hired Rachel Bernard as a consultant to bring me up to speed on growing better grapes and increasing income. Everyone in Napa knew Rachel. She grew up in the valley. Her dad had come over from Bordeaux and taught viticulture at Napa College. She earned a doctorate in oenology at the University of California at Davis and had worked as an assistant winemaker at Premiere Winery. Now she helps growers and wineries as a consultant, and serves on the Napa County Board of Supervisors, one of five members who run our county government.

We strolled back toward the house. The roasting lamb needed tending, and Rachel said she heard the kitchen calling her to prepare lunch. I turned my head at the sound of Buddy's big engine as he approached. Buddy drove a twenty-year-old red Corvette, which he babied.

"What's that great smell coming from the smoker?" Buddy asked as he came around to the backyard.

"I rubbed a leg of lamb with garlic and anchovy paste and smoked it with some grapevine cuttings and rosemary laid on top of the coals," I said.

"Bet it tastes as good as it smells. I'm sure glad I came for lunch. I know you have a few bottles of Pop's old Zinfandel to drink with the lamb. I still can't believe he's not here to drink his wine with us."

"For years, every time he sold grapes to the wineries, he made them bottle a few cases from our grapes just for us. After the wine aged two or three years down in the cellar, he would open one of the bottles with pride and tell us our grapes made the best damn red wine in Napa County," I said. "Let's go downstairs and pick out a couple of bottles."

"Where's Rachel?" Buddy asked.

I stepped closer to the heavy, old black iron smoker.

"In the kitchen making polenta and a salad to go with the lamb."

I turned to face him. "Do we want to take Fran's case and work for Franklin Reed?"

I opened the smoker and added a handful of rosemary twigs. Ah, I loved that smell. I closed the lid and walked with Buddy to the front of my house. We entered the cellar from a door next to the front porch. We ducked our heads as we passed through the low doorway. I pulled the cord to turn on the single light bulb.

Buddy took his time to answer my question. "Let's do it. Time for me to get off my ass and go to work for a change," Buddy said.

"As I told you on the phone, police are convinced that Fran Roberts killed her husband. You may remember her as Fran Phillips, Jack Phillips' daughter, when she went to school with Puck and me."

"I recall that you brought her over to our house with your brother, Robert. I sure don't see her as a murderer, no matter what her husband may have done."

We reached the bottom of the creaky, old wooden steps, and I turned around to face him.

I said, "It's been almost twenty-five years since I've seen her, but I knew her well. I could see her leaving him but not shooting the guy. The only way I sign on is if you can work on the case with me full-time for a month or two."

The musty smell of old wine permeated the cool air. Our footsteps echoed off the stone floor. We selected two dusty bottles to bring up from the cellar.

"Hell, yes. This retirement bores the heck out of me. How do you plan to start?"

"Let's start at the beginning. I'll talk to Fran, and you can start finding out who might have wanted to shoot Warren Roberts in the balls. Also, see what else you can learn about Fran and her husband. Now, let's go rescue the lamb from the smoker and see what Rachel's up to."

Buddy carried the wine into the house. I lifted the crusty

medium rare leg of lamb from the smoker onto a platter.

Ben Bennett, known throughout Napa County as "Buddy", ran the sheriff's department for thirty-eight years. I grew up with his son, Puck, and have known Buddy all of my life. Puck and I started riding with Buddy in his patrol car when we were twelve or thirteen. Funny how things worked out. I became the cop, and Puck runs his own restaurant.

Buddy recently reached his sixty-fifth birthday, the county's mandatory retirement age. The county's loss. Buddy would have fit the part at a Hollywood casting call for a middle-aged western lawman, sort of like John Wayne. He stood tall and lean with broad shoulders and long legs. Buddy was soft-spoken, but one look into his steel gray eyes, and you knew he meant business.

I called Franklin Reed to tell him we would take Fran's case.

"I'll take the case if you don't object to Buddy Bennett working with me. We'll share the fee," I said.

"That's a great idea. Buddy knows the county and he's still popular. He'll make a great witness if we ever go to court. Do you want a check now?" Reed asked.

"I'd like to make some inquiries first. I'll come by and pick up the retainer in a few days when we know more. We can discuss the case at the same time. By the way, I have one condition," I said.

"What's that?"

"I don't believe Fran is capable of murder, but if we find she did it, so be it. I won't help you pin the murder on someone else just to get her off. We'll find the killer if we can, but let the chips fall where they may. I won't help the police convict Fran, but I'm not going to lie either. If this is a problem, you need to get someone else."

"Look, Gene, I'm convinced Fran didn't do it. All I ask is that you bring me everything you find, and you and Buddy keep your discoveries confidential," Reed said.

"That's a given."

CHAPTER 4

TURNING OFF THE HIGHWAY TO SONOMA, I saw that Fran Roberts lived in one of the new subdivisions developed in the nineteen eighties west of town. Subdivisions had taken up more and more farmland. I guess people have to live somewhere, even on land that grows some of the world's best wine grapes. The Roberts' house sat back off the street like most of the houses in the neighborhood—a one-story brick with a good-size front yard, in a mock Spanish style with beige stucco on the front and a red tile roof. The new red Jaguar convertible in the driveway appeared out of place next to the modest house. I parked on the street and walked up the sidewalk. She saw me coming and opened the door.

"Hello, Gene. Franklin said you were coming. Wish the circumstances were different," she said.

I stepped inside.

The years had not been kind to Fran. Or perhaps I had just romanticized her image in my mind, as one does about a former lover. Fran stood about five foot five and carried about twenty more pounds than when I last saw her. She wore her brown hair short with feathered bangs that almost brushed her eyebrows. Her face featured high cheekbones, deep blue eyes, and a small nose that just turned up at the end, but now small lines appeared around her eyes and deeper ones on her forehead. As I had expected, her eyes looked sad, and she appeared older than her forty-five years. She wore a caftan of deep blue, green and turquoise that almost reached her ankles.

"I just made a pot of coffee. Come in the kitchen, and I'll pour us each a cup."

I followed Fran into a sunny kitchen at the back of the house. It had yellow walls and shiny white appliances and a tiled island in the center of the room. Sunlight streamed through large windows that faced the backyard. She invited me to join her in eating a warm cheese Danish that she took from the oven. The kitchen smelled of fresh-baked yeasty sweet bread. The pastry and French roast coffee both tasted delicious. Funny, I don't remember Fran knowing how to cook. We sat on facing benches in her breakfast nook.

"I'm so sorry about your husband, Fran. No one deserves to die like that."

"Warren was difficult in some ways, but I can't imagine anyone hating him that much. And I can't believe the police think I killed him."

"Buddy Bennett and I will find out what happened and see if someone tried to set you up."

"What do you mean, 'set me up'?" She looked puzzled.

"Because Warren was killed with a small caliber pistol just like yours and because of the sexual mutilation, it looks to some like you could have killed him for revenge. I hate to ask, but were you and Warren having problems, or was Warren seeing another woman?"

"Another woman? Not that I know of. That never occurred to me until now. Something was bothering him the past few months. He acted more remote, even for Warren, but I thought it was his work—something about an important research study."

We took our second cups of coffee with us and walked back to the family room. I sat on the sofa, and Fran sat on the other side of the wrought iron coffee table in a large, carved wooden chair covered with red velvet. She had furnished the room with a red Oriental rug and heavy, dark, Spanish style furniture. The room smelled of lemon furniture polish. I leaned forward with my hands on my knees.

"I know it's difficult for you to talk now, but tell me about Warren."

"A rather quiet man, Warren seemed almost like the stereotype engineer. We first met at Northwestern and lived in Chicago for twelve years after we married. Dad helped Warren get some contracts around here so Warren and his partner, Victor O'Connell, could open an office. We moved back to Napa six years ago. Dad had always wanted me to move back home and he usually gets his way," she said.

I stroked my chin and gazed beyond Fran at the gas log fire, remembering her dad, Jack Phillips. That bastard never thought me good enough for his daughter when Fran and I dated in high school. He had asked Fran, "Why are you going out with that nobody?"

My dad talked with an Italian accent and grew grapes for the wineries. Grape growers enjoyed little status back in those days—people considered us simple farmers. Phillips, on the other hand, owned Chateau Carneros Winery, one of the largest at the time, and he acted like a big shot. To separate us, he sent Fran to Northwestern for summer school right after graduation to separate us. She didn't come back until the following Christmas. By then, the magic had gone, or perhaps the youthful lust had waned. The separation worked, and Jack got his way. In retrospect, it worked out for the best, but I'll always remember Fran as my first love. Fran coughed politely, and my attention returned to the present.

"Tell me about Warren's work," I asked as I drained the last of my coffee.

"Warren and Vic knew each other at Northwestern. Both graduated as civil engineers. They joined the same Chicago firm. That company worked with developers and builders— land planning, designing utilities, soil testing, that sort of thing. But since coming to Napa, Warren and Vic moved more into environmental engineering. Both of them had done some of that with the firm in Chicago. They found a greater demand for that expertise in the Napa-Sonoma-Mendecino area and no competition. Their company grew a bit in the last few years," Fran said.

"How did Warren get along with his partner?"

"O.K., I think. When we first came out here, we got to-gether with Vic and Susan all the time. We gradually made other friends and saw less of them. Vic and Susan have since divorced. Warren and Vic got along but not as best friends. It became very different when they owned their own office. Vic was the salesman and wanted the company to grow faster. I think Vic cared more about making and spending big money than War-ren. As the technician, Warren loves to get involved in engi-neering projects and solve problems—I mean, he loved to—I still can't get used to Warren being gone."

Her eyes watered, and she fought back tears. I settled back into the sofa.

"Who else worked at the office with Warren and Victor O'Connell?"

"They couldn't afford any staff at first. Vic's wife, Susan, worked half-days for them. Sometime Warren would type the reports himself. Then three years ago, Susan left Vic and got a divorce. After that, I believe they would call a temp agency when needed. I've lost touch with the office and Susan the last year or two because I was helping Daddy. Warren didn't tell me much about his work. I don't know if they finally hired a secretary or not," Fran said.

"How about enemies? Do you know anyone who might have had a grudge against your husband?"

"People didn't have strong feelings about Warren either way. Warren was not the kind of person who stood out in a crowd. I loved him, but one could best describe him as average. Neither short nor tall, fat or thin, just an innocuous man no one would notice. No, I don't know anyone who hated Warren."

Because of the strange circumstances surrounding Warren's murder, I returned to the relationship question.

"I hate to pry, Fran, but I have to ask how you and Warren got along."

"Fine. Like any couple married a long time, we had problems to overcome through the years. But overall, I would say we got along pretty well. We loved each other."

"Tell me about the night Warren died. What did you do that day?"

"Dad had asked me to help him make an invitation list for the winery's 50th anniversary. I left his office at Chateau Carneros about four, stopped at Safeway on Clay, came home about five o'clock, and started dinner. Warren called and said he had a meeting after work outside the office. He did that often. I expected him home about seven or seven thirty."

"What did you do when he didn't show up?"

"I figured he became involved with his work and forgot to call." She gasped, "Could that have just been an excuse? I got tired of waiting, sat down to eat about eight thirty. The police came to the door an hour later with the bad news."

"Last question, Fran. Tell me about your pistol."

"Because Warren often worked late, he wanted me to have a gun at home for protection. He bought it when we lived in Chicago and registered it with the state when we moved here.

We kept it hidden in our bedroom closet up on a shelf behind some sweaters. When the police asked, I couldn't find it. Maybe Warren took it to the office. I don't know where it is."

Then she leaned toward me and clasped her hands between her knees.

With her blue eyes wide open, she raised her voice, "I didn't kill him, Gene."

I tried to reassure her.

"Buddy and I will get to the bottom of this. Try not to worry. We'll talk again soon."

I stood up and started to leave. She stopped me by reaching out for my wrist. Her hand felt warm.

"Wait a minute. Tell me about yourself. We lost touch after high school, and I haven't seen you in years. Where did you go after Napa Junior College? Are you married? Do you have any children?" she asked.

I took a step backward and rescued my hand.

"So many questions. I went to Napa J.C. to please Pop, but I thought growing grapes wasn't for me. I'd wanted to be a cop ever since I was a teenager. So I got a scholarship to San Jose State and then a degree in criminal justice. I landed a job with SFPD after college and stayed there twenty-three years."

"I see your still good looking with your olive skin and chiseled features, and still no wrinkles. So why did you leave the police department?"

I swallowed. I had a hard time continuing, but, for some reason, I wanted to tell Fran the rest of the story.

"I didn't get married until five years ago, and my wife was killed a year later. One morning, I took off work to drive her to the O.B. for a check up. We slowed down near a stop sign close to our house when this hired thug drove by and tried to kill me with a twelve-gauge shotgun. A psychotic bitch who blamed me for busting up her dope business had hired him. She's now in prison as is the shooter. Anyway, I lost my wife and unborn son, and I caught fourteen pellets in my left arm and shoulder and had two broken ribs. I stayed in the hospital for three weeks and in rehab for almost a year. I came back to the department and rode a desk for a year or so. Therapy helped my depression a lot, but police work was never the same, so I retired."

"I'm so sorry about your wife and son, Gene. Looks like we're both alone now. By the way, why did you come back to Napa?" Fran asked.

"After I got shot, Pop finally forgave me for leaving home. When he became sick, I came home on weekends during rehab and helped him. I found that I actually enjoyed growing grapes. When Pop died last year, I took retirement. So now I grow grapes and plan to open a P.I. office, too, probably with Buddy. But first, I want to help get you off the hook. Don't worry, we'll the find the real killer," I told her.

She walked me to the front door. We shook hands, and I told her I would keep her informed. Without thinking, I hugged her for a moment. It felt awkward for both of us.

As I left the Roberts' house, I wondered if Fran had told the truth about not knowing about any girlfriend or was she just in denial? Warren Roberts had on a disguise when they found his body. Why did he hide his identity? And what about her dad? If Jack Phillips knew his son-in-law cheated on his daughter, did he have something to do with Warren's death? I remembered Phillips as over-protective and a control freak with a bad temper. I'd better pay that old bastard a visit.

The question remained—why kill Warren Roberts? Was the murder a set-up or an act of jealousy or revenge? For Fran's sake, I hoped we found the answer before she was indicted and tried for his murder. I wanted to get her out of this jam. Finding her husband's murderer had become more than just a job. I still cared for Fran but in a different way now. After all, I had once asked her to marry me.

I drove home, and Rachel was waiting for me.

"How was Fran?" she asked.

"Pretty much as I expected, after her husband's death."

"How did she look?" Rachel asked.

"She looked sad. She looked frightened….. Oh, I know what you mean. She looked terrific, just as the day I last saw her all those years ago. Not a day older. Her figure's a little fuller, if you know what I mean."

She punched my good arm. "Be serious."

"OK. What you're really asking is how did I feel seeing her. I felt some nostalgia and I felt I honestly wanted to help her out of this trouble. But no spark. I couldn't wait to see you," I said I reaching out and pulling her to my chest.

CHAPTER 5

I THOUGHT I WOULD LIKE THIS PRIVATE DETECTIVE work. Starting this investigation reminded me of why I became a policeman in the first place. The suspense and curiosity always excited me.

The first private eye, Allen Pinkerton, started a private detective agency after serving as President Lincoln's secret service chief during the Civil War. Pinkerton used the slogan "We never sleep" and trademarked an open eye as his logo, hence the name "private eye."

The day after seeing Fran, I drove over to Terrace Street. The winter sun warmed my neck and sore shoulder. Six townhouses stood on the block where someone whacked Warren Roberts and another six on the next block. The alley extended only behind those two blocks. The development appeared be no more than a few years old. The architect designed all of the two-story houses in red brick with distinctive doors and a different color of trim on each one—window boxes and such.

I got out of the truck and walked down the alley. At the end of the alley, I went around to the street and came back up the sidewalk in front of the townhouses. Roberts almost certainly came out of one of these houses before he died. But which one?

I drove Pop's fifteen-year old, red, Ford pickup north on Silverado Trail toward the farm at dusk. The sunset cast a soft pink and orange glow on Howell Mountain, contrasting with the pastel blue sky and the puffy white clouds. Nature painted a portrait worthy of a world-class museum.

I spotted Rachel's navy Volvo in front of the house as I turned into the drive. I grinned, and my heart skipped a beat. I realized I felt that the blue car belonged there.

The house was dark. I opened the door and called out to Rachel but heard no answer. I walked down the hall and heard the sound of sobbing. I found her in the back of the house in the little sitting room I used as an office. She sat in the dark room with her head down on Pop's old mahogany desk. I gently touched her left shoulder, and she started crying. I put my arms around her and asked what happened. She lifted her face from the desk.

"I'm scared, Gene. They killed my dog, Danny Boy, and left a note saying I—moi— could be next." Rachel's voice quivered.

This stunned me. "Where did this happen?"

"I returned home from my office and found him in the back-yard. Someone had cut him open and the bastard nailed a note to his body saying I could be next! J'ai tr`es peur—I'm so frightened. I had to come out here. I hope you don't mind," Rachel said.

"Who would do such a thing? And why choose you?"

"I've been trying to think who could have it in for me. I can't think of anyone from the past. I haven't offended anyone that I know of since I started consulting, and all of my clients seem content. Maybe it has something to do with my role as a county supervisor, but I don't recall making any enemies during the campaign or since I got elected," she said in a soft voice, tears running down her cheeks.

I straightened up, resting my hand on her shoulder.

"Someone wants something from you. They'll let you know in good time. Let me see the note."

She passed it over her shoulder. The attacker had used a computer printer, and the stock looked like plain vanilla 20-pound stock that anyone can buy anywhere. Of course, no one had signed the note.

"I'll turn it over to the police for prints but I doubt it can be traced.

I kissed the top of her head.

"The threat is real. We have to take some serious precautions. I have an old Python .38 revolver with a two-inch barrel that will fit in your purse. I'll give you the gun to carry. You can stay here so you won't be home alone. You'll be safer away from your house."

"Pretty sneaky way to get me to spend the night."

She gave me a weak, tearful smile. I knew she felt a little better as we'd had this conversation before.

"Stay here just for a little while until we're sure you'll be safe at home. You can even bunk in brother Robert's old room, but I can't promise I won't knock on your door in the middle of the night."

"That's O.K. I'll sleep with you. I need you to hold me tonight."

"Let's go to your house to see if your visitors left anything we can use to trace them and we can bury poor Danny Boy."

On the surface, Rachel portrayed the cool, efficient professional as a viniculture consultant with great credentials. But she was a softy under that veneer; I knew Danny Boy had meant a lot to her. She had owned the Irish setter for years, and he moved with her from job to job. Rachel lost a best friend when some cruel son of a bitch slaughtered her innocent pet to make some sick point.

We buried Danny Boy in the corner of her backyard under a large plum tree. Rachel carefully placed his toys, feeding dish, and his favorite dog food next to him in the grave. I knew she was having trouble keeping from crying.

Not sure Danny Boy could use these items on his journey to the Great Beyond, she said, "It can't hurt. Better to be safe."

Even in the dark, we could see well enough with the bright porch lights and my police baton-type flashlight. I examined the yard, careful not to disturb the crime scene. I found no signs of the intruders, and they had not broken into the house, only the backyard.

I held her hand, and we walked back into her house. In a somber mood, Rachel sat in her family room. I lit a fire, and, in little more than a whisper, she told me about how a girlfriend at Davis had given her the newborn pup. She told me a story I'd never heard before.

She said, "I'm not proud of it, but I had an affair with a professor in grad school. He was my mentor and the wine grape guru at Davis, head of the acclaimed experimental vineyard."

She ducked her head in embarrassment. "I was easy pickin's," she said.

"I actually thought he would leave his wife for me. Anyway, when it ended, my roommate gave me Danny Boy."

I smiled and said, "I'm sorry you suffered, but he doesn't sound like the right kind of guy for you. You needed someone like me."

"Whatever you say, dear. As time went by, Danny Boy accompanied me out in the vineyards. His presence always made me feel more secure when working in the fields around strange men."

While she talked, I improvised a simple late pasta dinner that would have made Dean and DeLuca proud. I found a chilled bottle of Buena Vista Chardonnay in her refrigerator and opened it. The wine had a faint bouquet of lemon peel. I used a little wine to poach a few tiger shrimp she had bought just yesterday. After the shrimp were just done, I removed them and reduced the wine, adding some cream and herbs de Provence. I boiled a little dried linguini and sauced it with the wine-cream and topped it all with the shrimp. I sliced some beautiful fresh organic tomatoes that needed only fresh basil leaves, salt, and a grind of pepper. We drank the remainder of the bottle of wine and ate a little Hagen Daaz Coffee and Cream for dessert.

Rachel got up from the table and carried our dishes to the sink.

She turned her head and said over her shoulder, "I've been thinking. The only thing I can think of that someone could want from me is my vote on the proposed ordinance from Keep Napa Green that has everyone so agitated. They want a moratorium on vineyard expansion. The wineries have expressed strong opposition. But no one could be crazy enough to kill my poor dog and threaten me over only my one vote."

"It doesn't sound probable, but what's this ordinance?" I asked.

She came back to the table, moved her chair close to mine, and continued.

"Environmental interests have been trying to limit the growth of wineries in the valley for many years. Most of the agricultural land grew fruit and nut crops years ago, and only a handful of wineries existed then. The number of wineries exploded when they discovered that wine grapes grown here made some of the world's best wines, and the price for premium grapes soared."

"So how would grapes do any more damage to the environment than other crops?" I asked.

"Keep Napa Green ordered their own scientific study which suggested that more vineyards will cause soil erosion and damage the streambeds. Environmental interests want to stop the licensing of any new wineries and prohibit expansion of vine-yards from just north of the town of Napa all the way to Calistoga. That's the area of the best soil for premium grapes. The winery people call KNG's study bullshit. The Napa County Board of Supervisors is studying Keep Napa Green's report to determine its validity. Some people on both sides have become excited."

"So you think the threat might have come from extremists on either side of the issue?"

"C'est horrible penser ansi— to think so,' Rachel replied, ' but some of them have such animosity for the opposite side. Who knows?"

Rachel had shed some new light on the current environ-mental controversy, which I knew nothing about. She suggested a possible motive for Danny Boy's brutal murder and the threat to her.

The clock showed the late hour, and Rachel looked whipped after her hard day. While she packed an overnight bag to return with me to the farm, I mused on this county moratorium ordi-nance business. But my thoughts kept coming back to that goddamn note and how to protect her.

CHAPTER 6

Buddy called the following morning. I took the portable phone out to the deck. I didn't want the sound of my voice to disturb Rachel's sleep.

"About Warren and Fran Roberts,' Buddy said, 'it seems that Fran left out some minor details when describing their marital relationship. I talked to several of their friends and found that the Roberts had separated for a while two years ago," he said.

"For how long?"

"I couldn't find out, but they had a talked-about scene only last month at Rutherford Grill in front of Beaulieu Vineyards. It seemed their quiet dinner turned into a shouting match. I thought the rumor about flying ribs might have been something of an exaggeration. She left the table in a huff and drove off by herself, leaving Warren to find his own way home. I interviewed the restaurant manager and confirmed the story, but no one seemed to know what the row was about."

"Do you think she was deceiving us on purpose, or did she believe her marriage was O.K.?" I asked.

"Denial can be seductive. Warren Roberts' family attorney, not Franklin Reed, also works for Fran's father. The lawyer went ahead and told me about Roberts' will since it will become a matter of public record in probate anyway."

Buddy always had a way of getting people to tell him whatever he wanted to know.

"Warren left few assets other than his interest in his firm and a small insurance policy. The lawyer hinted that there had been a pre-nap and that Fran owned her trust fund and the house. Fran couldn't have had a financial motive to kill her husband, even though she was his only heir."

I thought this partnership with Buddy would work out. He loved the work, and retirement bored him. Buddy knew everybody within a hundred miles. His contacts and experience made him an ideal partner.

"Can you check further into Warren Roberts' bank and credit card records from before his death and also see if telephone records for the last six months show any strange calls?" I asked.

"Sure, Gene. Anything else?"

I perched on the rail of the porch.

"Hell, yes! Someone broke into Rachel's backyard yesterday and killed her dog. Left a threatening note nailed to the dog's body. I don't expect any prints on the note, but I would appreciate it if you would have the crime lab look at the note and examine Rachel's backyard, too. You'll get a quicker response than I would."

"Is she OK?" Buddy asked with great concern.

"She's upset and frightened and awful sad."

I then called the O'Connell-Roberts office and asked to speak to Victor O'Connell, Warren's partner. O'Connell didn't want to meet with me, saying he had told the police all that he knew.

"Talking to you is a waste of my time. I don't know who killed Warren," O'Connell said. He had a gruff voice.

"Jack Phillips is paying us for a private investigation of your partner's murder. I know Mr. Phillips will appreciate your full cooperation." (Well, maybe Jack Phillips wasn't paying me himself, but it sounded good.)

Jack Phillips referred a lot of business and served as an important contact. After all, they couldn't have even have gotten the company started without him. Many times, guys who fooled around got murdered for personal reasons, but maybe someone had a business reason for killing Warren Roberts.

"You said your name is Ventura? OK, I'll give you a few minutes tomorrow at eleven," O'Connell said as he hung up on me.

I wanted see if Victor O'Connell knew of anyone who might have had a reason to kill Warren Roberts. Just as much, I wondered if O'Connell knew who Roberts saw that night on Terrace Street. There might well be a connection.

The O'Connell-Roberts engineering firm officed in an old, converted, Victorian house on Jefferson Street, just south of where Jefferson crosses Trancas. They had done a good job of restoring the old place to its original condition. They'd painted it gray with white trim and shutters, and a wide porch stretched across the front. I walked in. No one sat at the reception desk. I thought O'Connell was there alone. I called to him, and he came out to meet me.

I don't know what I expected Victor O'Connell to look like, but he surprised me. A small-boned man, he only stood 5'6" or so and looked like a strong wind would blow him away. He couldn't have weighed more than 140 pounds. He wore his dark red hair almost to his shoulders, and a pencil-thin mustache grew on his upper lip.

He dressed up more than the typical casual Napa fashion for office wear. His double-breasted, silver gray, silk suit looked better than off-the-rack. He wore a simple gold chain over his snug, black, silk T-shirt, and his polished black calfskin boots must have had heels at least two inches high.

As soon as I introduced myself and told him I worked for Fran's lawyer, he repeated that he didn't know who killed his partner. He tried to end the interview right there, but I didn't let him off.

"I understand your reluctance to discuss Warren and Fran, but if I'm to help her, I need to know everything I can about them," I said.

O'Connell was reluctant but went ahead with the story anyway. He told how Jack Phillips had encouraged Warren and him to move to Napa and had referred engineering business to get them started in their own business. We still stood in the reception area.

"Do you know of any problems between Warren and Fran?" I asked.

He patted his hair in place.

"It was difficult being Jack's son-in-law," O'Connell said. Warren complained about Jack's interference and his pampering of Fran."

"What do you mean?"

"Well, first he wanted to give them a big house when they arrived. Warren said no; he'd buy his own house. Jack gave Fran major presents like the Jaguar convertible. Warren appreciated Jack's help, but resented the meddling. It threatened his independence."

O'Connell hadn't invited me back into his office yet. It was clear that he intended to cut the interview short. He leaned against the receptionist's desk, and I sat in one of the overstuffed chairs adorned with doilies. It smelled musty.

"Had Warren seemed unhappy in particular or said anything about Fran in the last few months?"

"Warren had seemed pretty satisfied. He hadn't complained about Fran for a while," O'Connell said.

I jumped on that. So he complained about her before?" I asked.

He didn't answer my question. Something else to think about. He hitched himself up to sit on the desk.

"How well do you know Fran?" I asked

"She was my partner's wife. We all ate dinner together some when we first moved to Napa, before Susan and I split up. I haven't seen much of her since then." He looked away from me as if something caught his eye outside the window.

"I'm trying to get a handle on their relationship. Didn't you see them together when you worked in Chicago? How did they get along there?"

O'Connell began to bang his heels against the side of the desk.

"Warren and I worked together at McKinsey & Smith. It was just business. He told me his father-in-law would get him some engineering projects out here and that he needed a partner who did client contact. I checked it out and agreed to move to Napa with him. I saw it as an opportunity to have my own business. But Warren and I didn't socialize in Chicago, so I can't give you an opinion about how he and Fran got along. I didn't know her well in Chicago."

"Have you and Warren made good money here?"

He hesitated, deciding whether or not he should answer.

"We do O.K now. And business has grown, but we had a good chunk of bank debt to pay back then. So Warren and I drew only a modest salary at first. Now that the debt is paid, I think the business will take off."

Now that I had him talking, I wanted to learn more.

"How do you propose to do that?"

"I want to expand our operation, open a second office in Sonoma, and hire another engineer."

"Did Warren agree?"

"Warren thought I moved too fast. He always came around in the end, but I always had to push him in the right direction."

"What about Warren's clients?"

"We worked our clients together. I did the marketing, and we discussed how to handle the projects. Then Warren took control over the work. We met every Monday morning and talked about how the projects were going."

Can you tell me something more specific about his jobs?"

Now he drummed his fingers on the desktop.

"He was planning the expansion of three wineries, a new, two-story, office building in Oakville, and a medical clinic for three surgeons in St. Helena. I just don't know how I'm going to get these jobs finished now. Warren also worked on that hush-hush study for Judy Harris from the county board."

My ears perked up.

"What hush-hush study?" I asked.

"I don't know much about it. Warren did that on his own. He just said Ms. Harris wanted him to do some research and asked me to keep the job a secret. I guess it's O.K. to talk about it now. Can we wind this up? I have to go," he said.

I continued, "Do you know anyone who might have had a grudge against Warren?" An argument? Or a dispute over a job or about money?"

"Nothing comes to mind. Warren was a quiet, serious type. I never knew anyone who didn't get along with him."

"Do you know why Warren was on Terrace Street that night? Is that where his girlfriend lives?"

"No, I have no idea why he went there. Warren wouldn't have told me if he had a girlfriend anyway. We didn't talk about personal things."

The phone rang in some back office. He turned to leave me and to go back down the hall.

"Just a minute, Mr. O'Connell. Would you give me a list of Warren's clients? Someone may know something that can help Fran, you know, Jack Phillip's daughter."

"I know Fran is Jack's daughter. I'll fax you that list if you promise to be discreet. Now just leave."

We both knew I could have acquired the list from the

building permit records at the county court house.

"Here's my card, Mr. O'Connell. If you think of anything else, please call me."

I knew the interview had come to an end. So what the hell, might as well risk pissing him off more.

"I hope you don't mind me asking where you were the evening Warren was killed?"

He raised his voice a notch or two and slammed his fist down on the desk.

"I resent that question. I don't have anything to hide and I don't owe you shit!"

I remained calm. (Cool detectives are supposed to remain calm. Says so in the Private Eye Manual, Second Edition.)

I said, "I'm not accusing you of anything. I'm asking this same question of everyone who knew Warren."

"Fuck you, anyway, Ventura," was his strident reply.

This time, he did turn his back to me and headed toward his office. I heard the door slam. I guessed he wanted me to leave.

I found it strange that not once did O'Connell talk about feeling sorry about his partner's death, not even when worrying about how to get the pending projects completed. He had known Roberts since college days. They had worked together for years, and Warren had brought him out to California to set up a successful business. Now he showed no remorse over Warren's death.

I asked myself about that partnership. Perhaps O'Connell didn't need Warren anymore. Warren's father-in-law helped them get their first jobs. O'Connell brought in the new business and now he could hire someone cheaper than a partner to ramrod the jobs. In addition, Warren hesitated to go along with O'Connell's expansion plans. O'Connell could now buy Warren's interest from the estate for a song. It seemed O'Connell, too, had a motive. What could Victor O'Connell's ex-wife Susan tell me about what went on in that office? Perhaps her feelings about her ex would color her response. Or maybe she wouldn't even talk to me.

I closed the door and left.

CHAPTER 7

OVER BAKED FRENCH TOAST FLAVORED WITH grated orange peel and made with thick slices of wonderful country raisin bread from Oakville Grocery, Rachel and I discussed my interview with Victor O'Connell.

"I can understand your surprise at O'Connell not expressing any grief over the death of his partner,' Rachel said in between bites, 'but perhaps he just didn't want to share his feelings with a stranger who sometimes can have an intimidating manner."

I sat up straight and proper.

"I assure you that I acted like a gentleman at the meeting and even wore a suit and tie. I remained calm even when he screamed at me and told me to fuck off."

"Gentlemen don't lick maple syrup off their plates," she said with a mock frown. "Did you learn anything from O'Connell?"

She used her napkin to wipe a drop of syrup from the right corner of my mouth.

"O'Connell didn't tell me much, only that Judy Harris asked Roberts to do some research and to keep the job a secret. O'Connell said he didn't know any of the details."

"Judy Harris? Mon dieu! She's one of my fellow county supervisors. I'll call her and see if I can find out what's so mysterious about the engineering study. What do you have planned for today?" she asked.

"I'm going to help Ernesto plant the cover crop and get started with the pruning and then I need to go downtown to see Franklin Reed."

"Speaking of pruning," she said. "There's a funny story of how pruning got started in France? By accident, sometime around the seventeenth century, the bishop's donkey in Tours, Saint-Martin, got into the vineyard. He started grazing on the young grapevines. Those particular ones produced much more fruit the next year than the vines that had not been chewed on. People have pruned the vines ever since. They celebrate every year in the Loire Valley by tasting the new wine on the Feast of Saint-Martin. They even carry an effigy of the donkey in the parade."

"Wine lore fascinates me. I don't think even Pop had heard that one."

Rachel went off to work at a vineyard near St. Helena. I kissed her goodbye and made certain she carried my pistol in her purse, cautioning her to stay around other people. Bad guys don't like witnesses. We both knew Danny Boy's killer would contact her again.

I called Buddy to inform him about my meeting with Victor O'Connell. I told him about O'Connell's attitude and repeated my surprise at his seeming lack of sympathy over the loss of his partner.

"I'm faxing you a list of clients I wheedled out of O'Connell. I don't know how interviewing them will help, but it seems like the logical thing to do."

Sometimes this scut work paid off. Buddy knew most of the names and began telling me about them. I heard the clatter and whine of my fax machine. A list had arrived from the Napa County Appraisal District, giving me the names of the owners of the twelve townhouses on Terrace Street. The person Roberts visited may not have been an owner but a tenant. This list gave us a place to start. Maybe we could cross-reference Warren Roberts' contacts or phone calls with the names on the list. I knew the police had interviewed every person in the neighborhood, but someone could have denied knowing Warren.

I spent the rest of the morning helping Ernesto Zuniga prune and sow crimson clover seeds between the rows of the Zinfandel vines. I always loved the rich aroma the earth gave off after a rain like we one last night. Ernesto had helped Pop take care of the vineyard for the last ten years or so. Pop said Ernie had the best feel for grape growing he had seen since he left Italy.

I asked Ernesto, "I paid twice as much for clover seeds this year. Is it still cost effective?"

"We plant clover because the blossoms attract the good insects that eat the destructive bugs on the vines. That way we spend less on chemical pesticides and protect the soil at the same time. The grapes are better, and the cover crop crowds out the weeds. In addition, the clover stabilizes the soil, keeping it from running off during the rainy season, a major concern when your vines are planted on a hillside."

We finished two acres and took a water break. I scraped the mud off my shoes and stretched. My shoulder muscles complained.

"We leave the clover in place until the harvest, right?" I asked.

"Almost. We plow the cover crop back into the soil at the end of the growing season to eliminate any remaining weeds and to fertilize and aerate the soil."

"Rachel said the grad students at Davis call it "green manure."

Ernesto went on, "Some wineries have gone all organic and use no pesticides or chemical fertilizers at all."

That afternoon, I showered and put on a blue blazer, gray flannel slacks, a crisp white dress shirt, and a silky maroon tie. I drove to Franklin Reed's office to pick up the retainer check. It felt good to get out of work clothes for a change. I had found out through the years that wearing a tie helps. You get more respect and appear to be in control, even when that's just an illusion.

Some private eyes charge a daily or hourly fee plus expenses. Reed and I agreed on a flat fee to investigate the murder. Buddy and I would receive half of the fee at the outset and the remaining half in thirty days, or sooner if we solved the crime. If needed, Franklin and I would discuss the progress and change the arrangement at the end of the month.

Franklin's firm occupied a smart-looking office in a new one-story building on First Street in downtown Napa. The office had that new smell of fresh paint. The receptionist gave me the check and a contract signed by Reed. She introduced herself as Terry Reed, Franklin's daughter. (I couldn't get used to my contemporaries having grown children.) I signed the document. She said her dad expected me to meet him in the conference room. He got right to the point as I entered.

"So, Gene, have you found anyone yet who wanted to kill Warren Roberts?"

"His partner didn't seem too broken up about the murder, but I don't know why anyone would have shot Roberts in the balls unless they were trying to frame Fran. We are still looking for the person Warren Roberts visited the night he was killed. By the way, Buddy found that all wasn't a bed of roses with Fran and Warren after all. She told me they had no unusual problems when I talked to her, but they had separated at least once in the last couple of years, and witnesses told Buddy about a big fight in public a few weeks before the murder."

"Lots of couples fight. Doesn't mean Fran killed him," Franklin said.

"No, but it gives the prosecution a motive to use at trial. What about Fran's dad? Do you think Jack Phillips could have had anything to do with his son-in-law's murder?"

Reed pushed back his chair from the conference table.

"That's ridiculous. Jack plays hardball in business but takes good care of his family. Besides, he's paying our bills on this case," Franklin protested, raising his voice.

"Yes, Jack protects his family. Let's say Warren screwed around with another woman. Jack finds out. He already blames his son-in-law for their marital problems. By killing Warren or having him killed, he gets his revenge and makes a point by shooting the man in the nuts. Then he throws everyone off by hiring you to defend his daughter."

"You sure you aren't suggesting that possibility because you still blame Phillips for mistreating you twenty-five years ago?" Franklin said.

In a low, calm voice, I said, "I don't think so. You asked about other suspects. I'm just suggesting other possibilities."

Reed backed off. "Don't get excited. I'm just doing what lawyers do, playing the devil's advocate. If you want to keep this job, be careful how you talk to Jack. He pays the bills, and if he says you're off the case, that's it."

"It's only logical for me to interview Jack to get information that can help clear his daughter. I promise to tread softly. Trust me, we'll get along fine."

He frowned. Not so sure he believed me.

Franklin asked me about Rachel and whether we would get married. I gave him some non-committal answer—"non-committal" as in no commitment. I loved Rachel, but was I ready? Did I still love Alexandra even four years after her death? And did I want to take the risk of getting hurt again?

I turned my gaze to the view outside the window.

Sometimes her memory came as fresh as yesterday. I looked

down at my ring finger and remembered that Alex and I met at a baseball game. The Giants had come back from a long road trip and played the Astros at Candlestick Park. A breeze cooled the evening. Most nights at Candlestick, you could taste the ocean. We both stood in line to get coffee between innings; progress was slow.

I made some casual remark. "How about this. We wait fifteen minutes just to get a cup of bad ballpark coffee."

She gave me that great smile of hers and said, "At least the bad coffee is hot."

I chuckled, and we chatted a bit about the weather as strangers do. I liked the way she looked and noticed she wore no wedding ring. But how do you ask out someone whom you just met in line at a ballgame without coming on too strong? I have always been kind of shy when it comes to women.

We reached the front of the line, picked up our coffee, and headed back to our seats. We walked in the same direction and turned down the same aisle.

"Why are you following me?" she asked.

I assured her I always sat in the same seat in the left field bleachers. We compared tickets and found our seats only one row apart.

She laughed, "Maybe we were meant to meet. Would you like to meet me for some good coffee after the game?"

Boy would I. We walked to a diner three blocks from the stadium and talked for hours. We went out for dinner the following night and saw each other every day after that until her death.

Our two years together were the best of my life. We lived together for a year to make certain our initial mutual attraction would last. Better than that, it grew even stronger.

I had grown to like Judge Crawford through the years for his wisdom and sensitivity. I asked him to marry us in his chambers. We honeymooned at a quiet lodge on the lower Oregon coast overlooking the Pacific. We watched a violent electric storm on our wedding night from our second floor window. We held each other, looking out at the hard rain, streaks of lighting, and tall waves crashing against the jagged rocks. Thunder provided the sound effects.

The sky had cleared and the sea calmed by daybreak. We watched white whales with our binoculars as they frolicked on the horizon in the midday sun. The graceful giant mammals leaped in and out of the ocean, throwing up thousands of droplets like showers of diamonds.

Alexandra's feminine appearance belied her strong, independent streak. Alex had risen through the ranks at BART, the Bay Area Rapid Transit system, and filled the position of Assistant Manager when I met her. She held her own in a male-dominated industry.

She almost reached my height at 5'9" when she wore heels. Her smooth olive complexion came from her Greek heritage as did her black hair and dark eyes. I didn't know where her long legs and slim body came from but I loved every inch of her.

By the end of our first year of marriage, she became pregnant. She took a leave of absence in the seventh month of her pregnancy. We couldn't wait to have a child at our ages—Alex was thirty-eight, and I was forty-five. Neither of us had been married before or dreamed we would ever have a family.

Pop loved her the first time he saw her. Pop adored Alex. She made him happier than I had seen him since Mamma died. He would take her on early morning walks through the vineyard and show her the land he loved so much. Pop would regale Alex with stories of his childhood in Calabria.

He would say, "Alexa, my dear, I cama to New York justa so I could meeta my wife."

Their walks would last for hours.

Alex served as a bridge between father and son. Pop had chosen to be distant since I decided to become a policeman instead of working with him at the farm. Our relationship had been more formal than either of us had wanted. But through Alex, Pop began to show his love for me. I know he forgave me at last for having gone my own way.

Alex's pregnancy thrilled Pop as much as it did us. He couldn't wait to become a "nonno". And he was devastated when Alexandra and our unborn son died. We tried our best to console each other. But it didn't help much.

Franklin Reed patted the desktop and stared at me, wondering why I had tuned out.

"Gene, Gene. Are you OK?"

My thoughts returned to the present, and I focused on him again.

"Yeah, sorry, I was back in San Francisco for a moment."

He must have thought I had a premature "senior moment." Chagrined, I got up quickly, shook his hand and walked out the door. We'd finished our business for the moment. I decided to try to find Susan O'Connell, Victor's ex-wife. She had worked in the O'Connell-Roberts office when they moved to Napa from Chicago and maybe she could shed some light on how the two partners got along.

CHAPTER 8

I FOUND SUSAN O'CONNELL WITH NO PROBLEM. She had kept her married name and had stayed in northern California. State employment records showed she was worked for Alice Water's renowned restaurant Chez Panisse in Berkley. I found her residence and phone number without any trouble. She seemed eager to talk about her life in Napa and invited me to come to her apartment after work.

She lived in a gated complex near campus. The project looked about twenty years old but was well maintained. The flower garden inside the gate sprouted reds and yellows and purples even in February. The perfume of jasmine came to me as I passed the flowerbeds.

Susan O'Connell greeted me almost as soon as I rang her bell. One could best describe her with one word, "compact", and not in a negative sense. She stood five feet tall but with all her parts in perfect proportion. Her stylish short blonde haircut crowned a pretty heart-shaped face. Her low voice seemed out of place with her short stature. As she led me to her dining table, I tried to break the ice.

"I found you through your job at Chez Panisse. We used to eat there often when I lived in San Francisco. My wife, Alex, used to get a kick out of the unusual way the chef put together different ingredients and flavors."

"Yes. Eating there is one of the great perks. I lucked out. Their office manager needed help, and I applied at the right time. Now I'm an assistant manager and have quite a bit of responsibility," she said.

She got straight to the point as soon as we sat down. No more small talk.

"I was sorry to hear about Warren's death. He was a sensitive man and a good person. But I'm not shocked, Mr. Ventura," Susan said.

"Why is that? And you can call me Gene, Susan."

"When I heard Warren was killed, I assumed Jack Phillips was responsible."

"Why did you think that?"

"Jack Phillips just hated Warren. He thought he could control his daughter when they moved back to Napa. But Warren interfered. And Jack went nuts later about the possibility of them getting a divorce." She spoke with her gray eyes flashing.

"How do you know this?"

"Jack came by a lot in the early days when we first opened the office. I got to know him pretty well. He welcomed Warren at first, but after a while their relationship soured when Jack realized he couldn't control things."

"What did Phillips want to control?"

"Jack called in favors and helped Vic and Warren get construction jobs when they first started and introduced them to his banker for financing. So Jack thought we all owed him. He also thought he could intimidate his daughter and son-in-law. But Warren stood up to him."

A pretty glass bowl of shelled, salted pistachios sat on the table; I nibbled on a few.

"But why would Phillips object to a divorce?" I asked.

"That would get Warren out of the way and free Fran to stay close to Daddy."

"I overheard the discussion when Warren and Fran had separated. Jack stormed into our office one day. It was hard not to hear Jack screaming at Warren. He called Warren an ungrateful son-of-a-bitch, said he brought Warren out here and saved him from a dead-end job. He said, 'don't you dare divorce my daughter.' Warren answered that Fran wanted the separation, too. Jack said, 'Well, you go back on your hands and knees and beg her to take you back. Do whatever she wants. There's never been a divorce in my family and there never will be. I'll not have it!'"

"But did you ever hear Phillips actually threaten Warren?"

"Not in so many words, except for telling Warren he'd be sorry if he divorced Fran."

"Sounds like you don't like Jack Phillips," I said.

"It's not that I don't like him. Jack's a bully, but I appreciate what he did for us, helping us start our own business. I just didn't like him picking on Warren. Warren didn't deserve it."

"How about Fran? Do you think her father caused their problems?"

"Jack didn't help their relationship with his interference, but that wasn't the issue. Fran and I had become pretty close at the time when we moved from Chicago. I got the impression that the spark had gone from their marriage, that they had grown apart and were just going through the motions."

I scratched my head. Susan and Fran close?

"So you don't believe Fran killed Warren?" I asked

"Not at all. Who said that? She didn't hate him, just didn't love him any more."

"The police suspect Fran because Warren was killed with a pistol like the one they kept around the house. And Fran has no alibi."

"I don't believe for a moment that Fran did it," Susan said. I munched on some more nuts.

"Lets talk about the business. Is there any other person who might have wanted to kill Warren? Maybe a client or a competitor?"

She clasped her hands together on top of the table.

"No one. At least not while I worked there. I started working in the office when we opened. We couldn't afford to hire anyone. After a couple of years, I couldn't take living with Vic any more, so I left him and got a divorce. But Warren was a nice guy. He didn't make enemies."

"I'm sorry about your divorce."

"It worked out for the best. I should have bailed out long before. Vic meant well but went through spells. He was gregarious and outgoing most of the time. Then he'd get depressed and become nasty. I'd have to get away for a few days. He got worse over the years. I tried to get him to go to counseling or see a doctor, but he wouldn't hear of it."

"How did Vic and Warren get along?"

"OK. They had a business relationship, with each one bringing his own strengths to it. They needed each other, but I'm not sure they liked one another. Vic considered Warren weak like Jack did, but he wasn't. I know Vic had more ambition than Warren and was more of a risk-taker."

"Do you think Victor wanted to dissolve the partnership?" I asked.

"Interesting question. Vic got frustrated with Warren sometimes. But I don't think it ever came to that."

A clock chimed in the living room.

I thanked her for taking time to see me and reached across the table to shake her hand. I stood up and pretended to leave. I wanted to gauge her reaction to my next question. I walked toward the door, paused two beats, and turned around—a trick

I learned from watching Columbo on TV.

"Would it surprise you to hear that Warren may have had a girlfriend?" I asked.

She lost her composure for a moment. Her face fell, and she hesitated.

"I guess not."

"I don't mean to pry, Susan, but I need to know everything I can about Warren to help find the person who killed him. Did you have an affair with him?"

She delayed for about five seconds and looked away from me.

"How did you know? Did someone tell you?"

"No. It was the way you spoke about him; I had a hunch there was something more."

She faced me again.

"It didn't last long. I was going through my divorce, and Warren and Fran were separated at the time. Warren wasn't very cool, but he was a good listener and helped me out. We were both lonely and needed someone at the time. Sex with Vic wasn't much to start with, and he became even less interested through the years."

"How did your affair with Warren end?"

"He broke it off when he went back to Fran," she said.

"How did you feel about that?"

"It was just short-term therapy; no love lost," she said.

Her words said one thing, but her eyes said something different. I hadn't thought of Susan O'Connell as a suspect before now.

"When did you see Warren last?"

"Oh, ages ago. Sometime before I moved here."

"Have you talked to him since then?"

"Maybe I called him a year or so ago. I don't remember for certain."

"Do you get to Napa often?"

"I see where you're going with this. I guess that's your job. No, I don't have much reason to go up there anymore."

"Do you mind if I ask you where you were the night of February 3rd?"

"Let me think. It happened last week. Mondays I stay home and watch "Allie McBeal". Tuesday night, my boss called a meeting at the restaurant. The third was a Wednesday; I always work on Wednesday nights."

I reached over the table to shake her hand again.

"Thank you for your time and cooperation. I know it couldn't have been easy."

Susan O'Connell's suspicion of Jack Phillips could have been well founded, regardless of what Franklin Reed said. Phillips wouldn't have dirtied his hands by killing Warren himself, but that didn't mean it was beyond him to hire a killer. Susan had tried hard to get me to suspect Phillips for Warren's murder. I questioned if she told me the absolute truth, or if she had another motive, like protecting someone else, even herself.

Maybe Susan waited for Warren to divorce Fran and come back to her. When he didn't but took a new girlfriend instead, could her jealousy have turned to rage? The upward angle of the shots to Warren's neck could have come from someone her size.

CHAPTER 9

I EXAMINED THE LIST OF TOWNHOUSE OWNERS in the two blocks on Terrace Street. I assumed the police had knocked on every door, but they reported to Fran's lawyer that they still didn't know where Roberts had been before he was shot.

Couples or single men lived in half of the townhouses, but the list named six owners who were or could have been women:

J. Houser
Pauline Edwards
Mrs. Oscar Fink
Ms. C. Greene
F. Linz
Shirley Street.

I waited until seven o'clock, after people came home from work, and started knocking on doors. "J. Houser" answered to Jerry. "F. Linz" was Fred. Mrs. Fink opened her door. She wore a tent-like muumuu and weighed at least 250. Pauline Edwards offered me coffee and wanted to show me photos of her grandchildren—probably not Warren Roberts' girlfriend. No one answered at the Greene house. The brilliant full moon shined in the clear sky. I felt a chill in the air and pulled my collar up. The next address belonged to Shirley Street.

Shirley Street looked like a fashion model—a definite candidate for attracting a middle-aged man. Quite tall, she exemplified classic Irish features: strawberry blonde hair worn shoulder length and fair skin and eyes resembling sparkling emeralds. I guessed she was in her mid-thirties. She wore black shorts and a tight black T-shirt. I introduced myself and asked her if she had known Warren Roberts.

"The police showed me a photo of the man shot in the alley. I told them I had never seen him before." Her voice sounded soft and melodious.

"Did you hear the commotion in the alley with all the police cars that night?" I asked.

"I missed it all. I had a book signing that night at my store, Bookends, and customers stayed until about 8:30. Joan and I closed the store about fifteen minutes later. All was quiet by the time I got home."

"Who is Joan?"

"She's my partner."

"So you'd never seen Warren Roberts around the neighborhood?"

"No, never."

"Well, thank you Ms. Street. I appreciate your time," I said as I started to leave.

She touched my shoulder.

"Wait a minute. Wouldn't you like to stay and have a drink? I hate to drink alone."

She gazed at me with those green eyes from under her thick lashes as if she had more on her mind than liquid refreshment. There's no accounting for some people's taste. Though tempted to stay with this beautiful lady, I declined. Monogamy has its price. I descended the steps and headed for home and Rachel.

I forced my mind back to business though it wasn't easy. Shirley Street must not have been Roberts' girlfriend. She was working at her bookstore at the time of the murder, so she had an alibi that could be confirmed. I left the townhouse complex and made a note to contact the missing Ms. C. Greene. I hurried to the truck as rain began to fall. Fat drops landed on my bare head. I should have known better and always carried an umbrella in February.

I opened the door and found Rachel waiting for me. She rewarded my not yielding to temptation and greeted me with a passionate kiss that said more than "welcome home." She led me to the bedroom instead of the kitchen.

"And here I thought I was coming home for dinner," I said.

"Well, dear, your dinner will just have to wait," Rachel replied.

"They say the way to a man's heart is through his stomach."

"I suspect whoever said that aimed a little high, don't you think?"

She lit two candles on the dresser and turned out the lights. I watched her take her time to undress with the soft glow of candlelight bathing her body. She knew how much I loved to watch her and the effect it had on me. I got up from my chair and picked her up and carried her to the bed. We held each other tightly, our bodies touching from head to toe. She smelled of soap and flowers from her perfume. We kissed for only a short time before she rolled me on my back and climbed on top. Sex can be O.K. It can be good, even extraordinary. But sex wins the Cordon Bleu and Le Grand Prix when it's with one who tugs at your heartstrings.

She rested her head on my chest after we made love, my right arm wrapped around her shoulder, my hand on the curve of her hip.

Rachel told me, "I've decided not to let those bastards win, Gene. They haven't contacted me yet and must hope to keep me on edge until they tell me what they want. It's a psychological ploy to soften me up. To hell with 'em. I'm not going to give in and change my lifestyle."

"You sound pretty cocky, and I'm glad you're feeling better, but you better take the threat to heart. Keep the gun handy and exercise caution during the day. I'm certain they won't bother you here at night."

"O.K., I'll try to be careful but I'm not going to give in."

We got out of bed, put on robes, and wandered into the kitchen for a late supper. We ate leftover lamb with Major Grey Mango Chutney and Caesar salad with basil croutons and a bottle of Cakebread Merlot. We finished and pushed our plates aside. Rachel served bitter espresso and brought out a tin of crunchy hazelnut biscotti.

"Did you have a chance to talk to Judy Harris about her project with Warren Roberts?" I asked.

"I met Judy for lunch, and she said she hired Roberts to do an independent study. It concerned the environmental impact of continued growth of wineries in the area covered by the proposed ordinance. She decided to keep the study confidential until he finished his report because of the intense feelings of both the winery people and the "green group". Each side hired experts who contradicted each other. She planned to distribute copies of the Roberts study to the other county supervisors."

Rachel got up and started clearing the table. I rinsed the dishes while she talked.

"Judy never received the report, so she didn't know whether he finished it or not. The five-member board has only two women, Judy and me. I believe we both hold a moderate position on the moratorium issue. We don't advocate unrestricted growth, nor do we believe in a complete moratorium. Neither of us has decided how we will vote on the ordinance as proposed."

I thought about Buddy before I fell asleep. What secrets might Warren's credit card, banking, and telephone records reveal?

CHAPTER 10

I CALLED BUDDY WHILE RACHEL AND I DRANK CUPS of coffee after eating breakfast.

"I have a check for you for half of the retainer. I went over to Terrace Street last night but couldn't find out who Warren Roberts visited that night," I said.

"Maybe I can help there. Warren Roberts' telephone records for the last six months arrived this morning. I'll bring them and meet you at Puck's restaurant for lunch at one, and we'll compare notes," Buddy suggested.

Rachel had overheard my conversation.

"How long have you known Puck?" she asked as she took a last bite of her spicy bacon and egg breakfast taco.

"He was my best friend growing up. I met Puck my first day of school in Mrs. Williams' first-grade class. Our old, scarred, wooden, school desks sat next to each other, and we both sneezed because of the chalk dust. We shared our anxiety about starting school. Mrs. Williams reminded us of Ichabod Crane from the 'Legend of Sleepy Hollow' with her Adam's apple sticking out to there. I remember that the new surroundings were too confining. She expected us to sit still all morning and not talk to each other. I recall we were ready to quit school after the first day and talked of running away to join the circus."

"I bet you didn't," Rachel laughed.

"No, we didn't. We stuck it out all the way through high school. Puck and I connected because our home lives differed from the other kids'. His dad raised Puck alone since his mother ran off after he was born, deciding that she didn't want to be a small town lawman's wife after all. And I grew up dominated by a stern old-world father who spoke with a funny accent. It was only later that I realized he loved me."

Rachel squeezed my hand and filled my coffee cup.

"One can see it was difficult for you both," Rachel said in her French way.

"It wasn't so bad. We had baseball. The greatest day of our young lives was the day the Giants moved from New York to San Francisco, only forty miles away. Puck and I were seven or eight, and we spoke of only one topic of conversation that magic summer of '58—our hometown Giants. All our allowances went for buying Fleers bubble gum with baseball trading cards in hopes of finding a Willie Mays or even a Johnny Antonelli, a paisan. Bruce Johnson, the kid with the most Giant cards, always got picked for our sandlot games, even though he couldn't catch flies in right field. That's where we always stuck the worst players."

I closed my eyes and could almost sense the distinctive odor of my worn sweaty Rawlings baseball glove.

"Pop came from Italy and didn't understand why everybody got so excited by baseball and the new hometown team. He thought it a waste of time. Better I should be hoeing weeds from around the vines than indulging in this baseball foolishness. Pop knew only one game, bocce, which he played behind Robert Mondavi's winery on Sunday afternoons with his cronies."

"Did you get to see any games?" she asked.

"Just a few. We listened to most every game after school on

Buddy's old Philco radio. The sound was tinny, and every few minutes you had to hit the radio to get rid of the static, but we could hear the crack of the bat and the roar of the crowd. Our version of paradise that summer was to sit in the left field bleachers at Candlestick Park on a sunny Saturday afternoon. A few times, Buddy took us to a game. Pop objected, but Mamma intervened on my behalf, as she did throughout my young life. Mamma had grown up in New York, and even in Little Italy they knew baseball. She negotiated a compromise with Pop: if I finished my chores around the vineyard, I could go to the game with Puck and his dad. She didn't worry about me going into the city with the sheriff and his son."

"It sounds like a magic time for you. You remember it so well," Rachel said.

I drained my coffee cup.

"Magic's a good word for it—sitting in the ballpark with our baseball gloves, hoping to catch one of Cepeda's home runs, clutching a quarter and waiting until at least the 5th inning to buy the world's greatest hot dog, standing and cheering with 40,000 others after the last out when the Giants won."

I imagined the voices of the venders hawking peanuts and sodas and the smell of the mustard and hot dogs.

"I'll always remember Willie Mays patrolling centerfield, running like a gazelle to the outfield fence and making one of his famous 'basket catches'. Everyone cheered when his baseball cap went flying off behind him. That summer began a life-long love affair with my beloved Giants. I made lieutenant many years later and bought season tickets in the same left field bleachers where we cheered like crazy in 1958."

"We've never talked about it, but did you play also?" Rachel asked, putting her foot up on a nearby chair.

"We lived for baseball as kids. Puck and I went through Little League and Pony League together and made our high school team. We dreamed of playing pro ball, like every kid did—for the Giants, of course. I never learned to hit a curve ball, and Puck never mastered the art of throwing one. He threw an acceptable fastball, but when he tried to throw a curve, strange things happened."

Rachel glanced up at the clock and said, "Are you two still close?"

"Puck and I went our separate ways after high school. I stayed home and started Napa Junior College, and Puck went off to Arizona State in Phoenix. He worked his way through college in restaurants—first as a bus boy, then as a waiter—an introduction to his life's work. We're still pals these days and take in a Giants game from time to time. I had hoped that we could recapture that camaraderie we had as children and team-mates. But it's not the same; you can never go back."

I saw the clouds in the turquoise sky go scudding by the window.

"You mentioned Puck's life's work. When did he open The Vineyard?" Rachel asked.

"Puck opened his own place about ten years ago after work-ing his way up in restaurants. He's converted an old brick ware-house just off Highway 29 in Rutherford into a restaurant. It stands near a long-abandoned train depot now occupied by Hacienda Hardware where tourists buy so-called 'treasures."

"I know where that is, just up the road about 13 miles. I had a consulting job up there last year at John Fox's farm," she said.

"Puck created an atmosphere of the early 1900's in the Cali-fornia wine country. He has decorated the place with antique winepresses and other memorabilia as well as a grand painted mural of early vineyards and wineries. In contrast to the decor, The Vineyard menu features 'new cuisine', whatever that is. But tourists flock to the place, and Puck has done well."

Rachel 's good-bye kiss tasted of bacon, spices, and coffee.

"I'll have to leave. I have an appointment in Santa Rosa," she said.

"Be careful, make sure the .38's in your purse, and your cell phone's turned on,"

I called as she went out the door.

I met Buddy at the appointed time. We pick up the scent of charcoal smoke from the grill even before we entered the restaurant. Puck sat with us a few minutes in a quiet alcove and exchanged pleasantries. Then he went off to supervise his lunch business, taking our orders to the kitchen. I realized I hadn't seen Puck in several weeks, and he didn't look like himself. He said he felt OK, but I sensed something bothered him. He looked haggard and pale, and his eyes didn't sparkle like usual. Lines I hadn't remembered seeing before appeared on his forehead and around his eyes and mouth. I thought I smelled bourbon on his breath, but maybe not. Buddy didn't say anything, but I could tell he noticed something as well.

Buddy and Puck enjoyed an easy-going relationship, more like brothers than father and son. I had always envied their good-natured bantering, unlike my more formal conversations with Pop. Buddy stretched his long legs under the table and brought me up to date on the victim's telephone records.

"I think I found a match," he said. "There were several phone calls over a six-month period made from Roberts' office to a strange number, one that didn't fit any normal pattern—not to his office, family, friends or local businesses. I checked these odd calls with my contact at Pacific Bell, and they all went to a number registered to a Carol Greene. And get this—she lives at a Terrace Street address, just where the body was found."

I pounded the table.

"Way to go, Buddy! She's the one Roberts visited that night. See what you can find out about her—where she works, her background, any criminal record, etc. I'd like to know something about her before we interview her. It's funny; I'd planned to call her today. 'C. Greene' was the only person I couldn't contact from my list of owners."

"I'll get on it this afternoon, Gene. I'll make a few calls and I should have the information to you no later than tomorrow morning. I know you'll want to talk to her before the police find her."

Our steaming polenta-crusted sea bass came to our table served with a cold bottle of Sterling Sauvignon Blanc. A colorful medley of grilled green beans, yellow onions, red peppers and purple eggplant accompanied the fish. I filled Buddy in on my meeting with Franklin Reed and his hesitancy about my interviewing Jack Phillips.

"I have to talk to Phillips. He might know of someone who had it in for his son-in-law. I promised Franklin I would be a good boy, not even hint at my suspicion about him."

"Reed sounds awful touchy about you contacting his client. It makes sense that we would want to talk to Phillips to see if he could give us any leads."

He took another big bite.

"Tell Franklin to call Jack Phillips and clear it with him. That will get the lawyer off the hook, and Phillips will be obligated to see you as part of our effort to find his son-in-law's killer," Buddy said. "Besides, he's paying our bill. He should want to be included."

Buddy sure knew how to play the game.

"How do you like the fish?" I asked.

"Pretty good, but I still prefer fried catfish."

"We'll have to cultivate your palate, old man. This sea bass came all the way from Chile, and I like the crunchy polenta crust, too."

Buddy muttered, "Maybe it's worn out from swimming all the way from Chile."

I went back to the noisy kitchen and complimented Puck

and his chef. Puck and I agreed to find time to see each other sometime the next week.

As we left the restaurant, I thought again about the threat to Rachel. I wanted permission to talk to someone in the crime lab, so I stopped at the pay phone to call to my friend, Police Chief Mike Edwards.

"Hi, Mike. Your crime lab should be finished investigating Rachel Bernard's backyard where her dog was killed. She's very important to me. I'm anxious to know what the lab found. Would you please call down and ask them to give me a copy of their report?"

"I'll call them, but you can't interfere with their investigation. You agree to tell us if you find anything on your on."

"Sure, I'll call you at once."

I drove south on into Napa and turned left on 1st Street. I came to a four-way stop. I looked up and around and admired the century-old houses with their gingerbread trim. Light shone through stained glass panels with their muted colors and intricate designs. Magnificent old trees shaded well-maintained yards.

I found the crime lab office on the first floor at the rear of the police station. Rivka Daled expected me. I had heard about the Israeli lab technician who had come to California on an exchange program, but no one had told me how exquisite she looked. I may have been in a relationship but I could still look. She appeared to be under forty with dark curls cascading down her neck. She had large, exotic, almond-shaped eyes that were as dark as any I had ever seen, surrounded by thick dark eyelashes. The brilliant white lab coat made a sharp contrast seen next to her tanned olive skin. The lab coat opened just a bit, revealing a lissome, firm body. But what a face—high cheekbones, flawless complexion, and a dimple in each cheek—perfection. I couldn't tell whether or not she had on any make-up.

"Good afternoon," she said with a white-toothed smile that lit up the room. She actually seemed happy to see me, even though we had never met. She extended her soft hand in greeting.

"Chief Edwards said you would come by, but you're not what I expected."

"How's that?"

"I expected someone Chief Edward's age, but you're younger," she said. "He said this dirty old man was coming to see me."

Her voice had a lilting quality with just the slightest trace of a foreign accent, and I noticed a twinkle in her eye.

I laughed. Mike and I had a habit of always doing this to each other.

"We're about the same age, only he's not as pretty. We went to school together."

I enjoyed the banter with this lovely creature but I felt I should ask her about what I had come there for.

"Did you find anything in the backyard where the dog was killed?" I asked.

"There's not much to tell. No prints on the note. The poor dog was mutilated with a serrated six-inch knife, a hunting knife that anyone can purchase anywhere. The dog must have put up quite a fight. We found a lot of human blood in the street near the curb. We figure the assailant held his bleeding arm or hand until he got to his car but couldn't help dripping blood as he opened the car door. The blood didn't match with up with any on COSID, the national DNA database."

"I know COSID. We used it at SFPD when it first came on board." I said.

"Chief didn't say you were a cop."

"I'm not anymore. I retired over a year ago."

"You're way too young to retire," she said.

I let the compliment slide.

"Is there anything else in your report?" I asked.

"The only other thing we found that might help was the unusual muddy footprint between the wet grass and the curb. The fresh footprint in the soft damp dirt was a size 16-EEE Adidas sneaker. Could that belong to the owner of the house?"

"I think not. She's a size seven-and-a-half."

She grinned.

"I don't mean to be personal, but is she your girlfriend or just a client?"

"Why do you ask?"

"I just noticed you aren't wearing a ring, that's all."

I laughed again. "I'm sure you could do better than a gimpy 'dirty old man' like me. But yes, Rachel Bernard and I are together."

"That's a pity," she said, her lips still smiling.

I thanked her and shook her hand and turned around in a hurry. It might have been dangerous to stay there any longer. What's the deal with these women? First there was Shirley Street and now Rivka in the same week! I never got that much interest while I was unattached. Maybe I had improved with age after all, like a rare '93 Heitz Cabernet Sauvignon.

CHAPTER 11

I KNEW JACK PHILLIPS WOULD BE HARD TO FIND that time of year. When activity slows down at wineries in the winter, owners travel the circuit selling their product. Phillips and his marketing people call on wholesalers and grocery chains, hoping to get them to carry his wines. They visit restaurants, bars, and country clubs around the nation, encouraging them to place Chateau Carneros on their wine lists. They set up special tastings for managers, sommeliers, and even waiters. They entertain customers and wine and food writers in an incredibly competitive market. They give them creative gifts on occasion to promote the Chateau Carneros label, like cash. I assumed even his daughter's legal problems would take second place to Jack's sales efforts.

I caught him between sales trips. It didn't surprise Phillips to get my call.

"My attorney told me about hiring you and Bennett as his investigators," he said.

"We're looking into every phase of Warren's life and trying to learn who might have had reason to kill him. You might be able to point us in directions we don't know about."

"Sure. I'll help any way I can. Come on over to my

office at the winery. I'm in the first old building."

I puzzled over what type of reception I might receive considering our past history. I last saw him almost thirty years ago when he hated me because he thought I was trying to steal his daughter, Fran, away from him.

Chateau Carneros Winery rested on the banks of Carneros Creek off Old Sonoma Road. The value of the land had multiplied at least fifty times in the forty years since Jack Phillips inherited the property. Wines from Carneros grapes grew in popularity over the years. They graced tables all over the world. Experts considered Carneros grapes special, even for Napa. They took longer to ripen, had a lively flavor, and developed crisp acidity because the Carneros locale, straddling both Napa and Sonoma counties, shielded the grapes from extreme heat. Each acre yielded fewer grapes but of higher quality.

I passed through the impressive, eighteen-foot-high, arched, white, stone entrance and up the winding drive. The facility had expanded many times. They had built a wine tasting visitor center with a parking lot, the newest structure. They had chosen a handsome, two-story, faux French chateau design. The stately building featured a peaked roof of dark slate. Leaded stained glass panels adorned the massive mahogany entrance doors. I looked up and saw a balcony with French doors above each side of the entrance.

I continued driving beyond the visitor center fifty yards or so and came upon a gargantuan metal building the size of a football field. Crushing grapes, fermenting, aging, bottling, and storing no doubt took place there. Chateau Carneros had come a long way since I saw it last.

They had added several storage buildings out of view from the visitor center. I figured they contained equipment associated with the growing and processing of the grapes. Chateau Carneros grew only fifty acres of grapes behind the winery, a small percentage of their total production. Growing grapes on the premises was for show, to create the impression of "estate bottled" wines for which all the grapes must be grown on site. They bought most of their grapes from other growers.

The driveway ended in a cul d'sac where the original winery remained. That stone building had been converted to office space now. Jack's dad started his business in this drafty building before World War II. They hauled the grapes to the roof in the old days and used gravity to move them down to the crusher. Then the juice flowed into storage tanks in the cellar. They bottled the wine there and moved it to racks for aging. Did they still use that dark, musty cellar where Fran and I used to hide and make out? We used to get high just breathing the fumes.

Jack Phillips stood on the front steps to greet me. Still the bulldog of a man I remembered, he reached only 5'8" or 5'9". He looked as wide as he was tall. He sported a full head of hair, now turned steel gray, cut in a flat top about one and a half inches high. He wore a mustache and goatee more white than gray. He dressed in a red windbreaker with a blue Chateau Carneros logo over his heart and a white turtleneck. He had his brown cords tucked into his glossy alligator cowboy boots. Diamonds surrounded the face of his big gold Rolex.

He shook my hand but with a grip firmer than I expected.

"I've been checking on you, Ventura. Franklin Reed tells me you've made a name for yourself down in San Francisco. You've grown up since I saw you last. Come inside my office."

A slab of highly polished black granite functioned as his desktop, held up by sections of massive Sequoia pines. He sat behind the desk in a chair covered in leather, so big and soft it could have made a thousand pair of kid gloves. I chose a barrel chair facing him.

"You haven't changed much, but your winery sure has," I said.

"Yeah, wines from the Carneros district became very

trendy, and we grew along with the demand. But I sell more Carneros wine than anybody."

He still liked to brag.

"So tell me, can you help Fran?"

"Buddy Bennett is working with me now that he's retired. Since the police are convinced Fran did it, they aren't looking to find other suspects. We intend to find the real culprit."

Phillips remained a bundle of energy. He fiddled with the stuff on his desk while we talked. Black and white photos from the early days of California winemaking covered the walls of his office. Winery workers looked down on us from scenes of Model T Ford trucks groaning under their loads of ripe grapes. Graceful young women stomped grapes in huge vats. Another image showed raucous celebrants at the end of the harvest. Antique pruning hooks also hung from the walls. I noticed one side wall covered with plaques and honors and photos of Phillips smiling with various celebrities and politicians. I'd never seen so much paraphernalia hanging in one office.

"People will tell you I disliked Roberts," he said. "He gave Fran a hard time and refused to have any children. But no one I know hated him enough to kill him."

He spun his chair around and retrieved a teak humidor and offered me a cigar. I declined, and he lit an eight-inch stogie with his gold lighter. The aromatic smoke of expensive tobacco made me wish I enjoyed the taste as well.

"Did he abuse her?" I asked.

"No, nothing like that. He left Fran alone a lot, worked all kinds of crazy hours. I wanted to make her life easier, give her a big house and stuff. Warren wouldn't hear of it.

And I got the impression from her that he wasn't often affectionate, if you know what I mean."

He looked at me most of the time while we talked, but his gaze kept moving around the room as if he had trouble concentrating.

"Do you think Warren had another woman?" I asked.

"I didn't before, just thought he was too involved in his work. But Reed gave me a copy of the police report. Warren went to a lot of trouble to keep from being recognized the night he was killed."

"My exact thoughts."

"Can you find out if he cheated on my daughter?" he asked.

"Roberts left a townhouse on Terrace Street that evening. We will find out which one, and that might give us a lead. Do you know anything about Warren's work that might have taken him there or put him in danger?" I asked.

"Why kill a damn civil engineer? Warren and O'Connell worked for a big firm in Chicago and gained good experience, but they had limited opportunities to make big money there. I wanted Fran to come home anyway. I called in a few favors and got them several engineering jobs to get started out here. Most of Napa is beholden to me. I can make or break anybody in the valley," he boasted.

"Did you keep up with their business after that?" I asked.

"No. Warren and I argued about me giving things to Fran eighteen months ago when I gave her the Jaguar. We haven't talked much since then."

"What about his partner?"

"O'Connell gets after it, more ambitious than Warren. But they needed each other. O'Connell sold the engineering projects, and Warren got the projects finished so they could get paid. I know of no bad blood between them."

The intercom on his desk squawked.

"Sorry to interrupt, Mr. Phillips, but Franklin Reed's is on Line 2 and says it's important."

He punched a button, listened for a minute or two, said, "Oh shit," and hung up.

"Franklin says the police have located a witness who saw

a woman hurrying out of the alley about the time of the murder. She couldn't identify the person in the dark but said she saw a female figure. Napa police are now even more convinced that Fran did it."

"They'll be talking to her a lot more," I said.

He frowned and then stared hard at me through slitted eyes.

"You better hurry up and find another suspect,' he demanded, 'or we'll get a big-name private eye from San Francisco to take the case."

I got up and thanked him for seeing me and started to leave. Phillips' mood shifted.

He said, "I often wondered if I made a mistake breaking you and Fran up after graduation. She was crazy about you, but I didn't want her to marry a damn grape farmer. I also hated you for screwing my teenage daughter."

"We planned to get married. How did you know?" I asked.

"Her mother found the birth control pills, and we confronted her. We shipped her off to Chicago the very next week."

I told him I would report our progress to Franklin Reed every few days and left the winery to go home. Phillips didn't really need to kill his son-in-law. He used money and power to get his way. He might have tried to buy Roberts off or to use his influence to crush his business, but he didn't need to kill him or have him killed. But who knows what evil lurks in the minds of men.

CHAPTER 12

I FELT DRAINED AFTER MEETING WITH Jack Phillips. I hadn't known what I would find. I had once hated him with a passion that enveloped me. I remember thinking up diabolic ways to make him suffer an agonizing death. I wanted revenge back then for his taking away the love of my 18-year old life.

Rachel and I drank a bottle of cold Kendall-Jackson Chardonnay on the front porch after I arrived home soon after dark. I grilled fresh Pacific snapper filets seasoned with extra virgin olive oil and oregano from the garden. We listened to an old recording of Julius Massenet's "Manon" that Rachel had brought with her. She had a strong affection for operas by French composers. I felt better after the wine and the fish, and the small lemon tarts Rachel baked from her mother's recipe made my mouth water all over again. I took a second tart and a splash of Quady Late Harvest Riesling that had been hiding at the back of the refrigerator. We ate too much—at least I did.

We watched the Golden State Warriors game on TV and tried to stay awake. The phone rang. Rachel answered a call from Judy Harris, who served on the board of county supervisors with her. Rachel had forwarded her calls to my number. She covered the phone with her hand and looked over at me.

"Judy wants to know if I've received a $5,000 cash donation from an anonymous donor. An ordinary brown paper bag filled with fifty-one hundred-dollar bills appeared in her mail box with no message inside, only the words "Campaign Donation" printed with a black marker on the outside. What should I do, Gene?"

"Tell her that you haven't received anything like that. Then let me talk to her."

"Judy, no one's contacted me nor sent me any money. I don't know what to say. Hey, Gene wants to talk to you. Here he is."

Rachel handed me the phone.

"Hi, Judy, this is Gene Ventura. Here's what you should do. Put the paper sack with the money inside a larger, clean plastic bag and don't let anyone else touch it so we can see if we can get any prints off it. Let's get together as soon as possible to talk about it."

"Gene, it can't be soon enough for me." Judy answered. "How about tomorrow morning at my office? I have nothing on my calendar, and we can take as much time as we need."

"That's good. Rachel and I will be there at 10:00. Meanwhile, be careful, keep your doors locked, all that sort of thing. Lots of strange things have occurred, and we don't know if they're related or not."

Rachel gave me some background on Judy on our way to the appointment.

"Judy retired from professional tennis and moved to the Valley from San Diego. She soon became enamored with the Napa community and seemed to join every organization. She has headed the United Way fund-raising drive, served as Girl Scout leader, and worked as a director of the Chamber of Commerce. Many people encouraged Judy to run for mayor of the City of Napa. After serving two terms as mayor, she won the open spot on the Napa County Board of Supervisors."

"She's bright, energetic, independent, and quite outspoken. Local men find her attractive as a celebrity athlete, and the women appreciate her caring personality."

"Sounds like a neat lady. Maybe she'll sell us some of those yummy Thin Mints Girl Scout Cookies."

"Smart ass. Behave."

Rachel and I met Judy Harris in her office at the Napa Tennis Club out on Silverado.

A glass wall allowed her to see every court from her aerie. Judy had left the pro tennis tour about ten years earlier and used her accumulated winnings to buy the club. I studied her— an attractive tall woman, wiry and muscular with short silver hair. She looked as if she could still go back on the tour. Her hazel eyes blazed. She was pissed.

"How dare they think they could bribe me, whoever the hell they are." She went on, "I called the editor of the Napa Register this morning and told him to print an announcement that I don't accept anonymous donations and that the money will be placed in escrow at the downtown location of the Napa Bank of America. The money will be returned to the donor when he or she describes the amount of money, the denominations of the bills, the parcel that contained the money, and how the money was delivered. The money will go to a charity selected by the Napa City Council if it's not claimed within thirty days."

We heard the muffled thwack of rackets hitting tennis balls.

I wished she had talked to me first to discuss another strategy.

"I don't think anyone will claim the money since attempted bribery is a second-degree felony in California, punishable by as much as twenty years in the pen and a fifty-thousand-dollar fine. No one will ever show up," I said.

"Oops, did I screw up? I'm sorry. I was so angry I couldn't

see straight. I wish I had asked you first about putting it in the paper when I called last night," Judy said.

"Why do you suppose they threatened Rachel and offered you what may be an anonymous bribe? Do you think it's just a coincidence, or do you see a connection?" I asked.

"Well, we're both on the county board of supervisors and also the only two women," Rachel said.

"I don't know if that's it. The only controversial issue before the board is the moratorium proposal. We're both undecided, but I know Rachel shares my reservations about it being in the county's best interest to halt all vineyard development," Judy said.

"One side or the other on the moratorium issue could be responsible for the attempted bribe. I doubt we'll find any fingerprints on the paper bag. Rachel, your threat doesn't have to be related, and there could well be another reason for the attempted bribe. Judy, they won't contact you; your announcement in the newspaper assures that. I just hope the bad guys make a mistake."

I took the paper bag from Judy to have the bag and the money checked for prints on either the bag or the money. Now I needed to contact people on both sides of the moratorium proposal.

I told Rachel as we walked to my truck, "I like Judy Harris. She's good people; a bright, gutsy lady. I hope we can get to know her better, maybe have her over for dinner."

"I don't know, Gene. She's pretty cute," Rachel teased.

"She's not my type. I prefer soft, cuddly, well-rounded women."

"Thanks a lot," she said as she tickled me.

CHAPTER 13

BUDDY COMPILED A COMPLETE DOSSIER ON Carol
Greene, Warren Roberts' mistress, from his various California
sources. His voice on the phone sounded calmer than unusual.

"I got all the details, but found nothing startling. Carol
Greene was born in San Diego in 1960 and raised there. She
earned a B.A. from San Diego State and a Master of Architecture from Berkley. She interned at a major San Francisco firm,
which she joined after graduation."

"When did she move to Napa?" I asked.

"Fontaine Associates, a small Napa firm, recruited her five
years ago, and she made partner just last year. Ms. Greene has
a reputation of being smart and talented. She has designed some
of Napa and Sonoma's better-known winery projects since coming to the area. Greene did that spectacular, if gaudy, Portafino
Winery with a 100-foot facade, an exact copy of a 16th century
Venetian palace. She even included gondolas on a canal running in front of the winery. Portofino has become a favorite
stop for the hordes of tourists who descend on Napa each year."

"Thank God, I've never been there. Does she have a husband somewhere?"

"Nope, never married, no children."

"Does she at least have a record?" I asked.

"No criminal record. I didn't even find mention of a California traffic citation. In summary, Gene, she's 'Miss Clean'."

I didn't call ahead. I waited in front of her townhouse until she came home from work and surprised her on her front porch.

"Miss Greene, my name is Gene Ventura. I'm a private investigator and

I would like to talk to you about Warren Roberts."

She didn't blink and wasn't about to let me in.

"I told the police I wasn't home the night he was killed and that I didn't know Mr. Roberts," she said as she tried to close the door in my face.

I placed my foot inside the doorway and told her, "We acquired copies of six months of telephone records showing calls from Warren Roberts to your telephone number. You can talk to me now, or I can give the records to the police."

I observed her in the light of the porch lamp while she absorbed this new information. Carol Greene appeared rather broad-shouldered with brown hair beginning to gray worn in a twist on top of her head. She wore round rimless spectacles with metal earpieces like the ones John Lennon made famous. The navy business suit and matching pumps created a professional image. Her freckled angular face included a small thin nose and soft brown eyes, red from crying. I wouldn't call her unattractive, just rather plain—not who you would expect as a middle-aged man's mistress.

She hesitated a long moment and then invited me in. I followed her to a sitting area where she put down her purse and brief case.

She changed her story and said, "I see no reason now to talk about Warren. I know nothing about the murder and I see no reason to reveal our relationship or to cause his wife any more pain, now that he's dead.

"But you didn't mind dating her husband when he was alive," I said."

"Their marriage ceased to be long before I met him."

"How convenient for both of you. Now tell me about you and Warren and the night he died."

She turned on a lamp, and we each sat at opposite ends of her sofa. She told me her tale.

"I met Warren a year ago when I designed the Silverado Springs Winery's Visitor Center. He engineered the project. We worked together on the plans and the application for the building permit. He impressed me as an excellent civil engineer and great to work with."

"Is that when you started seeing him?"

"No. He asked me out for several weeks. I told him I didn't date married men, though I liked Warren. We became friends."

"Did he ever tell you that he was getting a divorce?"

"Yes. He said his marriage was over and that they planned to get a divorce. I agreed to have lunch with him to celebrate after the Napa City Council approved our building permit. We drank a bottle or two of Iron Horse Brut. I love delicious champagne. I drank too much and succumbed. We wound up at my place. He came over about once a week after that for a few hours after work then he would go home to dinner. Our love grew as we got to know each other over the last several months."

The house smelled of Lemon Pledge.

"If his marriage had ended, why did he still live at home with his wife," I asked.

Her eyes began to water, and she said, "Warren feared that, if his father-in-law found out, he would try to retaliate by ruining the business. He said Jack Phillips would hate the scandal of a divorce in his family. Warren planned to build the business with new projects and to secure clients outside the sphere of Phillips' influence and then he would get a divorce."

She turned away and covered her face with one hand. "We talked about getting married," she sobbed. "After all these years, I finally met the right man."

I gave her my handkerchief to dry her eyes and asked her about the night Warren died.

"Not much to tell. He arrived about 5:15 like every other evening when we were together. We made love, shared a drink, and talked for a while. He put on his black outfit and left; I never saw him again."

"Did you see or hear anything after that? And what's the deal with the black outfit?"

"I returned to my bedroom after I saw him out the back door. I didn't see anyone nor did I hear any shots or any unusual noise. I heard a commotion in the alley an hour or so later. I went out back to investigate. I saw Warren's body lying in a pool of his own blood. It horrified me. I was like the statue of Commendatore in Mozart's 'Don Giovanni'—I had been turned to stone. How could he be dead! I don't know if I can ever get that nightmarish scene out of my mind. I saw no reason to tell the police about Warren and me. We had always kept our relationship a secret."

"What about the black sweat suit?"

"We joked about Warren's disguise. He parked his car blocks away and wore black sweats over his suit and pulled a black baseball cap over his eyes, hoping no one would recognize him. Napa's a small town, and Warren feared his father-in-law would find out about us."

"Was he afraid Phillips might hurt him if he found out?"

"No, not physically. Only that Jack Phillips still had the power in this community to influence companies not to hire Warren's firm and that could ruin his engineering business."

"What did Warren tell you about his partner, Victor O'Connell?"

"Warren and I talked a lot. We both understood each other's

business, one of our common interests. Some tension developed over the direction the firm should take. O'Connell wanted to borrow more money and open another office and hire at least one more engineer. Warren had felt great relief when they finished paying off the bank loan. He just wanted them to take their time building the business, and then hire new personnel as they could afford to. I'm not sure how serious the difference in opinion was. It appeared to be an ongoing discussion."

"How about their personal relationship? Warren and O'Connell had been friends since their college days."

Carol Greene thought for a minute or two and then replied, "Warren didn't talk about Victor as a friend, only as a business partner. I'm not certain they were ever close friends. Warren needed a salesman, and Victor could sell anything.

I asked her if Warren sensed any danger or knew of anyone out to get him. I noticed she had twisted my handkerchief into a knot.

"I don't think so. But he had been agitated and felt a lot of stress in recent weeks over the study Judy Harris had hired him to do."

"Tell me what he told you," I asked.

"Judy Harris didn't accept the environmental impact report submitted by Keep Napa Green nor the one from experts hired by N.V.V.A. The vintners' guys stated that, in building new wineries and expanding existing ones, they would use effective techniques to control soil erosion, run off, and pollution of the water table. Keep Napa Green's study said 'no way' could they accomplish that. Miss Harris wanted to know the truth, so she hired Warren to make a third study, objective and unbiased, of the moratorium proposal. He agreed to keep his research and findings confidential. He didn't even show a draft of his report to me or his partner."

"Did he tell you his conclusions?"

"I'm not sure he even finished. But someone found out about the study and started to squeeze Warren hard. He didn't go into details, but I think someone even tried to bribe him. He seemed under a lot of pressure.

I told her I regretted that Warren had been killed and that I saw no reason at that time to disclose their liaison, but I knew the police would find her, just as we did.

This damn environmental business kept cropping up. It also seemed Jack Phillips could have a motive after all. Maybe Warren's partner wanted out. And I still couldn't rule out his wife who may have been jealous after all. And I thought I might have let Susan O'Connell off too easy. She still cared for Warren long after their affair. Perhaps he promised her they would get back together when he divorced Fran. How angry would she have been to find out he had moved on Carol Greene instead?

For that matter, what about Carol Greene? I believed her story, but then I wasn't there. She could have told Roberts to let himself out of the back door. While he changed into his disguise, she could have gone out the front door and walked around to the back. Perhaps she killed him and added three shots in the balls out of vindictiveness because he told her that he wasn't getting a divorce after all or that he had found someone else.

Maybe all these years of police work had made me too suspicious.

CHAPTER 14

I THINK WE CAN AFFORD TO PUT IN DRIP IRRIGATION at least on the five acres closest to the house," Ernesto Zuniga said. "I know we can save money on water in the long run and control our irrigation better,"

I replied. "It's just concerned about the up-front cost."

I found it hard to balance my time between the vineyard and the detective work even with Buddy's help.

Ernesto asked me to meet with him to discuss installing drip irrigation. Water has an essential role in the vineyard. Too little water and the vines may get stressed and stop producing sugar, and grapes become dehydrated in hot weather. Too much water and they yield too much sugar. He came to the house the day after I talked to Carol Greene.

Rachel and I had finished breakfast and were talking about the economics of drip irrigation when Ernesto knocked on the front door. He wore his usual faded blue overalls with a red-checked flannel shirt and a Red Man baseball cap. I poured him a cup of coffee, and he spread out the irrigation brochures on the breakfast table. Drip irrigation consists of long plastic tubes running down each row of grapevines with one dripper at each vine. The water source is programmed to deliver the right amount to each section of the vineyard.

"We'll need to rent the giant sprinklers like in the past if we have a summer as hot and dry as last year. Dripping will save us that cost, tambi'en," Ernesto said.

I began to study the irrigation material.

"Those hot, dry summers are part of the magic," Rachel said. "The dry heat ripens the grapes without the humidity they would get in the East. That helps make Napa Valley a unique growing environment. At UCal/Davis they call it a Mediterranean climate with plenty of rain in the winter and spring. The summer days grow hot and dry, but the breeze from the ocean refreshes the nights, and the early mornings get the cool summer fog. Such a climate exists on less than one percent of the earth's surface. This unique climate makes Napa grapes prized throughout the world."

I looked up from the brochure and said, "I've never heard it referred to as a Mediterranean climate before."

Ernesto turned to Rachel, "Mis ancestros came from Spain. That is on the Mediterranean, no?"

"The Spanish Franciscan missionaries expanded north from Southern California and settled in the San Francisco Bay area around 1817. They grew grapes for their altars and their tables and knew they'd created something special. The Russian trappers in the settlement near Fort Ross made some of the first wine in northern California about the same time," Professor Rachel offered.

"But our local wine industry got started in the late 1840's and the early 1850's," I added. "George Yount, a farmer from Ohio, may have been the first Napa winemaker. He liked his table wine so much he considered selling it to the public. Around the same time, an English brewmaster, John Pritchett, may have been the first to sell Napa wine. He shipped some wine to San Francisco for two dollars a gallon. Pritchett built the first real winery in 1859 at what is now the corner of First Street and Monroe in downtown Napa. Local history books refer to Charles Krug, who worked with both Yount and Pritchett, as the father of Napa wine." I concluded her history lesson.

"Es muy interesante," Ernesto said. "I didn't know about the Spanish missions."

I tried to bring the discussion back to irrigation.

"Pop never got around to buying a drip system. I agree we need to do the whole vineyard. Let me see what terms I can get at my bank to finance the irrigation, and I'll let you know next week, Ernesto. I know we have to finish installing it by the middle of March when the vines begin to grow."

The telephone interrupted our discussion. Franklin Reed spoke only a little above a whisper.

"The police located the gun they believe killed Warren Roberts; looks like the gun described by Roberts in his permit application. They sent the gun to ballistics for testing. Some kids found it in the cypress woods about a half-mile from where the murder took place. Police dusted the gun for prints and found none," Reed said.

I heard Jack Phillips shouting in the background, something about "lazy-ass detectives". We better get a break in the case soon. I left a message for Buddy, telling him about the pistol.

I said goodbye to Franklin and replaced the receiver. Even if the pistol belonged to Warren and the police could prove the couple fought, no direct evidence existed to charge Fran. Franklin could expect her to be questioned again. Maybe we could learn something from Paul Martin at Napa Valley Vintners Association or at the Keep Napa Green office.

I left Rachel and Ernesto talking about water and things and climbed into the truck, heading down the mountain to talk to my banker at Westamerica Bank in Napa. All we needed was more debt. But starting drip irrigation made a lot of sense.

I had driven about a hundred yards down Howell Mountain Road when I heard a popping sound under the truck and saw a wisp of smoke.

I touched the brake pedal as I came to the next curve. Oh shit! My brakes had gone out.

The truck gathered speed as the road curved down to the right.

Again, I stomped hard on the brake pedal. I tried the emergency brake—nothing. About two miles to go before I reached the bottom and a level road. And I still had no brakes.

I tried turning the engine off. No help there.

The truck picked up more speed, and I tried to keep from going off the road and down the mountainside.

Just made it around the next two turns, tires screaming all the way.

I ran out of options. And I damned sure wasn't ready to die.

The truck continued to pick up speed as I rounded the next bend.

And there, before me on the right, Providence had provided a solution. The California Highway Department—bless them— had created a turn-off lane for vehicles in trouble. The gravel ramp inclined at about a thirty-degree angle, forcing runaway trucks to decelerate. I turned onto it and started to slow down as the ramp rose. An embankment made of the same gravel stood about three feet high at the end of the rise, about 400 feet away. The truck hit the barrier at about twenty miles an hour. It stopped with a jolt. My head snapped back and forward. Thank God, the barrier held.

I sat still for about five minutes and caught my breath. What incredible luck. I called for help on the cell phone and then got out of the truck. The front bumper was jammed back, touching the tires. I saw no discernable damage otherwise. Brakes go out a little at a time, not all at once like this. My brakes worked fine yesterday. And emergency brakes hold. When I could think straight, I felt certain my mechanic would find that someone had monkeyed with the brakes. I might not have such good fortune the next time.

My sweat-soaked shirt clung to my body, and my hands shook. I had never thought of myself as a coward. But trying to keep my pickup on the road and not go over the precipice scared me just about as much as anything I'd ever known. Only twice before had I felt such gut-wrenching terror: the drive-by shooting of Alexandra and one other incident.

CHAPTER 15

I TOUCHED THE SCAR BENEATH MY RIGHT EAR, remembering that first time I experienced nameless fear. I was just a rookie cop at the time, only seven months out of the academy. We were patrolling up Powell Street. Sergeant Ralph Karl drove the black and white. I rode shotgun.

We noticed a shiny black '74 Camaro, the latest model, with the twin-cam interceptor engine still running. Someone had left it parked sideways in front of a 7-Eleven. All that and seeing no one in the car made us suspicious.

"Maybe just some guy in a hurry to buy cigarettes or a six-pack' Karl said, 'but we'll check it out since we've had a rash of convenience store robberies lately."

We caught the robber red-handed, interrupting him cleaning out the cash register. He had his .38 revolver aimed at the frightened clerk. My partner and I drew our pistols and forced the robber to lay down his weapon and hit the floor. This is when procedure dictated that we cuff him—mistake #1.

Sergeant Karl unhooked his walkie-talkie from his belt. "Have robbery suspect apprehended at 7-11 store, 1401 Powell Street. Request backup."

It seemed we had caught the serial c-store bandit and looked forward to the "atta boys" that they would give us when we returned to headquarters. Just then, a second robber came from the back of the store carrying a 12-gauge sawed-off shotgun— mistake #2. He fired over our heads and said, "Drop your guns!"

I put down my service revolver, but Karl hesitated. The shotgun-wielding bastard fired at Karl's chest. Kaboom! Karl wore no chest protector—mistake #3—and died at once.

The first robber then got up and finished emptying the register. Sirens screamed in the distance. The two robbers hurried out to the Camaro, both herding me with their guns. My ears still rang from the shotgun blast. They called me "baby faced cop" as I looked young for my age, and told me to go with them or they'd shoot me on the spot. After what they did to Karl, I knew they meant it. They chose to take me hostage as a bargaining chip. We had fucked up big time by not checking the back of the store and the bathroom.

"Mr. Shotgun" got behind the steering wheel, and his fellow asshole got in the back seat with me. He pulled a long, sharp hunting knife from his belt and held it close to the right side of my neck. This crazy licked his lips, and I knew he was eager to stick me. Fun time for him. The driver floored the gas pedal, and the hot Camaro took off like a shot, tires screeching, rubber smoking.

Where was our backup?

I realized the stew I was in and became more scared than I had ever been before. I knew they would kill me, once they got away and no longer needed a hostage. I could I.D. them, and the penalty for killing two cops was the same as for killing one. They had nothing to lose.

I broke into a cold sweat, and my stomach jumped up into my chest. Strange things crossed my mind. I realized I would never meet the woman I might have married and never get to know the children I might have fathered. Nor would I ever get the opportunity to reconcile with Pop.

Where's the backup?

The driver sped east over the San Francisco-Oakland Bay Bridge, smashing the tollgate. He crossed over to Highway 24, heading toward Lafayette. He made the mistake of picking up a California Highway Patrol car; I guessed he thought he could outrun it. He gunned the engine and drove like a mad man. He ran the red lights in Orinda and passed cars on the right as well as the left. Sheriff's and police cars pulled in behind us.

I told myself, "So you'll get killed in a car wreck instead of being shot. Great."

"Mr. Shotgun" changed his strategy.

He told his partner, "Take the cop's radio and tell the dispatcher we have taken patrolman #4930, or whatever the hell his number is, as a hostage, and we'll kill him if everybody doesn't stop tailing us."

The second banana did as he was told. The dispatcher, to my enormous disappointment, acquiesced, and the patrol cars backed off. What the hell, I knew these guys would kill me anyway.

The driver relaxed and slowed down to only ninety. His partner placed the knife back next to my neck.

I couldn't have known the highway patrol had set a trap, but it didn't surprise me. We climbed a good-sized hill on the highway about forty-five miles east of San Francisco.

As our car reached the top of the hill, the driver shouted, "Oh shit, there's a roadblock at the bottom of the hill!"

We saw a row of four patrol cars parked end-to-end all across the highway and the shoulder, too. Three patrolmen stood next to two sawhorses set up as a checkpoint. The same space existed between two patrol cars parked just behind them. Two more sheriff's vehicles pulled in behind us, creating a box and keeping the driver from turning around.

The driver stomped the gas again, throwing us backwards and causing the hunting knife to nick my neck just below my right ear. He pushed the hot Camaro to over 100. He aimed to go through the gap.

He hit the sawhorse on the right, shattering it to pieces and flinging chips and splinters high above the cars.

I knew I was finished. I didn't even notice the blood from the knife wound dripping down my shirt.

The Camaro flew up in the air, crash landed on the highway shoulder, and rolled over three times, coming to rest upside down.

Somehow, I was thrown clear. I landed hard on the highway, breaking my right arm and scraping some skin off the side of my right leg. Both robbers died in the crash. But I came through it alive!

I somehow survived that first instance when I experienced total terror. Fortune had smiled on me that time, too.

CHAPTER 16

RACHEL TOOK ME IN HER VOLVO TO THE auto repair shop to pick up my wounded truck. My mechanic confirmed my suspicion that someone had sabotaged the brakes.

He reported, "I found the brake linings undamaged, so I checked further. They poked a small hole in your brake fluid tank, causing the fluid to leak out. This mischief was much more difficult to locate than if they had simply damaged the brake lining."

He raised his voice to override the noise of the other mechanics working inside. We paused outside the mechanic's office. I gave him a check.

I told Rachel, "It's hard to believe the environmental dispute had anything to do with Warren Roberts' murder or Danny Boy's death or sabotaging my truck. California has a reputation as a hotbed of environmental activity, and activists have targeted the wine industry for years, but killing an engineer or me seems a little extreme."

"Most winery owners, on the other hand, only cooperate with each other on a sporadic basis. And their lobbying never includes violence. The two sides have argued about growth and pollution, perceived or actual, on and off for decades," Rachel said.

We sat down on a nearby bench, not yet ready to go our separate ways.

"I recall Pop telling me how growers and wineries complained in 1973. The supervisors voted to limit the size of new vineyard lots to a minimum of forty acres in the hills watershed. This was meant to eliminate the numerous small vineyards, slow down the growth of wine production and keep the streams from silting up more in Napa. But no one reported any incidents of intimidation that time."

She turned around to face me.

"But someone threatened me and tried to bribe Judy Harris, both of us members of the board of supervisors. Maybe there's a connection with the proposed ordinance, maybe not. Keep Napa Green has proposed a moratorium on new wineries and on the expansion of existing ones. Napa Valley Vintners Association opposes the moratorium. Most of the wineries in Napa Valley belong to the vintners group. Go see Paul Martin and find out what he knows."

We got up from the bench, and I kissed her goodbye. I noticed purple storm clouds rolling in over the Mayacamas Mountains.

I got in my truck and called Buddy on the cell phone. "Hey, Buddy. I got my truck back, so I'm headed for Paul Martin's. I know nothing about Keep Napa Green. See if they have local leaders, look at their reputation around town, and find out if the police or FBI knows anything about them. Mr. Martin runs Napa Valley Vintners Association, and, after I meet with him, you and I will compare notes and decide how to approach KNG."

I watched the first fat raindrops make muddy streaks on the windshield. I reviewed what I knew about NVVA.

Early leaders of the Napa Valley wine industry, like John Daniel and Louis Martini, organized NVVA before World War II. Perhaps "disorganized" would be a better word. Winemakers love their independence but gather together as a united force only when faced with some emergency. Paul Martin runs the organization these days—the only individual respected enough by the various factions. Mr. Martin keeps them united the best he can, raising money for friendly candidates, lobbying in Sacramento, and mediating disputes. He cajoles members to donate funds and to present a united front on most issues.

I turned on the windshield wipers and listened to the steady rhythm.

Paul Martin also maintained a tenuous relationship with the grape growers and their organization. Wine grape growers find themselves in a schizophrenic relationship with wineries. Growers need wineries to buy their product, but each views prices from its own perspective. Growers want limited production and high prices; wineries want more grapes at lower prices.

The growers held Paul Martin in high regard despite their differences of opinion.

I had called him "Mr. Paul" since I my childhood when Pop sold grapes to Martin Brothers Winery. Pop and Mr. Paul were friends in the old days and negotiated—or argued—every year about the price of the grapes. It always seemed to me like good-natured bantering, usually over a bottle or two of wine. One year they couldn't agree on a price—two proud men refusing to compromise. Neither spoke to the other for all those years after. Both men missed the fellowship.

Mr. Paul seemed glad to see me. He ran NVVA from an old white, frame, Victorian house in downtown Napa on Jefferson Street. He and his wife had moved there after he retired from the winery.

"Young Ventura, what brings you to the lion's den? Heard you'd returned to Napa, but I haven't seen you around town since you came home. How about a cup?"

He looked pretty much as always, except his snow-white mustache now matched his short curly haircut. He had the same alert dark brown eyes and smooth, tanned, olive skin—not a wrinkle in sight. A small man, muscular for someone in his seventies, he had answered the door with a black coffee mug in his left hand.

"Black, please. I've stayed pretty busy at the farm getting the place back into shape, so I haven't socialized much. Poor Pop had a hard time working that last year when he was sick."

The inside of the house retained its Victorian character. They had polished the hardwood floors to a gleaming finish and laid down quality Oriental rugs. Over-stuffed chairs invited one to sit and stay awhile.

I followed him from the entryway down the hall to his office, which had once been a bedroom. He poured me a cup of coffee from a shiny chrome thermos, and we both sat in matching armchairs upholstered in burgundy leather so old it had begun to crack.

"I always thought you would come back and take over the Zinfandel fields," he said. "I knew your brother Robert hated farming, but you seemed born to it. Your dad grew some of the best Zinfandel grapes in the state."

"It took many years for me to realize I liked to grow grapes. I have no regrets about my years with SFPD; I liked being a cop until I got shot. It seemed natural for me to come back home after I recovered."

"Does your arm feel any better?" he asked.

"I suppose it's a little stronger now than it was at first. It's fortunate I'm right-handed. I've pretty much gotten used to the limitations of a bum left arm."

"Such a tragedy about your wife and child. I'm so very sorry."

"Thank you, Mr. Paul."

"Now, what brings you to see me today?" he asked.

"I'm doing a little private detective work, Mr. Paul. The police suspect Fran Roberts, an old friend from high school days, of her husband's murder. She's Jack Phillips' daughter. His attorney hired me to investigate. Seems a county supervisor retained the victim for an engineering study about the proposed moratorium. We're checking to see if that had anything to do with his death."

"I read about the case in the paper. I can't imagine a connection," he said, "The growth issue has gone on for almost forty years, and we've never had any real violence. Some fanatics have vandalized wineries in other parts of the state, but not here, and no one has ever been hurt. They put sand once in the gas tank of an irrigation pump down near Santa Barbara. Many of our guys feel environmentalists have targeted our industry without justification. Some growers have been experimenting for years with organic farm methods, searching for ways to control pests and plant disease without depending on chemicals. Most vintners and growers live on the land they work and value it."

"Have you noticed any more emotion this time than in past efforts to control vineyard development?" I asked.

"The Napa economy depends on the wine industry, but some folks have always tried to hold us back, sometimes organized and sometimes not. We always manage to meet somewhere in the middle, but this time an outside agitator came in to excite trouble. She's the one behind the ordinance."

"Who are you talking about?"

"Sky Leonard. She doesn't know shit about our business. She worries about soil erosion, but hell, our future depends on protecting the soil. And what about our grandchildren? We can't plant vines today and harvest grapes tomorrow if we deplete the soil. We've spent millions at U Cal/Davis on research and have reduced soil erosion by two-thirds in the last ten years— you can check that out with the county. And we damn sure don't want to pollute our water. We all live here. What do they think we are—dummies? We don't need an ordinance to tell us what needs to be done."

I recognized the sweet smell of onions frying and heard an oven door closing. Mrs. Martin's perfect grandmother's face appeared in the door of the office and invited me to stay for lunch.

"Good to see you again, Mrs. Martin. It smells delicious, but I need to leave soon to get back to the farm."

She returned to her kitchen.

Mr. Paul continued, "Some of our guys make a lot of noise, but none of them are stupid enough to break the law. But she stirs up folks pretty well. It wouldn't surprise me if Sky Leonard bends the rules. Have you talked to her?"

"Not yet. I don't know her. Can you tell me something about KNG?" I asked.

Paul Martin took a sip from his coffee cup and thought for a long moment.

"I first heard the name Keep Napa Green a couple of years ago. We had small groups in the past with different agendas, but all of them worried that wineries were growing too fast. Some objected to increased traffic by tourists, others believed the Napa River was dying, wildlife folks thought we were driving the critters away when we cleared woods for farming. They all wanted things to stay the same. They didn't understand that we sat on one of the only two or three spots in the world where the best wine grapes could grow."

Mr. Paul pulled the cord to turn on the reading lamp between our two chairs. Raindrops fell from the dark clouds and pinged against the windows.

"Anyway, some of the local groups got together and contacted a national environmental association."

"What happened then?"

"They got them to send down a hired gun to organize all the opposition under one umbrella. They called it Keep Napa

Green. That's where Sky Leonard came in. What kind of name is that anyway—Sky?"

"Do you know where KNG gets its money?" I asked.

"I've looked into that some. The growers made donations, and those folks I mentioned held a chili cookoff fund-raiser. They get most of their funding from the Living Institute for the Environment, or LIFE. They wrote the so-called "research report"—total bullshit, by the way. You ought to talk to Casey Hammon, a reporter from Sacramento. He's doing research for a series of articles about the radical environmental movement."

'Thanks, I might do that. Would you poke around meanwhile and see if you hear of any winery guys taking matters into their own hands?"

"Gene, I miss your old man. That friendship lasted 40 years, even though we argued some. It was stupid to let one silly argument ruin that."

He gave me a warm handshake—the kind with two hands—and asked me to keep him informed of our progress.

I heard the cell phone ringing when I got back to my truck. The caller's muffled voice sounded like it came from the bottom of a deep well.

"I watched you come down the mountain," he said. "Go back to your grapes. Stop sticking your nose where it don't belong. I won't fail next time."

CHAPTER 17

THE NEXT DAY GOT OFF TO A BAD START. The sky looked milky gray. The wind blew a cold fine mist from the Pacific. My left shoulder hurt like hell, like a vise gripped it and kept squeezing. The artificial device works fine most of the time, but I feel it when the weather turns cold and damp. Spring can't come too soon for me. I wanted to stay in bed but I had an appointment with Sky Bennett. Buddy agreed to meet me first for breakfast to fill me in on KNG.

Buddy met me at Mrs. McDonald's Home Cooking on Solano Avenue just off Highway 29. It was a block from the Marriott Convention Center in north Napa. Mrs. McDonald's opened in 1987 and became an institution. Hungry regulars ate breakfast at all hours, ordering from a gigantic menu of fifty-two breakfast items. They moved to her present location when the first place became too small. The new free-standing restaurant featured a wine grape theme. Grapevines adorned the border high up the walls. Clear covers protected white tablecloths decorated with grape clusters and grapevines festooned the entryway.

Buddy loved Mother's biscuits and had had breakfast there daily at seven o'clock ever since she opened.

We walked in the door. The pleasant middle-aged hostess greeted Buddy with a radiant smile.

"Hey sweetheart, you look fine this morning."

"This morning and every morning. How was your date last night, Midge?"

"Ha! Some date. The old man's fallen asleep in front of the TV at 9:00 for thirty years."

We followed her to Buddy's regular table near the window. Sam Painter, who owned the hardware store in the next block, patted Buddy on the shoulder.

"Good morning, you old fart," Sam said. " She couldn't keep you in bed after the roosters crowed?"

"No, I wore her out last night."

Sam laughed and gave Buddy a high five.

Just before we got to our seats, Buddy stopped to speak to a tired-looking young woman with two kids. He bent down close to her and, in a soft voice, asked how they were doing. She said they were getting by. I notice he picked up their breakfast check.

We sat down, and a cute young waitress jiggled over to our table. Buddy reached out and put his arm around her waist.

"Where are we going tonight, honey bunch?"

"What's this 'we' business? My boyfriend's Ferrari only has two seats."

Buddy laughed. She put down a platter piled high with biscuits.

"You're not going to eat all of those by yourself, are you?" I asked.

"Hell, yes. Get your own."

Buddy removed a document from the inside pocket of this coat.

"I've received a report from my pal in Sacramento," Buddy said. "I found Sky was born in Marin County, California, in1963 to a Zina Leonard. The birth certificate listed no father. Keep Napa Green first registered with the State in

1995 as a non-profit organization, listing Sky Leonard as executive director. My friend thinks KNG is affiliated with an international organization operating out of Canada—Save Air, Nature, Earth, or SANE."

"My God, first there's LIFE and now SANE. I wonder if they have a vice president in charge of acronyms," I remarked.

"I've asked my contact in Washington to run down information on Sky Leonard and SANE and LIFE," he said.

I wished I knew more about the organization than I did but I felt it necessary to talk to Sky Leonard ASAP. I wanted to explore the possibility of any connection to either Warren's murder or the threat to Rachel or both.

Keep Napa Green operated out of a circa 1940's, two-story, white, frame house near an old section of downtown Napa. Surprise—they'd painted the shutters the color of fresh spring grass. The old house was built close to the street, and the front yard consisted of only a narrow bed planted with herbs and native plants. I found the door open. I knocked twice and entered the house. I found a large meeting room with perhaps fifty folding chairs and a podium and blackboard at the far end of the room. You could tell they'd remodeled and removed the wall that once separated the living room from a dining room. Two open doors at the back of the meeting room led to a small office on the left and a refurbished kitchen on the right. Sky Leonard came out of the office to greet me.

"My name is Gene Ventura, Ms. Leonard. We're investigating the death of Warren Roberts and have discovered a connection between him and the moratorium proposal that Keep Napa Green advocates."

I gave her one of the private eye business cards Buddy had printed for us. I noticed the faint smell of perfume.

Her appearance startled me. The description from the old fairy tale "Snow White and the Seven Dwarfs" surfaced from the deep recesses of my memory: "her lips rose red, her hair like night, her skin like snow." She stood five-foot-five or so with hair the color of ebony. The ends turned up well before reaching her shoulders. Soft milk-white skin, red lips, and a matching hair ribbon all contrasted with the black hair.

Her costume suggested naiveté. She wore an ankle-length outfit, a yellow skirt and a blue top buttoned from the waist all the way to her throat. Puffy short sleeves had alternating red and blue panels. Gold slippers adorned her feet, completing the Snow White image. Modesty personified. Her costume could have come off the rack in seventeenth century Merrie Old England. I found the get-up sexy for some reason. I suspected other men did, also. She led me back to her private office.

"I've never met anyone named Sky before. It's a beautiful name. How did your parents come up with something so unusual?

She fluttered her onyx eyes at me.

"What can I say? I was a child of the 60's. My folks lived in a hippie commune in northern California when I was born. It was quite the thing in those days, naming kids Star, Earth, Sunshine, etc. Everyone thought Sky was a nickname when I attended Northwestern."

She spoke with a soft, melodic voice and had huge black eyes that seemed to hang on my every word. I thought the sincerity act just a tad overdone.

"What does Keep Napa Green do?" I asked.

"Our mission is to protect and preserve the air and the earth and the wildlife. We envision a pollution-free world with trees left to grow, streams and rivers pristine, and animals free to roam."

"What has KNG done to influence the board's vote on the moratorium proposal?" I asked.

Sky said in a sweet voice, "Why like any other caring, non-profit organization, we just tried to show the county supervisors how important it is to stop ruining the Napa River. And where will the birds and animals live if all the land is cleared and there are no more woods for them to live in?"

"Just how did you go about showing them the light?"

"We asked a group of distinguished scientists to come here and evaluate the environmental damage first of all. Their research report showed a definite need for a moratorium." Her voice was so soft I almost couldn't hear her.

"I assume you gave a copy of the report to each of the five supervisors. What else did you do to convince them?"

"We held a chili cook-off and invited them so we could show the strength of the community support for the measure. Our members also called on each of the supervisors a time or two."

"I understand you raised money at the cook-off. Was that where you got your funding to pay for the report?"

The sugary sweetness began to dissolve. "What does that have to do with your investigation?" she asked in a voice that began to rise.

I changed the subject. "Did you know that a civil engineer, Warren Roberts, did independent research on the moratorium issue for one of the county supervisors?"

"No. That shouldn't have been necessary. We had already furnished the board with extensive expert material," Sky Leonard said.

"It seems that one of the board members wanted findings from a disinterested source," I said.

"Well, I can't see what any of this has to do with Mr. Roberts' death. None of us knew him or even met the man."

"I didn't imply that you did," I said in a cool voice.

Sky Leonard had told me what she wanted me to hear. And what about that goody, goody, two-shoes-act? I suspected there was an iron will behind that sweet façade. And Northwestern came up again—what a coincidence. The victim, his wife, his partner, and now Sky Leonard all had attended college in

Evanston. Sky must have gone there at a different time than the others since she was at least ten years younger, but I asked myself again about a connection.

I asked as I got up to leave, "By the way, Ms. Leonard, do you have any men working with you or KNG members around six-foot-five or taller? (No one shorter could wear a size 16-EEE shoe.)

"What a strange question, Mr. Ventura. I don't think we have anyone fitting that description."

CHAPTER 18

"I THOUGHT YOU OUGHT TO KNOW, GENE. It looks bad for your client. We have located a witness who saw a woman leaving the alley the night of Warren Roberts' murder. It was too dark to ID her, but the witness said she wore a long dress," my friend Mike Edwards, the Napa police chief, said on the phone.

A motive, locating the gun, and now finding a witness who saw a woman at the scene created a triple whammy against Fran. The circumstantial evidence continued to pile up. I wanted to tell Franklin about the witness in person and update him on our investigation, so I called him. He said he could see me right away.

I asked Buddy to come with me for a show of strength. I honked in front of Buddy's house. Who was that man walking toward the truck? I almost didn't recognize him. He wore a dark western-cut suit, a white starched shirt with a bolo tie, and a XXX gray Stetson hat.

Franklin had anticipated our arrival by making a fresh pot of coffee and ushered us into his private office. He already knew about the witness. Not a happy camper. I noticed a new twitch below his left eye.

"One of the secretaries in the DA's office called me. She told me they'd found a witness who saw an unidentified woman coming out of the alley about the same time as the murder. But my contact didn't know how much the witness saw."

"That detective John Lawrence will try to squeeze Fran some more," Buddy said.

A cloud of gloom hung over Franklin's office. At least the coffee smelled good and strong. Franklin filled our cups.

"I know, but Fran will come through OK," Franklin replied. "She's won't crack. Any other developments?"

"One of the county supervisors hired Warren to research the effects of the proposed winery moratorium," I said.

"Emotions are running pretty high on both sides of the issue. Maybe someone believed Roberts' report could hurt their cause," said Buddy.

"I met with Paul Martin at NVVA—I'm sure you know him. And I went to see Sky Leonard, who heads Keep Napa Green. She proposed the moratorium. Martin said the proposal has created heated discussions on both sides. If his report made strong recommendations, maybe someone wanted to silence him," I said.

"That's a reach, but I guess you need to follow it up," Franklin said. "Jack told me about your meeting with him. I'm glad you behaved yourself. You impressed him. He said you turned out OK after all. It's been three weeks now since you were hired. What else can I tell him?"

"Well, we found Warren's girlfriend. You decide whether to tell Jack now or not. I'm convinced she had nothing to do with Warren's murder. His death tore her up. She believed Warren and Fran would get a divorce and that she and Warren would ride away into the sunset together," I said.

"Who is she? How did you find her?" Franklin asked with excitement. He rose from his chair.

"Buddy found her by tracking telephone calls Warren made over the past six months. Her name is Carol Greene. She's an architect. Nice lady. She and Warren met while working together on a project the end of last summer. He told her that he and Fran planned to get a divorce. Of course, that could have just been a line."

"Are you certain there's no connection between the murder and the girlfriend?" Franklin asked.

Buddy responded, "We checked her out every which way—her background, her reputation, even other men who might have been jealous. She's squeaky clean."

I said, "Carol Greene is sort of attractive in a wholesome kind of way but not at all glamorous. It's almost as if Warren were her first boyfriend."

"Don't count her out yet. Double check to see if she at least had a motive, like maybe getting dumped by him, and got mad. I have to tell Jack that you found the girlfriend. Any work-related matters that could have gotten him killed? Like kickbacks with inspectors or fraud or whatever?" Franklin asked.

"I talked to Warren's clients and the people he worked with from the Building Permit Office. Warren maintained a professional image. Everyone said he did everything by the book; no one seemed to dislike him," Buddy replied.

"Warren's partner, Vic O'Connell, remains a big question. He didn't seem grief-stricken over his partner's death. I got the impression he thought he made a greater contribution to the partnership than Warren did since he brought in the jobs and thereby generated the income. Warren did the nitty-gritty and saw to it that the work got finished," I said.

"Do you think he would have killed Warren for that? Why not just buy him out?" Franklin asked.

"I don't have an answer to that question yet," I said. "Maybe he didn't have the money. I got the impression that Warren may not have had any interest in selling. He loved his work. I asked O'Connell where he was the evening of the murder, and he got pissed and walked away," I said.

"Wonder if he had an alibi? Anything more?" Franklin inquired.

Lightning and thunder rattled the windows. I know February rain makes the grapes better, but I could have used a break from these storms.

"I'd like to spend some of your expense money, Franklin, and make a trip to Northwestern University in Chicago. Warren and Fran, Victor O'Connell and now Sky Leonard all attended Northwestern. I want to see about any history there that could have a bearing on our case. It will only take a couple of days. I'll go on the cheap, fly coach, stay at Motel 6, and even take all of my meals at Burger King."

"You're running the investigation. If you think it's important, go ahead. My secretary will get you a plane ticket with an open return. She'll book a rent car and get you a hotel reservation in Evanston. Not many Motel 6's in Evanston."

Franklin ushered us out of his office. I took Buddy home and drove back to the farm to help Ernesto build trellises.

Franklin Reed had frowned about the witness the police had found, but otherwise seemed pleased with our report. Now he could tell Jack Phillips we'd located others who might have had reason to kill his son-in-law. And finding the girlfriend answered the question of why Warren Roberts visited that address that night. Now if we could only find who did it. But we all recognized that the DA might already have enough evidence to indict Fran.

CHAPTER 19

I AWAKENED AROUSED THE MORNING I WAS TO LEAVE for Evanston. No great surprise as I found my right hand cupped around Rachel's breast. I recalled when I had my final thorough physical exam after recovering from the shooting. The internist asked if I woke up in the mornings with an erection. Surprised, I asked, 'How did you know?' He replied that it happened to most men my age—and his.

Back to the matter at hand, no pun intended. I tapped Rachel on the shoulder to determine her interest. No response other than the rhythmic rise and fall of her chest. Undeterred, I lifted her soft, silky nightgown to just under her chin. I started kissing her shoulders and arms in a gentle way and worked my way over to her breasts. She smelled of lilacs. Then she awakened. She purred, and, in just a whisper, said, "C'est si bon—it feels so good when you touch me that way." She pulled my head up so she could kiss me. Her warm tongue parted my lips.

I then resumed my body kissing, taking each breast into my mouth until the nipples glistened and stood erect. Only fair that I shouldn't be the sole person with parts in that position. I let my lips travel downward. She sighed and called my name. I stopped my kissing as her hips started moving and I felt her excitement. I lifted her night-gown over her head.

I pressed my body tight against hers. We remained still, holding each other. She started to move. I raised myself and stayed motionless, allowing her more latitude. Then we began moving in unison and came together in a wild crescendo.

She shuddered, and, after catching her breath, said, "C`'etait magnifique, cheri. If this is how you leave me when you go out of town, you need to make more trips. It was wonderful. I love you, Gene."

"Me, too. I'm sorry you are in danger, but I sure like having you around every day—and night," I said.

"Maybe if this nightmare ever ends . . . . .," she started to say.

"It will be over soon. I won't let anything happen to you," I promised.

I remembered that I promised the same thing four years ago before they killed Alex and the baby.

We clung to each other and dozed for a while. The alarm went off, and we showered together, soaping each other's back. We made our way to the kitchen.

My plane didn't leave until early afternoon, and Rachel had no appointments that morning, so we cooked breakfast together, making a vegetable fritatta. I sautéed onions, mushrooms, and strips of poblano peppers. Rachel cut very thin slices of buffalo mozza-rella and warmed a baguette. I added four eggs whisked with a few tablespoons of cream when I had finished with the veggies. I cooked the eggs until just set on the bottom of the skillet. Rachel topped the egg/vegetable mixture with the cheese slices and placed the iron skillet under the broiler for two minutes until the eggs were firm and the cheese had melted. The first bite burned my tongue. We had just finished our second cups of café au lait when the telephone pulled us out of our reverie.

A distraught Fran Roberts spoke on the other end of the line.

"Gene, the ballistics report confirmed the shots that killed Warren came from the .25 caliber pistol Warren brought from Chicago to California."

"I'm sorry," I replied. What else could I say?

"The police picked me up yesterday afternoon for questioning and kept me at the police station until after nine o'clock when they allowed Franklin to take me home," Fran said. "They kept asking me where I was the night Warren was killed and when I last saw Warren's pistol. And I told them over and over that I waited at home for Warren and that I don't remember the last time I saw the damn gun because I thought it was still in the closet," Fran said.

"Just because that gun killed Warren doesn't mean you did it. I know the lab found no fingerprints. They have no proof," I replied.

"That's what Franklin told me. But that damn fat detective John Lawrence kept accusing me because he said he knew Warren and I didn't get along. I'm exhausted. Please help me, Gene."

Detective Lawrence had neglected to tell Fran about the witness who saw a woman coming out of the alley after Roberts was killed. He'd chosen to save that tidbit for the bombshell he would drop on her the next time he grilled her.

"The search goes on for other possible motives, and we have a lead or two, Fran. Just hang in there, do what Franklin says, and don't let the bastards get you down. Buddy and I will work around the clock to find the killer. Buddy's on his way over here now," I said, trying to reassure her as I hung up.

The sky finally cleared, and bright sun warmed the valley.

Buddy came to pick me up in his Corvette to take me to the airport in San Francisco. He waved at Rachel standing on the front porch. She waved back and blew me a kiss. I scrunched into the passenger seat, and Buddy took off. The drive gave us a chance to compare notes and to determine where to go next with the investigation.

As soon as we got on the highway, Buddy started telling me about the report he had received from Washington. It concerned Sky Leonard and Keep Napa Green.

"The size of the file the FBI has accumulated on the group amazed me. Sky's employer, Save Air, Nature, Earth (SANE), has the dubious honor of making the bureau's 'watch list' of eco-terrorists. These are militant folks who commit illegal violent acts in the name of environmentalism," Buddy said.

"What else?" I asked. "And can you speak up? I can't hear you over the roar of your fancy engine."

"Remember, I told you her parents had her on a commune where they lived in Marin County? The birth certificate only listed a mother, Zina Leonard."

"Does Washington know anything about a father?" I asked.

"Her father's name was Samuel Leonard. Her parents moved to Chicago in 1967. Both parents taught in the school system and became organizers for the local teachers union. They participated in politics and voiced loud opposition for Democratic Mayor Daly as not liberal enough for their taste," Buddy said.

"What happened to her parents?"

"Samuel Leonard suffered permanent disability from breathing tear gas in the anti-Vietnam rally at the 1968 Democratic National Convention in Chicago. They arrested him, and he spent several weeks at County General. He died in 1980 of lung disease at the ripe old age of 42. Sky's mother still lives in Chicago and teaches school," Buddy said.

I felt confined in the Corvette. I pushed the seat all the way back.

"What else do we know about Sky?" I asked.

"Not much until college. She earned an academic scholarship to Northwestern and took active part in campus socialist activities. Sky spent a year after leaving school training at SANE headquarters outside Toronto, and then they assigned her to do field work organizing environmental activist groups. She worked in Boulder, Falls Church, and Austin before coming to Napa. They incorporated under a different local name in each community, like 'Keep Napa Green."

"What did the report say about her activities in those cities?" I asked.

"Typical stuff," Buddy said. "They stirred up their followers, raised money, and got involved in local politics, advocating environmental measures. That's all legal. Problems arose when they did mischief to promote their causes, like sabotaging equipment used to cut down trees or threatening some poor farmer."

"Has Sky ever been convicted?"

"She's been suspected a number of times, but they've never pinned her down. She has no police record, but everywhere she goes trouble ensues. It seems the crimes have become more serious with each succeeding new assignment. The threats and activities so far have been only against property, but the FBI has expressed concerned. They believe she's such a zealot, and perhaps somewhat deranged, that she might hurt someone."

Spring comes early to northern California. We saw wild almond trees just beginning to sprout their white blossoms as we sped south on Highway 29.

"Sky puts on a good act. You'd never think her capable of violence when you meet her. What does the FBI know about SANE?" I asked.

"It's an umbrella organization of a bunch of quasi-environmental groups that have different agendas. Some advocate cleaner air and water, others want to protect animals or forests, and global warming's now a hot button, too—all admirable objectives. The FBI is only concerned about harm to people and property, illegal methods used in pursuing these goals, and the potential for illegal conspiracy."

"What else have they learned?"

"Well, for instance, their research company is a phony. They call it LIFE, Living Institute For Environmentalism. Some concerned scientists believe they should go to any lengths to save the world, such as fabricating alarming research and signing fraudulent reports. Some of the so-called 'scientists' signing the reports have credentials that can't be verified. The bureau has a file of fictitious reports LIFE has submitted to support local political efforts where they have operatives. They have a 'No Oxygen For Our Children Due To Lumber Industry' and 'U.S. Running Out Of H2O.' They particularly like cancer scares, such as 'Skin Cancer Epidemic Proven Tied To Auto Emissions.' My friend at the FBI assured me they must have created research masquerading as fact when I told him about LIFE's scientific report supporting the Napa moratorium."

We crested a hill. The city sparkled like a bowl of jewels against the navy blue backdrop of the Pacific. This view still gives me wonderful goose bumps, even after all these years.

"This is a bit out of my area, but aren't phony research reports against the law?" I asked.

"I asked the same question. If such a report causes a crime to be committed, those responsible can be held for conspiracy. But this is a gray area, and bogus research is hard to prove. The other problem is that LIFE maneuvers out of Canada even though most of their activities take place in American communities, so authorities can only go after local groups."

"Pretty damning stuff, but I'm not certain how it could tie into Warren Roberts' murder. KNG may have a motive to threaten Rachel or to bribe Judy to get them to vote their way. You and I will have to keep our eyes on Sky Leonard when I return from Chicago," I said.

Buddy pulled up at the United terminal. I grabbed my bags and stuck my head in the car window to thank him. He said he planned next to go meet with the police in both Oakland and Berkley. He wanted to check their DNA files to see if he could find a match with the blood found at Rachel's house. Any guy sick enough to kill Danny Boy could have killed Warren Roberts, too.

"Maybe you'll turn over a rock in Chicago and find something we can use."

I straightened up as Buddy drove off. I wondered again if any of the puzzle pieces would ever fall into place.

CHAPTER 20

I SAT ON THE PLANE NEXT TO A MOTHER WITH a year-old son who lived in Sausalito. We chatted a bit after take-off. She told me her parents had sent her a ticket to Chicago so they could meet their grandson. The child kept reaching for me and giggling.

She asked me at one point, "The baby likes you. Will you hold him while I go to the galley to have the flight attendant warm a bottle of milk?"

I enjoyed the cooing sounds the baby made while sitting on my lap.

The memory of Alexandra and my unborn child flooded back and I felt a wave of powerful emotions. Had I missed out by not ever having children? Did I stay single all those years after because I thought a family would hold me back in my quest to become a captain at SFPD? Maybe I'm not too old. I fantasized about having a child with Rachel. Maybe there was still time.

The mother returned with the baby bottle. She took the child back.

"Do you have any children?" she asked.

"I said, "No.""

I soon saw that both the mother and son were sleeping. I took a paperback out of my briefcase.

I drank two of those funny little bottles of Dewar's Scotch over four hours, ate six miniscule bags of over-salted peanuts, and passed on the typical airline fare. It always reminded me of the Swanson's TV dinners that they advertised on TV when I was a kid. We were taxiing on the O'Hare runway by the time I got through half of James Patterson's book, "Cat & Mouse".

"This is the pilot speaking. We flew over the storm, but get ready for cold weather, folks. The temperature here is 12 degrees with a wind chill factor of minus ten."

A new cold front had blown into the Windy City that day. The cold, damp wind blowing off Lake Michigan hit me in the face like a stinging right cross as soon as I left the terminal. I felt my nose and lips numbing. I asked myself if this trip to Evanston was as necessary as I had thought. But I warmed up in the overheated car rental lobby.

"To Evanston is easy, Mr. Ventura," the Avis man said. "Just follow 190 to the Northwestern University sign."

I followed Interstate 190 to Evanston without getting lost once. Northwestern University sprawls on the shore of Lake Michigan, accessed by Hinman Avenue. I planned to start at the Northwestern Police Department and go from there. One of my old FBI contacts in San Francisco who helped us on the Ludlow case now operated as a Special Agent assigned to the Chicago office. He had asked the head of the campus police as a favor to help me get access to otherwise confidential student records. I met with a Sergeant Nelson on campus.

"You must be special, Mr. Ventura. We don't get many requests for cooperation from the FBI."

"Not special. I just worked with Cyrus as a cop in San Francisco. Please call me Gene."

He offered me a welcome cup of coffee and a doughnut, the universal policeman's coffee break.

"I'm working on a murder case in California, and several
of the people involved, including the victim and perhaps a suspect or two, attended Northwestern. I need to know more about
them," I said.

"Go over to the Rebecca Crown Center where all student
records are kept. I'll call and introduce you. You'll get to see
whatever you want."

The doughnut tasted damn good. Must be Krispy Kreme.

"Thanks. That'll be a big help," I said.

"I can pull up any police records for you from here on campus or from Evanston and Chicago PD. And I suggest you look
at the old yearbooks from the appropriate years at the University Library. Surprising what you can learn from them," Sergeant Nelson said.

"I'll do that. I'll appreciate those police records, too. Here
are the names: Warren Roberts, Fran Phillips, Victor O'Connell,
and Sky Leonard."

"Is Sky a nickname?" he asked as he wrote the names down.

"Nope. Sky's her real given name."

I hurried across campus so I would have some time with
the student records before closing time. I passed the famous
purple quartz boulder know as The Rock. My guidebook described it as a former water fountain donated to Northwestern
by the Class of 1902. Students traditionally painted the rock
with slogans promoting campus organizations or events.

I smiled at "Stop Genetically Altered Corn Rally". What
happened to plain old "Save The Whales"?

The Rebecca Crown Center consisted of three administra-
tive buildings on a broad elevated plaza with a tall clock tower
in the center. The sergeant had told me to use the clock tower
as a landmark and that the clock face turned purple when the

football team won a game. The poor fellow turning on the purple lights hadn't had much to do until the last few years.

I stayed at the administration office reviewing the student files until they kicked me out at closing time.

The comely young woman joked, "Sorry, sir. We have to close. You must either leave or spend the night."

Streetlights cast their soft glow overhead as I left the building, but my watch said only five o'clock. It gets dark early in Chicago in late February. As I walked through the campus to find where I had parked the rent car. I heard a lot of noise in the distance, close to the lake, shouting and whistling and clapping. I veered off to see what the commotion was about.

The sign on the front of the clamorous auditorium said "Picks-Staiger Concert Hall". The building seemed to shake because of the enormous hullabaloo. I looked inside and walked in without needing to present a ticket. The crowd packed the hall like sardines in a can. Some even stood in the aisles. I guessed most of the people were students, men and women in their twenties and thirties.

I heard them chant, over and over, "AFFIRMATIVE YES! PENA NO!"

A woman in a yellow dress rang a cowbell at the end of each chant. I saw at least four hand-painted signs proclaiming, "PENA GO HOME!"

A middle-aged man holding a wireless microphone in one hand on stage peered out at the crowd from behind a podium. A Latino man of medium build, he wore his black hair long and frosty around the edges. He sported a salt and pepper mustache. Mr. Pena wore a gray flannel suit with a light blue shirt and a maroon paisley wool tie. Two older white men stood on either side of him. The speaker attempted to address the crowd, but they shouted him down.

I thought I got a whiff of body odor from the multitude.

I observed several campus policemen scattered about the auditorium and I saw Sergeant Nelson in the aisle in front of me. I tapped him on the shoulder to ask what was going on and had to yell. Nelson motioned me to follow him outside the auditorium.

"They don't want him to be heard," Nelson said.

"Who don't they want to be heard and why not?" I asked.

"The speaker is that regent from the University of California who's against affirmative action. The campus speaker's bureau invited him to speak. The crowd doesn't like his viewpoint, so they shout him down. They don't want to let him speak."

"And who are the two guys standing next to him?" I asked.

"The president of the university and the provost. They asked the audience to hear Pena out and then ask questions, but this crowd refused."

They screamed even louder, hurting my ears. They jumped up and down on their seats and spilled over into the aisles.

"They already know his opinion, and they don't want to hear any explanation or facts. I just hope it doesn't get ugly," Nelson said.

"I don't get it. Why doesn't the crowd appoint their spokesman to debate the speaker afterwards and then shut up and listen?" I asked.

"Not acceptable to the organizers of the demonstration. They don't want a debate. They decided to stack the hall and not to let him talk. The administrators find themselves in a bind. They don't want to empty the hall, denying the students freedom of speech, but they're embarrassed that the prominent speaker who came all this way doesn't get to express his views under the same freedom. I learned at the campus police convention that this tactic is now employed on campuses throughout the country."

"What will happen next?" I asked.

"The speaker and administrators will give up and leave at some point. Then the students will applaud and cheer, claim victory, and go home."

"I don't get it. I thought one main function of a university was the free and open discussion of ideas. I think this stinks. It's rude and crude, and they ought to discipline the rabble-rousers," I said.

An even louder response from the crowd drowned out my opinion as the college president raised his hand and asked for attention. I thought back to twenty years ago when we held strong opinions, too. We loved to argue with a speaker, but only after hearing him out. The crowd that night missed the point. They would tell you they were fighting for justice and freedom. They didn't even know the meaning.

I found my rent car and drove back to the hotel. I would obtain the information I needed the next day about Warren, Fran, O'Connell, and Sky. Then I could leave and stay away from a college campus for another decade or two.

CHAPTER 21

I HAD PROMISED MYSELF THAT, IF I EVER HAD occasion to be in Chicago, I would have dinner at Charlie Trotter's. Some claimed the restaurant came closest to Michelin Five Stars of anything in America. Alexandra gave me a copy of Charlie Trotter's cookbook for my birthday the first year we were together.

I remembered she said, "Let's try out one of the recipes to celebrate your birthday."

Chef Trotter's recipes combined ingredients I would never have thought would go together, but the finished product always exploded with flavor. They combined French techniques with American ingredients and Asian flavors.

I also needed a distraction after the disturbing demonstration at the campus. I headed straight for the restaurant. I knew the dinner would be out of my price range; I could just see Franklin Reed's face when he saw a two-hundred-dollar dinner on my expense account. What the hell, I didn't know when I would ever come this way again. I called and was fortunate to get a last-minute reservation for the second seating, a rarity, as people have to reserve tables months in advance.

"We've had a single cancellation, Mr. Ventura, otherwise we're fully committed," the manager said.

I found the restaurant with the directions he gave me in a circa 1908 brownstone near Lincoln Park.

"Can I interest you in our Kitchen Table Menu in which you taste fifteen small portions while eating in our enormous kitchen?" the maitre d' asked. "There one can watch our craftsmen at work and soak up all those wonderful aromas."

I opted instead for the Grand Menu of the day, and we walked into a handsome dining room decorated in shades of burgundy and cream.

Wine Steward Joseph Spellman came to my table before the first course.

"Mr. Ventura, we can serve you excellent wine by the glass since we have a sophisticated nitrogen system that keeps open bottles fresh. I know our selection will please you."

We discussed options for the first three courses. He had studied the day's menu and suggested a wine to match the flavors of each course. They stocked world-class wines; Spellman really knew his stuff.

"I'll take a glass of '79 Krug Brut with the scallops and oysters that will offset the caviar flavor—and give me the 10-year old Mayacamas Chardonnay with the turbot," I said.

"I'd recommend a Napa red wine with the entrée, Mr. Ventura. I have a very nice 1985 Opus to go with the wild game."

I approved. Opus is the product of a partnership between Baron Phillippe de Rothchild and Robert Mondavi. They bottle a blend I would compare with the better wines from Bordeaux.

"Now what do you suggest for my dessert?" I asked.

"Nothing beats Sauterne with chocolate. We have an open bottle of 1991 Chateau d'Yquem."

I agreed, and he took my order back to the kitchen.

My meal began with Maine scallops stacked with

Kumamoto oysters and butter clams dressed with crème-fraiche-Osetra caviar vinaigrette. The kitchen painted each plate as if it were a canvas. I almost hated to disturb the design, but I did so anyway and with gusto.

"That opening course may turn out to be my favorite," I told the waiter.

"The seafood tasted so fresh it must have been swimming around in the kitchen."

The chef took a Caribbean approach to the fish course. I found the fresh turbot filet interesting served with its green pineapple preserves over a spicy coconut sauce. I'm not generally a fan of turbot, and this presentation would have been a bit sweet for my taste had the acid in the Chardonnay not created a wonderful balance.

Next came roasted bobwhite quail and black buck venison. Veal sweetbreads and grits accompanied the quail, and the venison snuggled next to a bed of collard greens and wild mushrooms. The southern touch of the grits and greens at first seemed bizarre, but the merging of the flavors worked well. The bitterness of the greens stood up to the game flavors.

I cleansed my palate with green tea sorbet with tangerine gelee and preserved ginger and fresh plum puree. I wouldn't have minded a chance to cleanse my palate again with that combination.

The waiter approached me. "Are you ready for dessert, sir?"

Where would I have room to put the chocolate dessert?

The picturesque dessert came to the table with a rich, thick espresso I had never tasted before. The waiter placed before me a plate with a glistening dark chocolate dome. This sat on a pattern of dark and white chocolate swirls with puddles of blueberry and red raspberry puree off to the side. I bit into the grand chocolate cake and found a warm, liquid, chocolate center that felt like velvet on my tongue. Tiny scoops of firm hazelnut ice cream and chocolate sorbet surrounded the cake.

I called Mr. Spellman over to my table.

"You made an exemplary recommendation. The chocolate dome capped off the feast, and the d'Yquem tasted like liquid sunshine."

He thanked me and made an almost military about-face in leaving.

I lifted the coffee cup to my mouth and remembered Alexandra and how she would have loved this dinner. You want to share a special meal like this with someone you love. I thought of Rachel. I missed her that evening.

Charlie Trotter's had lived up to its reputation. I was sated. I drove back to the hotel and fell asleep almost as soon as the old Bogie movie came on the TV screen.

I drove back to the Northwestern campus after I awakened and ate a light breakfast. I located yearbooks for all the different years Fran, Warren, Victor, and Sky attended the school. I found nothing startling but learned a bit more about each one's background. I went back to meet Sergeant Nelson and thanked him for his assistance.

"I appreciate your help and advice. I wouldn't have had access to the local police records without you."

"I hope you don't judge our university by the mob you saw last night," he said by the way of apology. "I'd put ninety percent of our students and faculty up against those from the best colleges in America. Every campus has its share of malcontents and assholes."

"You're right. We have more than our share in California," I said.

"Those demonstrators last night don't understand that when a minority kid applies for a job in the future, the employer will wonder whether he got his degree on merit or because of affirmative action," Nelson said.

I used a phone in a vacant office and made a collect call to Buddy at his house in Napa.

"The school records and the yearbooks revealed little of importance about Fran Phillips or Warren Roberts. Fran graduated in four years in 1977 with a degree in history. She had been a C-student, belonged to a social sorority—Pi Phi—paid a few parking tickets and cheered with the Wildcat Pep Squad," I told him. "Warren Roberts carried a 3.2 grade point average, pledged SAE and, in keeping with his major, belonged to the Civil Engineering Society. He graduated in five years in 1977."

"How about your pal Victor?" Buddy chuckled.

"Victor O'Connell was a different story. He attended Northwestern for two years from '71 to '73, when he was suspended for one year for an honor code violation. He came back from '75 to '78 and graduated with a solid 3.8 GPA. He belonged to the Civil Engineering Honor Society and was a member of the same fraternity as Warren."

"Did you check out Sky Leonard?"

"Sky Leonard's collegiate record came as close to bizarre as I could have imagined. She left school after her junior year in 1986. Her record indicated many incomplete courses, which she had dropped, but she made A's in almost every course she finished. It didn't surprise me to learn that she majored in both political science and drama. The Young Socialists Club elected her president, and the university placed her on disciplinary probation for one semester after her club took over the university president's house."

"They didn't expel her?" Buddy asked.

"She led a demonstration against the firing of an avowed communist assistant professor who lied on his employment application. The Young Socialists lost their charter and got kicked off campus, but Sky conned her way out of expulsion."

"Did any of our friends have a police record?" Buddy asked.

"Sergeant Nelson got us police records from campus, Evanston, and Chicago. We hit absolute pay dirt when I reviewed the police records. They had arrested Victor O'Connell for beating his wife in 1976. Neighbors heard a domestic disturbance and called the campus police who found the couple in a violent argument. The wife tried to hide several bruises about her face. She refused to press charges, and they dropped the matter. The record also listed O'Connell as an assault suspect in a bar fight, but witnesses changed their stories, and the grand jury issued no indictment."

"I didn't know O'Connell was married back in college. I didn't think he and Susan had been married that long."

I waited a minute or so for effect.

"I didn't either. So I rushed down to the Cook County courthouse and looked up the marriage records. A Justice of the Peace married one Victor O'Connell and one Fran Phillips in that courthouse in 1976. Surprise, surprise. How about that?"

"Dynamite!" Buddy yelled.

"They divorced a year later in 1977. Fran just happened to forget to mention her earlier marriage to O'Connell, and it's clear old Victor lied to me about not knowing his partner's wife well. He damn sure did know her," I said.

I continued. "Warren Roberts and Fran Phillips had no police records. Sky Leonard had several arrests for disturbing the peace when demonstrations got out of hand and for trespassing during the takeover of the university president's house. They never could convict her."

"We ought to send Sergeant Nelson a present. I'll see you at the airport at 4:30. Goodbye, Gene."

I needed to research one more thing before leaving Chicago. I wanted to check out the employment records at the engineering firm where Warren Roberts and Victor O'Connell had worked for so long. Perhaps I could talk to an associate who knew them.

I went to one of those quick copy places and ordered

business cards. I smiled at the young woman with the pink hair behind the counter and turned on the charm.

"Miss, I would appreciate your help. I'm from out of town and in a hurry. Could you please print my cards while I wait?"

I identified myself on the business card:

Eugene R. Ventura
Regional Personnel Director
General Service Administration
United States Government
425 Geary Street
San Francisco, California 94101

Not exactly honest, but they wouldn't release any records to me otherwise, and it wouldn't do any real harm. I'd keep the information confidential except for its possible bearing on Warren Roberts' murder. I didn't expect to learn anything new that would help us, but, while in Chicago, it made sense to check with McKinsey & Smith. And now I had a burning desire to learn as much about Victor O'Connell as I could.

I decided not to call first in case someone wanted to check on my new credentials. I hoped I could get to see the top dog in personnel by using my brand new business card. It always amazed me at how doors opened to someone presumed to be a federal official. I also hoped McKinsey & Smith worked on GSA projects or might bid on some from time to time.

I found the office high up in the rarified air of the 85th floor of the Sears Tower. Looking down at the ground made me a little dizzy.

I offered my bogus business card to the receptionist, saying, "I happen to be in downtown Chicago on another matter. Could I see your VP/Human Resources? I didn't make an appointment. Please give him my card and see if he can spare a minute or two."

The receptionist came back and said, "You can see Lucy Waters if you don't mind waiting fifteen or twenty minutes. And Lucy's not a him."

The business card had done the trick.

Lucy Waters came out to greet me herself. She wore a pale green corporate suit with a white blouse, no tie, and her hair pulled back.

"I appreciate you seeing me, Ms. Waters. A Victor O'Connell, who used to work here, has applied for a job as Senior Project Manager for GSA's Northern California Region. I found myself in downtown Chicago anyway, so I decided to drop by to get some employment information about him."

She said, "I only have a few minutes, but let's go back to my office."

I followed her. I started the conversation by telling her how her company had impressed me.

"You have quite an operation here, Ms. Waters."

"Yes, we are now the third largest engineering firm in Chicago. One-hundred-seventy-eight engineers work here."

"I appreciate you seeing me without an appointment. Did you know Mr. Victor O'Connell?"

"Seems that I met him at a quarterly staff meeting when I first came here. Slight build, dresses well, rather short?" she asked.

"That's him. He and a partner do utility and environmental projects in Napa, California. We're considering bringing him on board," I lied.

She moved behind her desk. I took one of the chairs facing her.

"Right, I think he left here with another one of our engineers to open their own shop."

"Do you remember anything about the quality of his work?"

"He must have been competent because, as I recall, he worked here a long time. Let me see if I can still find him in our computer files."

She took a few minutes to access her computer. She must have had at least a twenty-inch monitor on her credenza. She turned the monitor around so we both could see.

"Here it is," she said. "That's odd. He never made partner. Most engineers who work here as long as sixteen years do. He came to work here after college in '78 and left in '94."

That got my attention. I raised my head.

"Do you know why he didn't get elected partner?" I asked.

"No, it doesn't say. After training, he worked on some minor projects and ended up supervising them. He headed up of one of our presentation teams the last five years he worked here."

"What's a presentation team?" I asked.

"That's a group of our sales engineers responsible for bringing in new business. They find new clients and make detailed presentations," she said.

"O'Connell must have been a good salesman," I remarked. "He seems experienced. Why did they pass him over for a partnership?" I asked.

"I'm certain he was well qualified. Nothing in our file indicates poor performance. Could just have been a personality thing. Sometimes one of our engineers does a good job but has difficulty relating to someone on our executive committee. Perhaps a personality conflict. I would recommend him as an asset to the GSA," she said.

I knew that was all she had to tell me. I thanked her and left her office.

My two-day trip to Chicago had produced major results. The research about Sky Leonard's college years fit the information Buddy had found in the FBI files. She was bright, radical, and dangerous; she wasn't above breaking the law when it served her purpose.

I also learned that Fran Roberts and Victor O'Connell had been married before she married Warren Roberts. Fran hadn't mentioned this, and O'Connell lied about only having a casual social relationship with his partner's wife. And O'Connell had a history of violent behavior. And also, something significant must have happened at McKinsey & Smith that kept him from rising in the firm.

CHAPTER 22

CHICAGO TURNED OUT TO BE A GREAT CITY to visit. It resembled a seaside city but in the middle of the continent, with Lake Michigan and the Chicago River meandering through. I would like to go back and spend time there with Rachel, showing her the picturesque downtown with its spectacular architecture. And then there's stylish North Michigan Avenue, one of the most exciting promenades in the world. But not in February. The cold weather made my shoulder hurt. The doctors had told me this would happen, but, living in Northern California, I rarely noticed it. It gets cold on occasion at home but nothing like Chicago. I appreciated getting back home after two days and nights there.

Buddy met me at the San Francisco airport, and I climbed into the Corvette. I told him what I had learned in Evanston and Chicago on our way back home.

"I don't like the fact that O'Connell lied to me about knowing Fran, but that doesn't mean he killed his partner," I said.

"Why don't you confront O'Connell and let him know you caught him in a lie, then gauge his reaction?" Buddy suggested.

"I plan to do just that."

"Sky Leonard borders on sociopathic," I told Buddy.

"She's capable of doing almost anything for her cause, even killing somebody."

"To most people it would sound crazy, but maybe in her mind she could justify killing Warren Roberts. She couldn't afford to have his report defeat the proposal," Buddy said.

"We need to know more about Sky's activities and what's going on at the Keep Napa Green office," I said.

"We could bug her office and tap her phone," Buddy suggested.

"We could also buy a shitload of trouble if we got caught. The former Napa County Sheriff and an ex-police lieutenant found breaking and entering? No, thank you very much, I'd rather just keep an eye on her."

"I'll set up surveillance of her office for a week or so. We might learn a lot by seeing who comes to her office and watching where she goes. One of my old deputies is also bored to death of retirement, and I bet he would help us out for a case of good Scotch. He and I can take turns watching her."

I arrived home before dark and opened a bottle of Clos Du Bois Pinot Noir. I took a sip. I thought I could taste a hint of wild cherries. Rachel had left a message that she would be at a dinner meeting in Sonoma. I missed her. I also hoped I could reach Fran Roberts by phone after she came home from work. She picked up on the third ring.

"Hi, Fran. I just got back from Chicago and learned that you and Victor O'Connell were married while you were college. Why didn't you tell me? That history could have a bearing on finding Warren's murderer."

"That was so long ago and it didn't last but a minute or two. Besides, what could it have to do with Warren's death?" she asked.

"I'm not sure yet. You can't hide things from us, Fran. It's important for us to know all about the people close to Warren and how they're connected. This could help us discover who might have had a motive to kill him."

"OK. I was young and stupid. He was older and smart and said all the right things. We ran off and got married and kept it a secret. That felt quite romantic at the time. We even lived apart. If Dad had found out, he would have shipped me off to Siberia or some place even farther away. Then Vic got weird and started to push me around and rough me up. I had money, so I hired a lawyer and got a quiet divorce. It all happened in less than a year."

"Did Warren know about your marriage to O'Connell?"

"No, I didn't tell him. Remember, Vic and I never lived together. Warren knew that Vic and I dated and he thought that I dumped Vic, not the other way around. Vic agreed to keep the marriage a secret if I would drop the assault charges. I suspect you know about that, too."

I drank a little more wine. Maybe wasn't not cherries after all, but blackberries.

"Why do you think he beat you?"

"I thought about that for a couple of years afterward. I think maybe it just made him feel important that he could overpower someone, maybe because of his size."

"Well, why would you then let Warren bring him out here to be his partner?"

"Dad wanted to set Warren up in business so we could move back to Napa. Warren needed someone to front the business and meet with clients. He was a technician and good at designing and completing the jobs but not a salesman. I knew Vic was a sleaze, but he could sell that proverbial oceanfront property in Arizona. Clients liked him. He proved he could charm customers at McKinsey & Smith in Chicago."

I finished my glass of wine and poured another while still talking on the phone. I thought the second glass surpassed the first. A little oxidation always helps the bouquet.

"Wouldn't Vic take advantage of Warren?"

"I thought Vic would appreciate the opportunity to become a partner in his own company with clients brought in by my father. I also figured Daddy could intimidate Vic and keep him in line. Daddy could bring in business and he could take it away. If I saw Vic hurting my husband, I knew I could just tell Daddy and he could pull the plug and ruin Vic's chances of being successful here in Napa."

I shifted the phone to my right hand.

"Last question, Fran. I assume your dad knew nothing about your marriage to Victor?"

"We married outside the Church since Vic was Protestant. I figured someday I would get up enough courage to tell Daddy. Then, when I saw it falling apart, I saw no reason to tell him. It was over. If he knows, he didn't get it from me and he has never brought it up."

"Thanks, Fran, we'll keep you posted."

"The police say a witness saw a woman coming out of the alley that night. They told Franklin today. It wasn't me, Gene. I've never been there in my life."

After I hung up, I took plastic containers of leftover veal cacciatore and Parmesan polenta from the freezer and transferred them to the microwave. Momma always taught me to make more than I needed and to save the rest for another meal or two. I sliced a cucumber and a tomato and drizzled the veggies with a little olive oil and Balsamic vinegar. Not a bad quick dinner. I was pleased that the veal tasted better than when I had prepared it the previous month. One glass of Pinot Noir remained.

I decided to call on Victor O'Connell unannounced this time. I wanted to see his reaction when I confronted him with the lie he'd told me. I assumed the best time of day to catch him in his office was first thing in the morning.

I parked behind a U-Haul truck in front of his office. A guy came out of the office, walked to the truck, and returned to the office carrying a computer. I didn't recognize him.

Again, no one was in the reception area, so I walked down the hall and knocked on O'Connell's door.

"I'm sorry to bother you, Mr. O'Connell. I have just one more question, if I could have a moment of your time," I said in my most polite manner.

"You're back; I already told you to leave me alone. I'm quite busy this morning and I don't know why you keep bothering me."

"It'll only take a minute."

"Come in, then, but I've told you all I know about Warren's death."

I looked in my notebook as if something were written in it.

"I must have misunderstood when we talked last," I said. "You told me, according to my notes, that you barely knew Fran Roberts when you lived in Chicago."

"That's right. But what does that have to do with your investigation?"

"I just wondered if I had misunderstood you since you and Fran were married in 1976."

"Did she tell you that?"

"No. We found the record at the Cook County courthouse."

"It's none of your business, and I resent the hell out of you scrutinizing me. It's an invasion of privacy, and I may sue you."

"Sorry, Mr. O'Connell, it's a matter of public record. Anyone can look it up. I just don't understand why you would deceive me."

"Fran and I were college kids and we made a mistake, that's all. We agreed to keep our brief marriage a secret."

"But you didn't have to volunteer the lie that you didn't know Fran well."

I studied my blank notebook again. "To repeat my question: Did you see Warren and Fran together when you worked in Chicago, and how did they get along? You replied that you didn't socialize with them. Why not just leave it at that? That answer would have been enough."

Victor O'Connell stared at my face, his body shaking with anger. His eyes became hooded in darkness, and he leaned forward aiming his chin at me.

He yelled, "Get out of here! And don't come back! You better stop checking up on me. If you have any more stupid questions, contact my attorney."

Oops, I'd made Victor O'Connell angry again. But I didn't mind; I didn't like the guy. I still didn't know why he chose to lie to me.

I came out the front door and paused on the porch, watching the man move more equipment into the office. I waited outside for him. I introduced myself and told him I had business with Victor, which was not entirely untrue.

"I'm Ken Brandt, the company's new engineer," he said, "Victor hired me from San Francisco to ride herd over his projects out here. I'm glad to meet you."

He shook my hand. Victor O'Connell had wasted no time in replacing his dead partner.

CHAPTER 23

I GOT HOME FROM O'CONNELL'S OFFICE. Rachel sat at the pine table in the kitchen paying bills and sending out invoices. I hugged her neck and went back to my office. An hour later she came down the hall and stuck her head in the door.

"I forgot to tell you. Casey Hammon of the Sacramento Bee called. He asked you to call him at the Marriott in Napa."

"I wish you had told me when I first came in, dear." Sometimes that woman .....

I recalled Paul Martin mentioning that Hammon was doing research for a series. It had some tie-in with the proposed Napa County moratorium, I thought. I returned his call. The phone rang twice.

"Casey Hammon," he answered.

"Hello, Mr. Hammon, this is Gene Ventura."

"Call me Casey. I write for the Sacramento Bee, and Paul Martin suggested I get in touch with you. I came to Napa last night and hope you and I can get together to discuss Keep Napa Green. I understand you met with Sky Leonard."

"Yeah, just the other day."

"How about coming over to the Marriott bar later this afternoon and meeting me for a drink? We can talk then," he suggested.

"O.K. Let's try four o'clock, before the happy hour crowd invades the bar."

I walked across the lobby of the Napa Marriott to the bar. It featured a sports theme. Old black and white photos of sports stars and memorabilia from past eras adorned all four walls. Mays and Mantle, Joe Louis and Rocky Marciano. They all looked so young. A Pittsburgh Steeler "Terrible Towel" from the days of the famous Iron Curtain defense held a place of honor next to the door. I counted eight TV's strategically placed around the room. I appreciated that they had turned down the volume, so you had to read lips when the announcers came on.

One person sat in the bar at that early hour—Casey Hammon. He occupied a booth near the rear wall, well away from the long, light oak bar. I noticed two frosty bottles of Red Hook Ale in front of him along with two of those funny little glasses most bars choose to serve with bottled beer. I've never understood why. They never hold more than one or two good swallows and they don't keep the beer cold. Hammon rose from his seat and called me over. We shook hands.

"I hope Red Hook's O.K. The bar's not open yet, but I managed to get us a couple of beers. I've become a good customer here since I've been working on this story."

Casey looked spare and wiry, a classic tweedy ectomorph. His hair had started to gray even though he looked under forty. He reached only five-seven or eight with a thin frame—one of those guys with narrow shoulders, a slim waist, no discernable hips, and minus two percent body fat. He wore tinted wire-frame glasses. I thought he looked more like a teacher than a reporter. But, then, what's a reporter supposed to look like?

He had a mellow voice, like a 20-year old single malt.

"Thanks for meeting me. I'm an environmental writer for the Sacramento Bee and I'm researching a series about eco-terrorism."

"O.K. How do KNG and Sky Leonard fit in?" I asked.

"Our research has lead us to them. I understand you also have an interest in Ms. Leonard. Mr. Martin told me that you are a detective and that she may be involved in one of your cases."

"I spent less than one-half hour with her in connection with a case, so I don't know her all that well."

"Can you tell me about the relationship between her and your case?" Hammon asked after taking a long pull on his beer and wiping the foam from his upper lip.

"I don't mean to cast suspicion on her. I have no real reason to believe she's guilty of anything but acting different and dressing funny and pretending she's Snow White. I interviewed her looking for a link between KNG and the murder of an engineer. Keep Napa Green submitted a moratorium proposal to the Napa County Board of Supervisors for consideration. The engineer was preparing an analysis of the potential effect of the proposal."

"Did you find any connection?" Casey asked.

"She said she didn't know the engineer, and no one had told her about any study of the proposal. My partner and I haven't found out if she told the truth or not. What in particular do you mean by 'eco-terrorism'?" I asked.

"Various extremist groups use protecting the environment and saving wildlife as excuses to damage facilities whose owners they consider to be their enemies. We've traced many incidents involving fires, bombs, and sabotage in Western states back to various such vigilante groups that appear to have only loose alliances."

"Why would an environmental writer like yourself get involved? You must share some of the same objectives," I asked.

"I used to teach botany at Cal State-Fullerton and have involved myself in efforts to protect the land since my college days. I realized these nut cases had begun to affect mainstream activists who utilize acceptable legal and legislative means. They hurt our public image and effectiveness. The public begins to think of all environmentalists as criminals or crazies when those guys burn down research labs that use animals or destroy logging equipment or blow up outdoor recreational facilities," he said. "I decided I could do more as a reporter by exposing those fanatic fringe groups."

The cold beer went down easy, and I didn't mind when the waitress opened the bar and brought us another round. She had loaded the popcorn machine for happy hour. We could hear the corn popping and smell the buttery oil.

"I didn't realize eco-terrorism had become such a problem," I said.

"It's getting worse in fact. The most active group is the Earth Liberation Front, or ELF. The terrorists justify their destructive acts in the guise of concern for the planet."

"Have they caused much damage or taken many lives?" I asked.

"The most costly event so far was the ski facility fire at Vail in 1998. ELF said it torched the resort to keep the owners from developing an adjacent forest, a known habitat for the lynx. The damage exceeded twelve million dollars."

"That's pretty impressive."

"We don't know that they've killed anybody yet. So far, they've targeted the logging interests for cutting down trees and labs that use animals for research. They're against the fur industry, and one ardent group even burned a meatpacking plant in Oregon. They've incinerated labs working on genetic engineering, and their newest deal is destroying houses under construction on land they want to protect."

"Seems I read somewhere that most incidents have taken place in the West," I said.

"Yes, while most terrorism has taken place in the western states, ELF has taken credit for burning houses in New York as well as some in Colorado and Arizona. They usually spray-paint graffiti at the home sites: 'if you build it, we will burn it'."

"Have you traced Sky Leonard to any criminal activity?" I asked.

"Not outright, but, wherever she goes, acts of violence and sabotage occur. They sent her to Napa because they have targeted the wine industry for a long time. One cell in Santa Barbara advocates sabotaging vineyards in Napa, Sonoma, and Santa Barbara. The wine industry is a small fish in the pollution pond, but winemaking is so damn visible and makes for such good press. You don't hear about a farmer who cuts down trees to plant wheat or corn, but let someone do it to plant grapes, and the radicals come running," Hammon said.

"You sound like you're defending the wineries. I know our wine industry has done a piss poor job of communicating how we protect our water and soil. But, as a grower myself, I know we've come a long way in restoring the land," I said.

"On the contrary, I prefer that the wine industry not clear any more land, and I have concerns about polluting the Napa River. I would support any moratorium on expansion, but not destroying someone's bulldozer to achieve that end. Destroying property and bribery and intimidation have a negative effect in the long run, as I said before. I plan a series of articles detailing the crimes and featuring the players. That's why I've come here to investigate KNG."

I rubbed my index finger in the puddle of condensation from my beer glass.

"My partner, Buddy Bennett, is the former sheriff, and he ran a check on Sky through the FBI. Are you familiar with Save Air, Nature, Environment or the related Canadian group, Living Institute for the Environment?" I asked him.

"LIFE & SANE? Oh, yes. We're digging for more information about them. Some legitimate environment people charge that foreign money pays their bills so they can cause dissension and create havoc in America. Our financial editor is trying to trace the money flow for my series."

"Well, you know a lot more than we do. How can we help?"

"I'm looking for suspicious incidents in this area. Do you think Sky or her group may be bribing or intimidating officials involved in the moratorium vote?"

"Someone killed County Commissioner Rachel Bernard's dog, and she received an anonymous threat. But so far there's no connection tracing it back to Sky or KNG. Oh yes, and another commissioner, Judy Harris, received from some unknown source a sack full of money labeled 'campaign contribution."

"That looks like Sky's footprint."

"Speaking of footprints, we did find a footprint at the scene of the dog's murder at Rachel's house—a man's size 16-EEE. Police haven't found a match, but it sure as heck wasn't hers."

"I'll bet you find that he knows Sky when you catch him," Hammon said.

I thanked him for the beer and promised to share with him any information that might help his story. The happy hour crowd began filtering into the bar. I finished my beer, shook hands with Hammon, and left for home. He hadn't hidden his disdain for Sky Leonard. Did he know more about her than he had revealed?

CHAPTER 24

I PICKED UP THE PHONE ON THE fourth or fifth ring. Who calls at 7:00 o'clock on Saturday morning?

"You sound like you were asleep," Puck said.

"Can't understand why. Anything wrong?" I said, holding back yet another yawn.

"Not especially. Let's go for a jog. We haven't done that in a long time."

"But it's dark outside. What are you doing up at this hour?"

"Couldn't sleep. I've been up for a while. Just be glad I didn't call at five."

"OK, Puck. Give me a chance to open my eyes and grab a cup of coffee. I'll meet you at JFK Park at 8:15. I'll park next to the golf course clubhouse. Sure you're alright?"

"Well, I've seen better days. I'll see you at the park."

John F. Kennedy Memorial Regional Park abuts Napa College with frontage on both the Napa River and the Napa-Vallejo Highway. Puck and I have always run here since the days when we played high school baseball. The last time we ran must have been at least a month or so ago.

We stretched a bit and began running through the park. Puck and I ran our customary slow pace for about an hour without much discussion, which was our custom. We picked up bottles of cold water at the

clubhouse where golfers stood in groups waiting to tee off. Boy, that water tasted good. In my neglected condition, I needed to cool down after four or five miles. We walked a few minutes and found a park bench. We peeled off our jackets.

"You seem preoccupied. Everything all right at home?" I asked.

"Not really. Marian threw me out of the house again. I've been staying in the room I keep above the restaurant."

"I'm sorry. How are your kids?"

"All right. This is nothing new to them. This is either the third or fourth time, I forget which. At fifteen and seventeen, they understand. Besides, teenagers get pretty wrapped up in their own lives."

"What happened? Did Marian catch you with one of your waitresses?" I teased him.

"No, no. Same ol', same ol'. 'I spend too much time at the restaurant. I'm not home enough. She has no life. Blah, blah, blah."

"So hire an assistant manager and be home with your family more," I suggested.

"I'm making some money at last, after years of struggling, and I'm afraid to let anyone else mind the store. You know what happens to a restaurant when the owner's not around. I have to stay 'til closing and get home around eleven during the week, later on weekends."

I turned to face him.

"I know you, Puck. There's something else going on. Is it drugs or women?"

"You know I got over that coke thing five years ago. I don't party with that restaurant gang anymore and I go to meetings. I've met someone, though, since we've been separated. You know her—Sky Leonard."

I slammed my hand down on the bench. Damn it.

"Oh, no. She's crazy, Puck, and she's dangerous."

"Well, I'm not sure I agree, whatever. But she sure is fun."

"I can imagine. Buddy and I are investigating her and KNG as part of the Warren Roberts case."

"I know. She says you're harassing her, watching her house. She got a call from Chicago saying you went there to check up on her background. She's done nothing wrong, Gene. She didn't kill Roberts."

"We don't know that, and how can you be so sure? Sky's making a big push to get a moratorium passed to stop the growth of wineries. Warren's report could have caused the defeat of the proposal. Also, someone saw a woman her size leaving the alley where Warren' body was found."

"She wouldn't kill him just for that. I can't see her killing anybody. It's not her style," Puck said.

"You should see the FBI file on her. Bad things happen to people who oppose Sky everywhere she goes. Where'd you meet her?"

"At my restaurant. I couldn't resist approaching this exotic-looking woman. We chatted and got to know each other, and one thing led to another. She told me how people who oppose her environmental efforts have spread rumors and framed her," Puck said.

"Just be careful, Puck. She has a record of using people, getting them in trouble, and Sky always comes out smelling like a rose."

"So I can't get you to lay off?"

"No reason to panic. It's our job. If she's innocent, she has nothing to worry about. All your dad and I want is the truth. Buddy's never told me that he's seen you come to Sky's house."

"I don't go there. We always meet somewhere else, or she comes to my room at the restaurant. She told me that someone had her house under surveillance."

I couldn't help wondering if Sky was manipulating Puck to influence me or to pump me for information about our investigation. I hoped Puck wouldn't get further involved with Sky Leonard and that it wouldn't affect our friendship.

We heard a commotion. Several people in the park seemed to be congregating over near the boat-launching ramp and pier. I stopped a man holding a dog leash with a greyhound attached.

"What's going on?"

"It's almost 10:00 o'clock, time for Mother Murphy's Saturday morning poetry reading," he said.

Terrance P. Murphy, a.k.a." Mother", at one time taught English at Berkley until his eccentricities got too much for the administration. He drifted up the road to Napa and taught for a while at Napa College. "Mother" never outgrew the hippie movement and remained one of the last vestiges of Haight Asbury. You could hear him walking around town reciting Kerouac or Allan Ginsberg or some of the old 60's Bob Dylan poems—not any of Dylan's "new" stuff.

"How about listening to a little Mother Murphy, Puck? A little culture wouldn't hurt."

Puck laughed. "You go ahead, Gene. I need to shower and get back to the restaurant."

"Are we OK about Sky?"

"Sure," Puck said squeezing my good shoulder. "I know you have to do your job."

Mother Murphy stood at the end of the pier closest to the park. About twenty adults of various ages sat in a semicircle around him. Murphy wore his silver hair and beard long. His loose blue T-shirt and bell-bottom pants hung from his thin frame. Two rows of beads adorned his neck.

"Ginsberg loved Walt Whitman," Murphy explained in his clear baritone voice. "Allan thought of himself as Whitman's protégé."

He proceeded to read Whitman's "A Woman Waits For Me"

and " Once I Walked Through a Populous City". Next, from Allen Ginsberg's book HOWL, Mother Jones began to recite from memory,

I saw the best minds of my generation destroyed by madness,

Starving hysterical naked,

Dragging themselves through the negro streets at dawn looking for an angry fix,

Angelheaded hipsters burning for the ancient heavenly connection to the starry dynamo in the machinery of night . . . . . .

The audience clapped with enthusiasm, and Murphy ended his program as he always did with the Dylan anthem, "The Times They Are A-Changin".

All together a most thought provoking Saturday morning.

Chapter 25

Rachel poured us glasses of chilled Bouchaine Gewürztraminer that evening. We sat on the front porch and looked down at the green hills from our perch on Howell Mountain. The air tasted briny and we shivered as the wind blew off the Pacific— a novel seasoning for the spicy fruit flavor of the wine. Bizet's "Carmen Suite Number 2" could be heard from the stereo just inside the house.

Rachel said, "Your brother Robert called to invite us to come to San Francisco to hear Pl`acido Domingo sing 'Otello'. The performance takes place tomorrow, Sunday night, February 14th."

She looked at me coyly out of the corner of her eye.

I got it. Valentine's Day was tomorrow.

Robert held the position of assistant manager of the San Francisco Opera and he knew that watching and listening to Domingo always thrilled me. Robert and I grew up listening to opera. Mamma loved the melodies of Verdi and Puccini and cherished a collection of scratchy 78's recorded in Italy. Sunday afternoons we would sit on the porch, Pop with his pipe and Mamma with her sewing, and listen to the old RCA Victor phonograph.

Rachel turned her creaky wooden porch rocker to face me.

"How did Robert get into opera?" she asked.

"Robert knew even as a small boy that he wanted to grow up to be a famous tenor. He realized after years of lessons and auditions that he didn't have the voice. So he became an opera company administrator. Robert hung out around the opera office in San Francisco during the summers in high school and college. He found odd jobs, despite Pop's objections. He studied performance management at San Francisco University and later earned an MBA in their two-year weekend program. He started as an apprentice, then an intern, and joined the company after college. He worked his way up to the number three management spot at the San Francisco Opera under their brilliant, innovative General Director Lotfi Mansouri. Robert now heads marketing, in charge of ticket sales and promotion. I think he's seen every opera produced in San Francisco in the last twenty-five years."

"Why did your father object so to Robert's interest in opera?" Rachel asked.

"Robert's relationship with Pop suffered even more than mine. Pop didn't mind listening to Mamma's old records, but he couldn't relate to his son being a professional singer. 'Whata kinda work isa that for a man?' he would ask. Mamma understood Robert and encouraged his opera career but she never was able to turn Pop around. I understand his disappointment that neither of his sons followed the family tradition of raising the exceptional Zinfandel grapes that meant so much to him."

Rachel went inside to get a sweater, and I refilled our glasses with Gewurztraminer.

I called Robert back and asked him to have an early dinner with us at Tadish Grill before the opera. Robert and I had met often at the famous old seafood restaurant, the oldest in San Francisco, when I lived in the city.

Rachel returned wearing a blue wool sweater and carrying a large bowl of salted pistachios. She set them down on the table between us.

She settled again in her rocker, and said through a mouthful of nuts, "Tell me more about Robert."

"I can't remember a time when my brother Robert didn't hate the vineyard—unusual for children in Napa born to the life. He had wanted to live in San Francisco ever since he first saw the city. 'Why can't we live in San Francisco?' he would ask Mamma. Robert wasn't lazy; he just hated farm work. He worked as hard in school as I did. As you know, growing grapes requires a great deal of prepatory work in the months before the harvest. Weeds needing pulling, and spraying for insects was critical back then, but we didn't have the mechanization we have now. And Mamma's half-acre vegetable garden required attention, too. Pop expected Robert and me, even as small bambinos, to pitch in, and there was always work to be done."

I grabbed another handful of the salty nuts, which balanced the sweetness of the Gewürztraminer.

I munched some more and continued, "I figured out early on that the sooner I finished my chores, the quicker I could grab my glove and bat and find my friends to play baseball, so I did my tasks without much complaining. I didn't mind the work most of the time. The metamorphosis from barren black branches in January to beautiful clusters of grapes in the fall fascinated me. Not so Robert. He grumbled and helped me finish our daily work, but he didn't like it. He escaped whenever he could to listen to Mamma's records. He hitched rides into the city while he was in junior high and went to the opera office. He ran errands in exchange for voice lessons."

"Didn't he get in trouble when he got home?"

"Yes, but he didn't care. It was worth it to him. Pop never quite understood Robert. His family had farmed and grown grapes for generations in Italy. Pop's identity lay in raising grapes. The land was his life. He expected his children to till the soil just as the Venturas always had. As his sons, we would work in the vineyard; that's all there was to it. We awakened early and worked before school and came home after school to work some more. But Robert rebelled. Pop would say to Mamma, 'What'sa wronga with dat boy?'

"So your mother became the peacemaker?"

"Just one of her roles. It seemed that all activities at harvest time revolved around Mamma. She was part cheerleader, peacemaker, full-time cook and bottle washer. Mamma would flit everywhere: helping out, ministering advice, urging us on when we felt exhausted, and making certain to feed everyone well and supply them with cold beer and soda. We had help from hired pickers as well as neighbors. I'll never forget the big harvest incident when I was sixteen and Robert fourteen. It affected Robert and Pop's relationship for the rest of Pop's life."

Rachel leaned forward, interested and wanting to see my face in the soft, fading light at the end of day. I reached over and struck a match to light the hurricane lamp on the table.

"Why that particular year?" she asked.

"Our harvest was the culmination of an entire year's work, literally the fruits of our labor. It began sometime in September and lasted well into October."

"How well I know," Rachel said. "I've been there enough times. You have to pick each section of a vineyard just when the grapes reach perfect maturity."

"That year—1967, I believe—the San Francisco High School for the Performing Arts invited Robert to audition. They held the auditions in September over a five-day period—Monday through Friday—right in the middle of harvest time. Pop said he couldn't spare Robert; he needed him in the vineyard. Neither Robert nor I had ever before missed even a day of harvest. 'There will always be another audition,' Pop said. And

Robert said, 'I've worked and prepared for this audition for over a year. No way can I miss it'."

"No room for compromise existed. Mamma got caught in the middle. She knew Pop lived and worked for the harvest. At the same time, she supported Robert's ambition and knew what acceptance at the performing arts school meant to him. 'Giorgio,' she said, "just this once we can hire an extra hand.' But Pop wouldn't budge. 'My son belongsa ina the vineyard during harvest. The famiglia pays itsa bills for the year from thisa one time'."

"Mamma tried another tactic. 'Call the school, Roberto, and see if they can make an exception and have you audition after the harvest, or on Sundays when we don't pick grapes.' The school did not offer such options. Robert had to audition at the prescribed time or not at all. The crisis came to a head. Pop gave Robert an ultimatum. 'If you neglecta the harvest, Roberto, I will never forgiva you'."

Rachel let out a deep sigh. She'd held her breath all during my story.

"Who won?" she asked

"I guess no one. Robert went to the audition, and they accepted him—and Pop never forgave him. For the rest of his life, Pop believed Robert had betrayed him. And the guilt Robert carried with him weighed like a stone around his neck. He came home weekends, and the two occupied the same house but as strangers. Robert left after high school and never lived at home again. He came back from time to time to see Mamma or for family occasions, but he and Pop continued to avoid each other. Now and again, Mamma would slip away to meet Robert in San Francisco. I had expected that, in time, father and son would reconcile, but it never happened."

Rachel put her cool hand on my arm. I could feel her compassion in that touch.

CHAPTER 26

WE BEGAN OUR CELEBRATION OF VALENTINE'S DAY the
night before. I called Chef Curry, the new executive chef at
Domaine Chandon, and garnered a reservation. I had met him
before his promotion from sous chef. Rachel and I celebrated
special occasions at Domaine, her favorite restaurant—of course
she's French. The venerable French champagne house Moet-
Chandon had opened the restaurant some twenty-five years ago
adjacent to their 335-acre vineyard and winery in Yountville.

Rachel insisted, "Tonight the dinner is my treat and your
Valentine's Day gift."

We dined well on Paine Farms squab served with chantrelles,
wild mushrooms au jus, and a sweet onion tart accompanied by
warm, fragrant baguettes. We shared a bottle of their fine brut—
toasty nose with just hint of pear—and selected chocolate
mousse cake from their famous dessert bar. Chocolate goes with
champagne like basic black and pearls. The romantic dinner
diverted Rachel from our recent concerns.

We planned Valentine's Day that Sunday as a day of
R & R. We slept late, ate a relaxed brunch at home, and
headed for the city. I drove Rachel's Volvo. The weather
cooperated, a crisp, cloudy day with temperatures in the

low sixties. I later wished we had stayed home, but that was Monday morning quarterbacking.

Just like tourists, we spent two hours at the zoo and wandered around Golden Gate Park. Rachel wanted to window shop on Union Square.

"Look at that high fashion floor-length dress," she said in front of Neiman-Marcus' window. "That's not me."

I matched her for bad taste with ugly square-toed loafers at Johnson-Murphy's. We stopped for drinks at Fisherman's Wharf and met Robert at Tadish just before six.

Tadish grills swordfish like no one else. The crusty waiters, as always, acted like they themselves had opened the restaurant 150 years ago.

Robert regaled us with opera anecdotes.

"I remember a famous European conductor who refused to go on without his lucky batons. The Cardinal of Milan had blessed the batons, and his valet had misplaced them and couldn't find them in time for the performance."

"Did he conduct the opera anyway?" Rachel asked.

"No, he refused to go on, and the concert master filled in."

We laughed at the stories and shared his enthusiasm for the evening's opus based on Shakespeare's dark tragedy.

This production of Otello was one of the best I'd ever seen. We had ideal seats in the War Memorial Opera House. Robert knew I preferred to sit about fifteen rows back from the stage in the center, just far enough away from the orchestra pit to see the whole stage. I always marveled at the grand old auditorium, its impressive rotunda glowing with gold leaf on the walls and ceiling. The glittering crystal chandeliers in the lobby sparkled as patrons entered the hall.

This production featured spectacular military scenes and depicted strong feelings of love and jealousy. It's a story of betrayal. Otello looks on Iago, his best friend, as a brother. Iago lies and convinces him that his wife, Desdamona, is unfaithful, and Otello kills her in a jealous rage. Betrayal was a common theme in Shakespeare's tragedies, but I believe Iago's perfidy of Otello was even sadder than Brutus turning on Caesar.

As Otello, the Venetian general, Domingo's voice warmed up to perfection by the end of the first act, and the talented young baritone played Iago with just the proper degree of miscreancy. I was so consumed by Verdi's music that I hummed the melody from the final aria as we left the theater.

"You're off-key, as usual," Robert commented.

Robert hugged Rachel and me.

"Thanks for the Tadish dinner, Brother."

"And thank you for the opera. We should get together like this every month."

"We found the Volvo in the parking garage a block away. We had enjoyed a perfect day—until we drove home.

The digital clock on the dashboard said 11:52. The black moonless sky towered over us. We headed north on Highway 29 after turning off Interstate 80 just past Vallejo. No cars passed in either direction. The radio played Mozart. Rachel dozed, her head on my shoulder.

Out of the quiet, I heard a powerful engine rev up behind us. All of a sudden, we were hit from the rear. I felt a hard bump, jerking my head forward. Rachel awoke with a start.

A large dark shape appeared in the rear view mirror. No headlights.

Rachel screamed. I floored the gas pedal.

"Did you bring the gun?" I asked, as if that two-inch barrel would do us any good.

"No, it wouldn't fit in my evening bag."

Thank God, we both had on seatbelts, which we always used.

I zoomed to ninety. He was still on our tail.

I swerved to the left as there was no oncoming traffic. No net gain.

We couldn't outrun him. I heard the high-pitched whine as he gunned his engine. He came on us again.

I told Rachel, "Hold on. Brace yourself."

I hit one hundred, and the Volvo strained.

"Gene, I'm scared!"

A third time he plowed into us. White-knuckle time. I gripped the steering wheel with all the strength I had. I was having a hard time keeping the car on the road. Rachel was hysterical and crying.

Once more we felt a jarring impact.

I heard the trunk lid pop open. It blocked the rearview mirror. The Volvo swerved to the right edge of the highway. I barely avoided losing control by turning the steering wheel hard to the left.

I felt helpless. The metallic taste of fear rose to my mouth. It looked like the end of the road for us.

It was over as suddenly as it began.

The black phantom of a large vehicle passed us on the left and sped away, still with no lights on. How strange. He could have forced us off the road and creamed the car, probably killing us both. Or he could have stopped our car and shot us. Instead he just drove off.

I pulled over onto the shoulder and stopped. I caught my breath and turned on the interior lights. My hands shook, I felt my heart pounding through my chest, and nausea made swallowing difficult. We held each other, relieved we had escaped death. Rachel's face had paled, as if all the blood had rushed away. Tears glistened. The mascara she'd put on for this special evening stained her cheeks.

"He's gone. The truck stopped hitting us," Rachel said, still dazed.

"Are you OK?"

"My neck hurts, and I have a headache."

She started to massage her neck with both hands.

I knew the Volvo, strong as it was, had suffered badly, too. I surveyed the damage with a flashlight. Both taillights looked as if hit by a hammer. One of the bolts holding the left side of the bumper had been severed, and the bumper hung at a cock-eyed angle. A major crease ran horizontally on the trunk lid.

I recognized the sharp odor emanating from the trunk as I approached it. You never forget the stench of death. I shined my light inside the open trunk. Judy Harris' body lay there, curled in a fetal position. She wore jeans and a teal sweater and a hole where her nose used to be. The killer had dropped her dead body in Rachel's trunk. There was no blood, indicating she had been killed elsewhere. This time, I couldn't hold back the nausea. I threw up in a ditch beside the highway. I wiped the residue from my mouth with my handkerchief and returned to the car. I hugged Rachel again and told her of my gruesome discovery but kept her from seeing inside the trunk.

The crippled car seemed just healthy enough to get us back to Napa. I called the sheriff's office on the cell phone and spoke to the night duty officer. I asked him to have the sheriff meet us at Queen of the Valley Hospital where they keep bodies for autopsy. Rachel pulled her knees up to her chin and pressed against the right front door of the car to keep from shaking more.

The sheriff sent a sleepy-eyed young detective to meet us at the hospital. I told him the story and asked that someone interview us in the morning so we could go home. He looked at Judy Harris' body and asked an attendant to take it away. We both noticed mud and grass matted on her jeans and boots.

"You can go, but I need to impound the Volvo for the crime lab. I'll ask a patrolman to take you home."

We started walking toward the exit.

"Judy and I were friendly, but only in a casual way. But

why kill her and leave her body in my car?" Rachel asked.

"It's clear the murderer wanted to frighten you again. The most obvious connection is that you and Judy both serve on the board of supervisors," I said. "I think you should leave town. Do you have a relative you can stay with until we know it's safe?"

"No, no one. I'm afraid, Gene. Can't you look after me?"

We decided that for now she would stay around the house and vineyard, guarded at all times by Buddy or me, with Ernesto standing by. We would have to take shifts during the daytime while one of us worked on the case. We tabled the decision about her leaving town.

The danger to Rachel's life also increased the urgency of finding Warren Roberts' killer. I suspected the same person or people had killed Judy Harris. After being calm and rational in our discussion, I could no longer contain my anger. I let out a scream, causing an attendant to look at me as if I should be in their loony bin. How dare they mess with me and mine! Besides, I liked Judy Harris.

Aristotle said, "Anyone can become angry, that is easy. But to be angry with the right person, to the right degree, at the right time, for the right purpose and in the right way—that's not easy. "

Well, my Greek friend, this was easy. I wanted this son of a bitch.

CHAPTER 27

WE HAD A HARD NIGHT AFTER THE DEPUTY BROUGHT us back home. Rachel and I pondered for hours what message the killer meant to send by murdering Judy Harris and placing her body in Rachel's trunk. Rachel couldn't stop shaking. I held her in my arms. I tried warm milk, three Advil, a foot message—nothing helped. It seemed like forever, but at last she dozed off. So did I.

I awakened to her piercing scream. Her nightmare was a replay of the scene on the highway and discovering poor Judy's body. I hugged her again. She pulled me to her, and I felt her desperation. She made urgent silent love to me. Her sad warm tears fell on my chest. She moved away, sated and weary, and fell back to sleep.

I took my old Colt .357 magnum revolver from my locked gun case and picked up the worn leather shoulder holster, also the box of special cartridges that I had had hand-loaded for me. I had used this pistol when I first joined the force. Later, they made Glock 9 mm automatics standard because of the greater number of shots they could deliver and their versatility. But I still preferred the stopping power of the big magnum. I had seen its bullets penetrate an engine block more than once. I was fortunate that the cool weather allowed me to wear a jacket to hide the large holster.

We had a visitor just before noon the next day, Dan Hanes, the county sheriff. Since we had discovered Judy Harris' body in Napa County, the investigation came under the jurisdiction of his sheriff's department.

Sheriff Hanes, who replaced Buddy after Buddy retired, came to get our story himself. Hanes was polite and solicitous since Rachel along with her fellow county supervisors paid his salary. The board hired the sheriff and approved his budget. Hanes recognized the additional pressure he would be under to find the killer as the victim had also been one of the five county supervisors. People seldom chose to get killed in the county. Hanes's small staff of deputies didn't include a homicide detective, and he would have to call in the Napa city police.

I told him of our Sunday activities and the horrifying experience on the highway. Rachel started crying again as she relived almost getting killed and how we discovered the body.

"We don't know where they killed Judy or when they placed her body in Rachel's trunk. I can imagine only two possible opportunities in the previous twenty-four hours. They could have done it at my farm in the dark the night before. Or the killer could have followed us to San Francisco and put the body in the trunk at the parking garage while we attended the opera. I didn't see anyone following us to the city, but I wasn't looking for anyone, either," I said.

"When did you last see Judy Harris alive? Hanes asked.

"We met her at her tennis club last Tuesday. Some anonymous person left a bag with $5,000 on her doorstep, and she wanted to discuss it with Gene and me," Rachel said. "Judy fumed about what she perceived as an attempted bribe."

"I don't expect to find any prints on the money or the paper bag, but the Napa police lab is running a check," I said.

"We're inspecting the Volvo from end to end for any traceable prints or fibers or fluids that the killer may have left. They will return the car in a few days," the sheriff said to Rachel.

I doubted Rachel would want to keep the car. It would always remind her of that terrifying night when we came home from the opera.

Sheriff Hanes cautioned me, "Let the authorities do their job and try not to get in our way."

I mumbled some acquiescence, but both of us knew I wouldn't leave it alone. They were going to get some help finding Judy Harris' killer, like it or not, so they better find him before I did. Hanes had worked as an assistant to Buddy, and they remained friends. I knew Buddy could keep us informed as to how they progressed in their investigation.

Rachel continued to shake and to feel depressed. I gave her a happy pill and sent her to bed after the sheriff left. I though about who might have killed Judy and if there was a connection to Warren Roberts' murder. I received a phone call before long from Mike Edwards.

"I just heard about your ordeal and wanted to see if you and Rachel were OK."

"Rachel's still in bad shape, and I'm plenty pissed off. I want to get my hands on that son of a bitch. This guy scared the shit out of us, and also I admired and respected Judy Harris."

"I'm sure I'd feel the same, Gene, but let us handle it. We'll work with the sheriff's department. We have the resources and we have the badges, and you don't. You'll get in big trouble free-lancing. We'll get him. Murder of a public official gets top priority. I've put my best men on it already. Let it go, Gene."

"I promise not to do anything crazy, Mike. If, by accident, I were to come across a suspect, I'd bring him in and hand him over to you—if he let's me," I said.

"Yeah, just by accident."

"It doesn't make sense, Mike, that Fran Roberts would kill Rachel's dog, threaten her, and try to bribe Judy Harris. And why would she want to kill me coming down Howell Mountain? I think we both agree she also didn't kill Judy Harris. Someone else is at least implicated for sure, and they may well be tied to Roberts' death, too."

"Maybe so, but maybe not. Detective Lawrence thinks Fran could still have offed her husband. She had the weapon and the motive, and our witness saw a woman at the scene. Judy Harris is another story, and I don't know who you ticked off enough to get your brakes cut or your girlfriend's dog killed."

The conversation was heating up, but I knew Mike was doing his job. I would do the same in his shoes, so I backed off.

"OK, Mike, I'll turn over any information I find as promised and stay out of your hair."

"That's better. We go back a long way, and I want us to continue to work together, now that we both live here. Sally wants to know when you and Rachel are coming over for dinner. How about tomorrow night about seven? It'll do Rachel good to be distracted," Mike said.

"I hope she'll feel better by then. Rachel's tough, but she's never been traumatized like this before. I want her to meet Sally and the kids, too. I think they'll like each other. Expect us, unless I call you."

No one at the sheriff's department or Napa P.D. spoke of anything but what happened to us and about Judy's murder. The dispatcher, one of Buddy's old pals, called him before I had a chance to tell him the story. Buddy came to the front door soon after my conversation with Mike Edwards.

Buddy asked the obvious question after I assured him we were unharmed.

"Why do you think they would leave you alive when you were so vulnerable?"

"My best guess is they wanted to send us a message. They were telling us they could kill us if they wanted to, like they did Judy. And they wanted to make damn certain we would find the body in the trunk. It was either a command for us to stop our investigation into Roberts' murder or another warning to Rachel from the same guys who killed her dog. Maybe it's all connected somehow."

Buddy said, "I learned something interesting about his partner, Victor O'Connell, speaking of Roberts' murder. I was having breakfast at Mrs. McDonald's and ran into a guy who runs the local ReMax office. We had coffee together, and he mentioned he had sold an old Victorian house to Ken Brandt, the new engineer you met at O'Connell's office."

"So what's wrong with that?" I asked.

"Well, get this. Brandt came to town looking to buy a house two weeks before Warren Roberts died."

"Hmm, let's think about that for a minute, Buddy. So O'Connell hired Brandt without Warren Roberts' knowledge or approval. O'Connell looks good as a suspect. He wanted to rid himself of a partner but couldn't afford to buy him out. He secretly hired an engineer to replace his partner even before the murder and he had no alibi for that evening. It would have been easy to borrow his partner's pistol. There's only one problem. The woman seen leaving the alley damn sure couldn't have been Victor O'Connell.

CHAPTER 28

WHAT STARTED OUT AS A MISTY DAWN TURNED into a beautiful late winter morning—much too pretty a day for a funeral. The high sun looked down on Judy Harris' graveside service from the cloudless powder blue sky.

Poor Judy was buried in old Tolukay Cemetery, off Coombsville Road. Tolukay first opened in the mid-1800's on a site that featured several grassy knolls. Faded inscriptions marked many old gravestones. Every street bore the name of a different tree.

Parked cars lined almost all the streets in the cemetery. A large crowd circled the funeral tent below Laurel Street. It looked as if the entire town of Napa came out to say goodbye. Rachel pointed out many people I didn't know: city and county elected officials and administrators, tennis players from Judy's tournament days, folks who served with Judy on various committees and charities, and many people who just knew her as a popular caring person. We saw Victor O'Connell in the crowd and Sky Leonard and Jack Phillips next to his daughter, Fran.

The funeral sounds haunted me: the low strains of a lone cello playing the Bach Suite for Cello, the Sarabade in D-minor before the service began, the minister's baritone eulogy, the crowd joining the minister in a soft recitation of the Twenty-Third Psalm—"The Lord is my shepherd…"—the mechanical sound as the coffin was lowered into the darkness, and the final thud of shovelsful of dirt landing on the pine coffin.

Rachel gripped my hand and silent tears fell down her cheeks. I fumed. The taste of revenge filled my mouth. I wanted to find the asshole that murdered that fine woman.

Chief Mike Edwards and Detective John Lawrence stood at the edge of the crowd. Mike called me over after the service. He reached out his hand in greeting. Lawrence's hand stayed by his side.

"The coroner finished the autopsy last night. Thought you'd like to know. No surprises, though," he said.

"What did he say?" I asked.

"Powder burns with jagged edges at the entry wound proved they used a forty millimeter and shot her at close range. They found duct tape residue on her wrists, ankles, and mouth, and mud and grass on her clothes. Someone must have waited for Judy Harris, maybe at her townhouse, subdued her, and took her somewhere quiet, killing her and then dumping her body in your trunk," Mike said. "They tried to get something out of her first. The coroner found some pretty good bruises on her face and body."

"Son of a bitch," I replied.

"I'm sorry this happened, Gene. You told me that you and Rachel knew and liked her," Mike said.

John Lawrence said nothing, just looked away. I knew he didn't approve of Mike sharing the autopsy results with me. They got in their cars and drove off.

I took Rachel to see Pop and Mamma's graves before we left the cemetery. We drove around Circle Drive to Maple Street. We parked and walked down the hill.

We buried my parents before a wide "Mr. & Mrs."

tombstone marking both graves. A single bare rose bush grew next to the marker.

"Why one rose bush?" Rachel asked.

"It's the custom here. Mourners have been planting one rose bush by the graves for decades. No one remembers why or when it started. It's a nice gesture to remember loved ones with living flowers. The roses make for a vivid display of color and perfume the whole area every May when they begin to bloom."

"I wish I could have met your parents, Gene. I know from your stories they were remarkable people. Your mother sounded so warm and outgoing," Rachel said.

"Pop had a different personality, but somehow they fit together and devoted themselves to each other."

I looked at Rachel in a different way that day. I had never seen her wear black before. She stood straight on the hill, small against the snow-capped Santa Rosa Mountain far in the distance. I might have known a lovelier woman in my time but I couldn't remember when.

I placed two stones on top of the tombstone and took Rachel's hand. We walked up the hill to my pickup.

Casey Hammon surprised me by greeting us at the top of the hill.

"I saw your truck and decided to wait for you. I hope you don't mind," Casey said.

"No, that's all right. Rachel, this is Casey Hammon. I believe I told you about him," I said.

Casey's eyes opened wider as he turned to look at Rachel. A look of admiration crossed his face.

"Yes, you're the reporter from Sacramento. Nice to meet you," she said.

"I didn't see you at Judy Harris' funeral. Were you there?" I asked Casey.

"I stayed in my car and watched the crowd. I wanted to

see who showed up. I didn't know Ms. Harris, either, and I wasn't sure it was appropriate," Casey said.

"Gene told me you came here to work on a story," Rachel said.

"How's your research on the eco-terrorism story coming along?" I asked him.

"That's why I came to talk to you. I interviewed Sky Leonard at last," Casey said.

I replied, "Bet that was an eye-opening experience."

"Yeah, she didn't want to see me at first. She changed her mind when I told her I would write about the coincidence that some properties were damaged in every town while she worked there. Then she wanted to tell me her side of the story."

"Can't wait to hear this," Rachel said.

"What did she say?" I asked.

"That the charges were unfounded. She believed that the 'misguided polluters'—that's what she called them—framed her to make her organization look bad. They started their own fires and such to implicate poor Sky in every case. She reminded me twice that no one had ever indicted her. We know that the police in Falls Church and Austin said she covered her tracks so well that they couldn't find enough hard evidence. Police in both cities said they were relieved when she had moved on."

"What else did you learn?" I asked.

"She gave me the same song and dance about sponsoring the Napa moratorium as her civic duty. Said her group just attempted to gain public support and persuade the members of the board of supervisors to see the light."

"What did she say about SANE?" I asked.

"At first she denied her involvement. I pressed her and told her about the FBI file and the fact that LIFE, an arm of SANE, had furnished her questionable environmental reports. She relented only a little bit and admitted she received occasional assistance from SANE because they both shared the same environmental objectives. She denied that she worked for them. I didn't get much else from the interview," Casey said.

"Did she bat those long lashes at you and hang on your every word?" I asked. Rachel looked at me in a strange way.

"Oh, yes. I felt trapped in Giopetto's workshop," Casey laughed. "I'm going out of town for a few days to follow up a lead. I plan to be back in Napa next week."

"Sky is a puzzle, Casey, and we still can't fit her into our investigation of Warren Roberts' murder," I said.

Casey held Rachel's hand a little longer than I would have liked.

"It's been a delight to meet you," he said.

He didn't hold my hand quite as long when we said goodbye.

CHAPTER 29

WE DROVE HOME FROM THE FUNERAL, and a cloud of sadness overtook Rachel once again. Her eyes welled up, and she crossed her arms, hugging herself. She hunched her shoulders and bent her head forward. She resembled a turtle pulling into its shell.

Rachel had a fitful night's sleep. Bad dreams of the horror on Highway 29 and Judy Harris' death kept waking her up. She looked exhausted when I woke her with a cup of strong coffee.

"How about making some of your famous croissants this morning?" I suggested.

I knew baking would act as therapy for her.

I left Rachel in the kitchen and took my coffee to the living room. I stared unseeing out Mamma's picture window. Looking down Howell Mountain Road, I realized how vulnerable Rachel was, isolated here at my farm. First, the senseless killing of Rachel's dog got our attention. Then murdering Judy Harris and putting her body in Rachel's trunk convinced me that they'd go to any lengths to get what they wanted. They'd made their point, whoever "they" were. Now that I had found her, I wanted to keep Rachel in my life and out of harm's way. I needed to bring up the difficult subject of her leaving town until the bastards were caught.

174

The scent of baked goodies filled the house. Rachel called me from the kitchen, "Breakfast's ready." She sounded cheerier.

We ate a continental breakfast like Rachel had eaten most mornings growing up in France: fresh fruit, coffee served with hot milk, fresh baked croissants, creamery butter, and raspberry jam. I tasted the first warm flaky pastry and took a glance at the basket to make certain she'd baked enough for both of us. Not to worry. Rachel ate only one croissant; I finished the rest.

I looked up from my chair at the large oven Mamma had reigned over all those years. She ran the family from this kitchen, and people throughout the valley knew of her cooking. Buyers who came to the farm to select their grapes always made it a point to show up around lunchtime.

Pop complimented her, "Alessia, I think they coma more for your light gnocchi thena for my grapes. Youra the queen of our cucina."

Rachel asked where my mind had wandered off to.

"I think it's time for you to visit your folks," I told her as I put down my coffee cup.

"France is so far away, Gene, and I have a lot of work to do here."

"No matter what precautions we take, no matter how hard we try to protect you, if somebody wants to get you bad enough, there's always a chance they'll succeed."

"I'm sure I'll be O.K. with you and Buddy and Ernesto around and I won't go off on my own this time. It's to their advantage not to harm me until they tell us what they want," Rachel said.

"How do we know whether Judy told them what they wanted or not? They still put a bullet in her head. You've not seen your folks since they moved back to Bordeaux. I want you to go now."

She cocked her head to the side and teased, "Getting tired of me already?"

"Yeah, right, I want you out of my hair—at least go until we catch the bastard that did this."

She chided, "You already want to send me away, all the way to France, and I've stayed here at your house only a few weeks."

We heard the shrill whistle of the kettle, and Rachel got up from the table to fill the Melitta coffeemaker.

I decided to change the subject and tried to make her a bit homesick. "You've never told me how your folks came to California."

"It was that famous blind tasting in Paris. Dad and his colleagues couldn't believe any wines from the U.S. could compete with French wines."

"I remember Pop telling me that story. I think I was still a patrolman at SFPD at the time. Wasn't it around 1976?" I asked.

"I was just fourteen, so it must have been that year. Stephen Spurrier, the English owner of a Paris wine shop, set up this blind tasting at the Hotel International. He wanted to compare the best French wines with a special group of California Cabernets and Chardonnays selected by Andre Tchelistettff. Nine leading Frenchmen from the wine establishment comprised the group of tasters."

"The California wines won the blind tasting, didn't they?" I asked as I reached across the table to intertwine my fingers with hers.

"Well, two Napa Valley wines scored the highest out of the twenty wines tasted. The judges rated the 1973 Stags Leap Cabernet as the best red over two famous Bordeaux that placed second and third. California whites were even more impressive. Chateau Montelena '73 Chardonnay won first prize, and wines from Chalone and Spring Mountain came in third and fourth. The French were astounded."

"That tasting gave our wines status, put us on the map."

"Some said you 'd 'stormed the Bastille'. That event

intrigued Dad. He wanted to see where in America they made such exceptional wines," Rachel said.

"Where did you live at the time?"

Rachel got up from the table and poured us another cup of coffee. I smelled the wonderful aroma from the fresh pot. Why doesn't coffee taste as good as it smells? She came back and sat down.

"We lived in Haut-Medoc on the left bank of the Garonne, near Bordeaux where I was born. Dad was a winemaker for a family operation for eight years. Then he and the owner had a disagreement about releasing a second wine from the chateau for that particular vintage. Dad didn't think the wine met his standards, so he quit and began consulting."

"And he just up and moved to Napa and started teaching at Napa College?" I asked.

"No, he first came over by himself. He had met Andre Tchelistetteff, the leading California wine authority at that time, in France. So Uncle Andre introduced Dad to a few Napa winery owners. Napa Junior College and the local winery association were trying at that time to start some basic courses in growing grapes and making wine. Dad knew wine and spoke good English, so he took the teaching job and sent for Maman and me."

"Napa was quite different then—a small town with a hand-ful of wineries. No tourists, no wine trains, no blue-haired gran-nies on tour buses," I joked.

"No wine train, that's for sure," she laughed. "Everybody knew each other. I would come home from school, and Dad would be sitting at the dining room table with guys like Louis Martini, Stag's Leap's Warren Winiarski, and Joe Heitz. They fussed for hours about aging in oak barrels and how long to leave the Cabernet in the barrels or whether or not to filter the wine. Dad loved the excitement and camaraderie here and stayed in Napa for fifteen years."

"Was that when you became a winophile, rubbing elbows with those pioneers and tasting many different wines?" I smiled and asked her.

"As a rebellious teenager, I had no interest whatsoever in wine. People talked of nothing but winemaking for as long as I could remember, and I thought I wanted something else kind of like you and Robert," Rachel said.

"You changed your mind of course. I'm thankful for that. I might never have met you otherwise," I winked.

"Lucky for you."

She looked at me across the table and grinned.

"It was the harvest when I turned seventeen that changed my mind. I'll never forget that."

"What happened?"

"They excused us from school for the harvest in those days, and we had to go to school well into June to make up the time we missed. Almost every teenager hired on to pick grapes. We accepted the hard work and had a good time and made enough money to last us through Christmas."

"You'd been picking grapes for a number of years by then. Why was this harvest any different?" I asked.

"Dad acted as consultant that year for the Oak Valley vineyard in Carneros, and we picked Sauvignon Blanc grapes for sale to Applewhite Winery. Applewhite's winemaker, a friend of my dad's, came every day to decide with Dad which grapes they wanted picked. They make the best wines from grapes with the perfect balance of sugar and acidity, as you know. They took me aside and taught me how to test the grapes for ripeness. I learned how to use the refractormeter to determine the sugar content. After following them around for a few days and watching, they took me to a section of the vineyard where the grapes hadn't completely ripened yet. They said 'Rachel, these are your grapes. You decide when they should be picked'."

"A lot of responsibility for a kid," I said.

"You bet. I'm certain they checked behind my back, but I made the critical decision when to pick over a ton of grapes. I must have done a good job. They picked the grapes that same night. Dad liked to pick grapes at night because the cooler temperature benefited the grapes and the pickers."

"So how did the wine turn out?" I asked.

"Great! It went on to win a prize or two in wine tastings. I was so proud that my decision had an effect on the quality of that vintage. Dad bought me a case and teased that it was 'Rachel's wine.' I saved a bottle or two until the wine had well passed its prime. My first consulting job. That hooked me. I knew then I would always be involved in some aspect of winemaking."

"Why did your dad return to France after living in California all those years?"

"He was diagnosed with gout six years ago. He loved it here, but I think he always wanted to retire near his family's home in Bordeaux. So he and Mom bought a small house and left their favorite daughter here so she could meet her Prince Charming."

"Flattery won't change my mind. You still haven't agreed to leave town until we find the killer."

"I don't want to go without you. I would like to visit my folks but I want to wait until you can come, too."

"We're not just talking vacation here. This isn't just a visit. I want to make certain you'll be safe. I don't want to have to worry about you while I need to concentrate on catching this monster," I said. "Of course, you'll have the pleasure of your parent's company, too."

"I'm not thrilled about it, but, OK, I'll leave in a week or two. It will take me that long to finish my work with Ernesto on the trellises and get ready. Meanwhile, I'll stay around the farm all the time except when I leave with you or Buddy as my bodyguard," Rachel pouted.

I got up from my side of the table and went over behind her and put my arms around her neck.

"I guess that's O.K. but I'd rather put you on a plane in San Francisco tomorrow."

CHAPTER 30

"DO YOU MIND IF WE GO TO MIKE AND SALLY Edwards' tonight for dinner?" I asked Rachel.

"I guess that's OK."

I could tell she still suffered from our misadventure on the highway four nights earlier, even though she felt a little better after talking to her folks and telling them of her coming visit. I noticed an occasional tremor of her right hand that was new, and she couldn't hide her sad expression.

"We need to get out. Maybe you'll feel better," I said.

I knew she would have preferred that I cancel the dinner but I encouraged her to go with me. It would do her good to be with Mike and Sally and their kids, taking her mind off of that harrowing experience. I wanted to ask Mike a favor and knew I would have a better chance if I asked him at his house instead of at his office.

Rachel and I took the pickup, as the Volvo had not yet been returned. Those days I always checked out the truck for sabotage and always brought my .357 magnum with me.

The Edwards had bought a two-story house off Highway 12 at the western edge of Napa County near the Vineyard Knolls Golf Course. The subdivision looked new, and only two vacant lots remained undeveloped on their street. Mike and Sally had selected a contemporary house built of white stone with a gray peaked roof.

"Uncle Gene!" Mike Junior and Annette shouted together as they bounded out the front door to greet us. Annette, a blossoming twelve-year-old, gave me a tight hug. Mike Junior, now fifteen, put out his hand. I grabbed him. "You're not too old for my hug!"

Both children looked like their mother, with almond-shaped eyes and high cheekbones. Mike and Sally came out the door behind them. Sally was still one of the most beautiful women I had ever known. She had the combination of the best genes from her black father and her Vietnamese mother. She came up to me and kissed my cheek. Mike shook my hand.

"Rachel, these are my best friends, Sally, Mike, Mike Junior and Annette. Folks, meet Rachel Bernard."

"I'm so glad to meet you, Rachel," Sally said, "You're even more beautiful than Gene said you were."

"Thank you," Rachel replied.

"We're so sorry about the other night. What a horrible ordeal! You could have been killed, and poor Judy Harris," Sally said.

"We'll talk about that later," Mike said. "Now come in and have a drink. I can't wait to taste Pop's old Zinfandel that Gene's holding in both hands."

The children excused themselves and went upstairs, saying they had homework to finish. Mike reminded them that there would be no telephone calls until schoolwork was completed. Mike and Sally believed in old-fashioned parenting and setting firm guidelines and boundaries, always knowing where their children were and what they were doing.

"I almost didn't recognize the children. They've grown up since I last saw them. I hope they like Napa," I said.

"Naturally, they miss their friends in Philly but they'll get along fine. I'm really impressed with the schools out here," Sally said.

Sally and Rachel went to the kitchen to put the finishing touches on dinner while Mike and I stayed in the family room. Mike opened a bottle of the Zinfandel and poured us each a glass.

"Rachel's delightful, Gene. I hope this works out for you. I've thought about your encounter the other night. We're dealing with some mighty crazy folks. I'm worried. I believe Rachel's in great danger after Judy Harris' murder. I could have one of my men guard her for a while," Mike said.

"I've convinced her to go to France next week to visit her folks. She'll stay with me at the farm until then, and Buddy or Ernesto or I will be with her at all times. I think we're OK, but thanks for the offer."

Sally had anticipated that I might bring some of our old wine. I smelled steaks grilling outside. She topped them off with Gorgonzola butter. Sally called everyone to dinner, and the six of us sat around the dining table. Our big wine was a perfect match for the red meat. And Zinfandel loves chocolate, too, like the flourless chocolate cake Sally served for dessert with a dollop of whipped cream.

"I've never asked you, Gene, why you only grow Zinfandel grapes? Chardonnay and Cabernet Sauvignon seemed to be much more popular back East," Sally said.

"I think at first Pop felt comfortable with Zinfandel, as it reminded him of the wine from Italy and that's what he knew best. But he soon also realized Zinfandel grapes grew particularly well on our farm. Grapes vary greatly by the location of the vineyard. I found it interesting that some of the best Zinfandel grapes in Napa grow on hillsides above the valley like Howell Mountain."

"So then Cabernet or Chardonnay would not grow as well on your property?" Sally asked.

"I'm not sure—we've never tried it—but Pop's ancient vines produce small bunches of little grapes that make wine with intense, concentrated flavor. We have a smaller yield per acre but we hope our grapes are more valuable and sell for a better price per ton."

After wine and dessert, Sally went in the kitchen and brought out a pot of coffee flavored with chicory and hot milk, New Orleans style.

Rachel perked up and became involved in the conversation,

"At Davis, they call Zinfandel the 'mystery grape' because no one was certain where it came from, and it seems to thrive only in California. Zinfandel has no tradition in Europe unlike all of the other popular California grapes. We know the name comes from the Czech 'Cinifadl'. Zin is related to a black grape grown in Apulia, Italy, but the grapes are not quite the same. Researchers have traced the first Zinfandel cuttings that came to California to a nursery in New England in the mid-1800's. But no one knows for certain where they came from before that."

"I had no idea. I just assumed Zinfandel came from Italy," Mike said.

"Carol Meredith at UCal-Davis compared the DNA of 150 different samples of Zinfandel grapes. She found that the Zin grape were related to the Plavac Mali in Croatia, but, just like Primitivo in Italy, those grapes are related to but not parents of Zinfandel."

Joining in the discussion seemed to cheer up Rachel somewhat.

We all cleared the table after dinner, and the women went in the kitchen to visit and do the dishes. The children returned to their homework. Mike and I grabbed our jackets and walked out the back door to his yard. Mike lit up. I think he tried not to smoke in front of Sally. I savored the smell of Mike's cigarette. The fragrance of the smoke still attracted me even though I had stopped smoking years ago. This gave me an opportunity to talk to Mike.

"I'm very curious about the witness who saw a woman leaving the alley the night Warren Roberts was killed, Mike. Any chance I could talk to her?"

"You know that's against policy," Mike said.

"What can it hurt in this case? We already know she saw a woman leaving the scene but couldn't I.D. the person. I would just like to know more about what she saw."

"You know I can't, Gene."

"We both are after the truth. If Fran is guilty, so be it, but I'm not convinced at this point. There's no real motive—it's not money, and divorce is a much easier option than murder. And we know that divorce had been discussed. They had been separated, and her dad knew divorce was a possibility. The only circumstantial evidence is the gun."

"And the witness," Mike said. "Detective Lawrence thinks Fran killed her husband when she found out about the girl-friend."

"Why would his girlfriend matter so much to Fran that she would kill him if they were splitting up anyway and money wasn't an issue? The woman the witness saw could have been someone other than the killer, just some woman out for an evening stroll," I said.

"O.K. So what about shooting Roberts in the balls?" Mike asked.

Mike put out his cigarette in the grass and put the butt in his pocket. I tried not to smile at the cigarette game, as if Sally could be fooled.

"The killer could have done that to throw you off."

"Anything's possible but not always likely," Mike replied.

"I would just like to know what she saw that night in order to satisfy my concerns."

"I can't allow you interview her, Gene, but I'll tell you what I can do. I'll let you see the videotape of Detective Lawrence interviewing the witness but only on certain conditions. First of all, you promise not to divulge anything to anyone—not Fran's attorney, not your partner, not anyone. Secondly, you agree not to contact the witness—not in person, by phone, by mail, not even by Pony Express. Finally, Detective Lawrence must be with you when you view the tape. He won't be happy about you seeing the tape, but I'm the boss, and there's not much Lawrence can do about it."

"I give you my word."

I raised my left hand and put out my right as if swearing on a bible.

We went back in the house and joined the women who sat close to each other on the sofa in the den and chatted in low tones. I suspected they were whispering about me; Sally knew all of my secrets from the past.

We bid them goodnight and walked back to the truck. Rachel put her arm in mine and she looked more relaxed than I had seen her since our terrible drive home from San Francisco.

"I'm glad we spent the evening with Mike and Sally," Rachel said. "I like Sally and I think we'll be friends."

"I knew you'd like them. They're two of the best people I've ever known."

CHAPTER 31

DETECTIVE JOHN LAWRENCE MET ME IN THE lobby of the Napa police station and escorted me to a conference room that was set up with a VCR and TV set.

I gave him a polite greeting, offering him my hand, and said, "Good morning, Detective Lawrence."

He ignored my hand and grumbled, "Follow me."

He didn't say a word until we reached the conference room. He closed the door, turned around, and put his ugly face about a foot from mine.

He said, squaring his shoulders and glaring directly at my eyes, "I don't like this one god damn bit! I don't give a shit if you are the Chief's asshole buddy; you got no business looking at a tape of a police interview."

I smelled his cigarette breath.

"I'm sorry you're offended," I said in a quiet tone.

"Chief says I have to show you the tape in spite of my objections, but I want you to know how I feel," Lawrence said as he retreated.

"A lot has happened since I came here last. Someone killed a fine woman. They've threatened people involved in this case, and they've almost killed me—twice— since I started my in-

187

vestigation of Warren Roberts' murder. We both know Fran
Roberts is not responsible for all of this."

"Doesn't mean she didn't kill her husband."

"Maybe not, but you've got a shaky case. No physical evidence. No DNA. No prints. All you have is the .25—and you
can't even prove who used it. You have a dubious witness, and
the motive sucks. Fran gets just a little money that she doesn't
need anyway because she's heir to Chateau Carneros. Friends
say divorce had been discussed, so why kill him? Divorce is
easier and less messy. And you don't have to be grilled by heavy-
handed cops when you get a divorce."

Lawrence ignored my jab and thought for a minute.

"What about his mistress? We know you talked to her.
Maybe Fran got so pissed off when she found out about the
girlfriend that she lost control?" he countered.

"Same answer. What difference does it make if you're getting a divorce anyway—surely not enough to commit murder.
At any rate, let's see the tape. Chief Edwards knows your case
against Fran isn't solid. He consented to let me see the tape on
the condition that Buddy and I agree to cooperate and turn over
anything we find to you in person," I told him. "I also promised
not to contact the witness or reveal her name or the contents of
the tape to anyone."

"Yeah, Chief told me. We don't need your help. But I
guess I have to live with it since you're getting paid to investigate Robert's murder. Just don't interfere with me. Give
me anything you find." He said, softening his tone and re-
laxing his shoulders.

Lawrence dimmed the lights and turned on the VCR.
Lawrence came on the screen wearing the same "Pollack" tie
and brown polyester pants that I assumed had become his trade-
mark. The woman sitting across the table from him looked
middle-aged. Her skin was the color of café au lait. She was

well dressed—in contrast to her interviewer—in a blue silk blouse and tan slacks. Lawrence showed he had a charming side to his personality when he chose to exert the effort.

He lowered his voice and asked the witness questions in a conversational tone.

Lawrence	Please state your name and address.
Foster	Margaret Foster, 1205 Terrace Street, Napa.
Lawrence	Your occupation?
Foster	I am the principal at Napa Middle School.
Lawrence	Are you married, Ms. Foster?
Foster	No, I am a widow.
Lawrence	I'm sorry, Mrs. Foster. Who resides with you at your address?
Foster	No one. I live alone.
Lawrence	I understand you saw a woman leaving the alley of Terrace Street Tuesday Evening, February 2nd last. Could you tell me about the circumstances?
Foster	I had come home from school about five-thirty, fixed dinner, and decided to take a walk. It was a beautiful night for a stroll, just cool enough for a sweater. I walked south on Terrace Street toward Imola Avenue. A woman came out of the alley behind those new townhouses and turned to the right in front of me.
Lawrence	So she was heading in the same direction as you. Approximately what time was that?
Foster	It was probably a little after six-thirty.
Lawrence	And how far is the alley from your house?
Foster	About two blocks.
Lawrence	Did you recognize the woman?
Foster	No, I never saw her face. She turned in front of me. I only glimpsed a side view and saw her walk in front of me.

Lawrence	How far away from you was she when she turned out of the alley?
Foster	Only about thirty feet.
Lawrence	Did you ever get any closer to her when you were walking behind her?
Foster	No, she was walking faster than I. She reached Imola well before I did. I don't know whether she turned on Imola or went straight."
Lawrence	So she walked fast. Was she running?
Foster	No, not at all. She just walked faster than I. My knees aren't so good anymore.
Lawrence	Did you get close enough to be able describe her? She tapped her fingernails on the table.
Foster	As I've already said, I didn't get close enough to see her face. It had gotten dark, and she was too far away. Only a little light came from the half-moon, and I just got a glimpse. I would say she was about medium height, maybe a little taller.
Lawrence	Would you say she was five-foot-five?
Foster	It's hard to tell. She was not real short nor was she real tall—about my size, I'dsay. I couldn't tell you exactly.
Lawrence	What about her weight? Would you say she was about one-hundred-forty pounds?
Foster	I'm sorry, Detective. I couldn't say. Her dress was rather loose.
Lawrence	Can you describe the dress?
Foster	I can't say which color it was, but it was a dark color and ankle-length.
Lawrence	Did she have short brown hair with bangs? (Fran's hairstyle.) I laughed at Lawrence's attempts to implicate Fran.

Foster	I didn't notice. I couldn't tell about the length. I think her hair was dark, but again I can't say what color. I only saw her for a minute or two, and she wasn't close to me at all.
Lawrence	Was she white, Black or Hispanic?
Foster	White, I think, but I can't be certain about that, either.
Lawrence	Is there anything else you could tell me about the woman you saw that night?
Foster	I recall noting one thing at that time. Her walk would not be acceptable at my school. We encourage our young women to walk with their backs straight, their heads up and back. This woman had bad posture and walked with an unusual step, certainly not feminine or attractive.
Lawrence	Did you see anyone else on Terrace Street that night?
Foster	No, no one else.
Lawrence	Is there anything else you can tell me?
Foster	No, nothing. I already told you that.
Lawrence	How about unusual noises? Did you hear anything from the direction of the alley?
Foster	No, not a thing. I would have told you, Detective Lawrence, if I had heard any shots.
Lawrence	Thank you very much for coming. We may ask you to testify. At this point, the witness frowned and looked Lawrence straight in the face.
Foster	I'll say what I saw, Detective, but I couldn't identify that person from that night.
Lawrence	Here's my card. Please call me if you should think of anything else.

The videotape ended, and Lawrence got up and turned off the TV/ VCR and flipped on the lights. He pivoted toward the conference table but continued to stand.

"Well, Ventura, did you get what you wanted?" Lawrence asked.

"She certainly couldn't I.D. Fran Roberts, despite your pointed questions."

"No, but Mrs. Roberts is medium height."

"So are many other people; that's why people call it "medium", average. Let's see, she said 'not real short and not real tall', what's left covers quite a range. Mrs. Foster also couldn't say for sure about the time. Isn't it possible the woman she saw leaving the alley wasn't coming from the murder scene at all but just some resident of another townhouse out for a walk, like Mrs. Foster?" I asked.

"Not very probable. I think your client was so enraged about hubby's girlfriend that she took her little pistol and killed him when she caught him leaving Carol Greene's house. Then she shot him where it counted," Lawrence said as he pointed his finger at my groin.

"Have you tried forensic hypnosis?" I inquired. "A witness will sometimes remember more under hypnosis. See, Lawrence, I'd like to know who she saw, too."

"I called an expert in San Francisco and explained the situation, and he said hypnosis wouldn't help."

Lawrence wiped his hands on his pants and tugged at his collar. Perspiration had collected above his eyebrows. I questioned his reaction.

"You must realize, Detective, that this is a weak witness. No wonder she didn't come forward right after the murder. She didn't think it was important because she didn't see much at all and couldn't make an ID. You DA won't indict Fran Roberts with no more physical evidence and only this witness."

"I'm not through yet," Lawrence argued. "I'll build such a strong circumstantial case that the jury will believe it wouldn't be possible for anyone else to have killed Roberts."

Detective Lawrence meant business. We needed to provide a viable alternate suspect to get Fran off the hook. I thanked him for his time and offered my hand. This time he took it. His hand felt moist and sweaty. I left the police building.

CHAPTER 32

BUDDY CAME OVER AFTER MY DISTURBING session with Detective Lawrence to see if I had learned anything important.

"Good morning, Buddy. How about some breakfast?"

"Thanks, anyway. Just some strong black coffee. I watched Sky Leonard's office last night until the lights went out. Didn't get to bed until two."

"Any news at Sky's?"

"Nothing out of the ordinary. She stays pretty close to home except for the usual errands. She lives in a small apartment behind her office. No special visitors, just the same KNG supporters we've already checked out. No evidence of a boyfriend, seven feet tall or otherwise. Maybe she's not inclined in that direction. We'll give it another week or so and then drop the surveillance. "What did you learn from your pal John Lawrence?" Buddy asked.

I poured us each a cup and told Buddy about the videotape of the police witness.

"The lady was credible. She saw a female figure leaving the alley about the time of the murder, but she couldn't identify the woman. She was too far away, and it was dark. The woman came out of the alley and turned away from the witness, walking ahead of her in the same direction."

"Could she describe anything about her? Color of her hair? The clothing she wore?"

"She said it was a dark dress and long and thought the hair was dark. Medium height. Medium weight. Only thing unique was the way she walked; said she walked funny."

"Wonder what that means, "funny"? She doesn't seem to have helped the police's case much," Buddy said.

"No. Lawrence kept asking her pointed questions that referred to Fran, but she didn't believe she saw anything that would help him."

"Is Lawrence still convinced Fran did it?" Buddy asked.

"Yeah. He refuses to entertain the possibility that the other stuff that's going on could be related to Warren's murder. He either has no other suspects or he's hot to convict Fran or both."

"What do you think of his case against her?" Buddy asked.

"Looks kind of weak to me. He thinks he can build a case on circumstantial evidence that the DA can use to indict Fran. I'm not sure," I replied.

"That could happen. Let's see: there's the Roberts' gun, she has no alibi, and we know the shooter was shorter than Warren. And the witness saw some woman about Fran's size leaving the scene," Buddy enumerated.

"And Lawrence's suggested motive is that Fran went berserk when she learned about her husband's girlfriend. Then she killed him out of jealous rage, putting three bullets in his crotch to make her point. They also have witnesses who saw Fran and Warren fighting," I said.

"Lawrence may be getting close to an indictment. But my friend in the prosecutor's office says they're not yet ready to take the case to the grand jury," Buddy said.

Buddy lifted the coffeepot from the table and refilled both of our cups. The coffee tasted strong and bitter.

"Jack Phillips sure wants us to find the killer before they can indict Fran. He reminded Franklin that Warren was killed three weeks ago and that we haven't gotten any closer to finding the killer. That may be true, but we've no shortage of suspects," I said.

"There's the partner, Vic O'Connell. And Sky Leonard may not have wanted Warren to finish his report on her moratorium, but that might be a stretch. We know from Susan O'Connell that Jack Phillips hated his son-in-law. We aren't really considering Warren's girlfriend, but she could have cooked up her alibi, and the sad story she told you could have been a great act. What if Warren was ending the affair and she went postal?" Buddy theorized.

"It might not even be any of these people. Maybe some hothead on the winery side of the moratorium wanted to suppress Warren's report. They could have even more motivation than weird Sky if they stood to lose big bucks. Or his murder could have been the result of something we haven't even considered yet, like a person from his past or maybe an old jilted lover. We know Carol Greene wasn't the first girlfriend Warren had had since he got married. There was Susan O'Connell, who by the way, may have been furious when our lover boy chose Carol Greene instead of coming back to her. These guys follow a pattern of cheating on their wives. But I have a hunch the woman the witness saw is important," I said.

"There's no question that we're making somebody nervous by our prying," Buddy said.

"You're right. They tried to kill me coming down Howell Mountain. That was no accident. And how does the killing of Judy Harris and ramming our car dovetail with the threat to Rachel and killing Danny Boy?"

"I don't know. Where do we go from here?" Buddy asked.

I responded with a quizzical look. Silence filled the room.

Rachel came into the kitchen a few minutes later and wondered about the stillness. She looked at me with a questioning expression, holding a sheaf of papers in her hand.

"The bills came in for the materials to build the new trellises. You're running short on cash," she said.

"More good news. I guess we've almost used up the money from Franklin Reed's retainer," I said.

"I can let you have some money until we get our final check from Reed," Buddy offered.

"No thanks, Buddy, we'll manage."

"What you need is a new contract to sell the grapes from your fall harvest. You won't have any trouble borrowing against a good contract, and you can pay the bank back after the grapes are in and paid for," Rachel suggested.

"I'll just have to take some time off from the Roberts case and do a little selling," I groaned.

"I don't think you'll have too much trouble. Your dad's Zinfandel grapes have a good reputation and almost sell themselves. You just need a buyer who wants to make premium wine. I've got some ideas and I'll make some calls tomorrow, but you'll have to meet with the winemakers yourself and take them out in the field to show them the plants. Wouldn't hurt, either, to break open a bottle or two of the old wine made from these grapes," she said.

"That reminds me, Buddy, you asked what we do next," I said. "Well, I'm going to tonight's Napa Valley Vintners Association meeting. I'm an associate member as a grape grower, and I still know some of the guys from growing up here. I want to take the pulse of their feelings about the moratorium proposal and see if I can find any hotheads who might take the law into their own hands."

CHAPTER 33

THE NAPA VALLEY VINTNERS MET EVERY MONTH, rotating the location amongst the various wineries. I drove to the Stone Valley Winery on Silverado Road for the seven o'clock meeting. The parking lot filled in a hurry. Pickup trucks sat unabashed next to late model Mercedes and BMW's. The proposed moratorium debate had generated an unusual high attendance.

Some thirty or forty men and women stood around the hospitality center in small clusters of three or four having discussions and waiting for the meeting to start. Paul Martin flagged me down as I entered the room.

"Hello, Gene. Good to see you. Have you heard any news about the board's moratorium vote?"

"Hi, Mr. Paul. Rachel believes the vote will be postponed due to Judy Harris' death. A county supervisor has never died before while in office. The county attorney is checking the charter. An interim member may be appointed to fill her spot until the next election."

Someone from the host winery came by with a tray and handed each of us a glass of Stone Valley Fume' Blanc. I tasted a pleasant hint of green grass at the back of my mouth.

"What else is new?" Paul Martin asked.

"We're learning more about Sky Leonard and her background. Napa's not the first town where she's organized environmental groups. That reporter, Casey Hammon, contacted me. He's doing research for a series of articles about radical environmental groups and seems quite interested in Ms. Leonard."

"You don't often come to our meetings. What's the occasion?"

"We haven't ruled out that someone is so hot about this vineyard moratorium issue that they have gone off the deep end and silenced Warren Roberts for good. I want to hear what the prevailing attitude is of your guys," I said.

"You're wasting your time. No winery owner would think of doing such a thing. Most people I've talked to feel certain KNG doesn't have the votes to pass the proposal anyway. Only County Supervisor Gabe Houston favors the moratorium. The other three board members are either riding the fence, like Rachel, or are leaning our way. I'm certain they will vote with us if we show them we'll do the right things.

"So you don't know of anyone who might have gotten stirred up enough to use violence?" I asked.

"No, of course not, Gene."

We heard the rustle of people entering the auditorium for the meeting. We followed them in, and I took a seat.

Mr. Paul presided and he attempted to follow a preset agenda, but everyone wanted to rush through the other items to get to the moratorium discussion. Paul Martin brought up the name of each county commissioner. He asked members who knew each one, how they thought he might vote, and what arguments to use to persuade him. He asked the people who knew them to lobby each supervisor in a temperate way except for Gabe Houston.

Some speakers rose to address the meeting and reiterated the potential detrimental effects of the proposed moratorium. One owner had purchased expensive acreage that he would be unable to plant under the new rules. Others voiced concern about their expansion plans. A woman said she belonged to a group that planned to open a new winery and had thus far invested over a million dollars in the project. It would be squashed should the moratorium pass.

I sat in the back of the room and listened and paid careful attention to each person. I gauged the response of those who didn't contribute to the discussion as well as the speakers. I saw various levels of concern, but no one stood out as acting too excited or emotional.

That didn't mean that someone who had a lot of money at stake wouldn't get violent. And what about some independent person who held a strong belief that government had no right to interfere with a person's property rights? I couldn't identify any such person by any action taken in the crowd. But such a person didn't have to be at the meeting.

A social hour followed the meeting. It surprised me that most of the people drank coffee instead of wine. I heard snippets of conversations as they milled around. Some people I knew greeted me, asked about my vineyard, and wanted to know who had contracted to buy my Zinfandel grapes. When I mentioned we had not yet made a forward contract, they assumed I was attending the meeting for that purpose. I took another sip of my coffee. I realized right then that I must learn how to sell my grapes. The one person I expected to see at the meeting hadn't shown up, Jack Phillips.

I drove home after the NVVA meeting. I saw Buddy's old Corvette parked in front of the house at that late hour. Someone had turned on every light in the house, including the spotlight I had installed over the front door to illuminate the porch and front yard.

"What's going on?" I asked as Rachel opened the front door. She wore a gloomy expression, and her mouth sagged at the corners. Her eyes looked like a deer's whose gaze had been caught in a headlight. A switch seemed to also have turned off the bright countenance I had come to know and love.

"They contacted me at last, Gene. It is the moratorium. The bastards want me to vote for it."

"Tell me verbatim what they said."

I hugged her to stop her from trembling. I felt the rapid beat of her heart next to mine. I guided her inside the front room and sat next to her on the sofa.

"The guy put on a fakey British accent. He said something like, 'We've warned you before, lassie. You know we can get to you, no matter who protects you. You'll be wantin' to support the moratorium ordinance and see that it passes; otherwise there be consequences.' He didn't mention Judy Harris, but the inference was there."

Buddy came over to us, bringing Rachel a snifter of the RMS Brandy from the liquor cabinet.

"Rachel called me right after you left for the meeting. She told me about the phone call, and I came over. Ernesto had stayed with Rachel, but I sent him on home."

"Rachel, can you get a flight and leave for France tomorrow?" I asked.

"I talked to Dad. He got the message I had left on his answering machine. He and Mom are winding up a visit to Spain. They'll arrive home a week from Friday. I didn't tell him why, just that I wanted to come for a visit. I didn't want to alarm them. They'll drive to Paris and meet my flight the day they return." Rachel replied.

"What do you think, Buddy?" I asked.

"I think Rachel will be safe as long as she's with one of us at all times. The danger would increase if she went down the mountain and out in the open. I'll get Max to take my shift watching the KNG office. Things are quiet after Sky goes to bed and until about ten in the morning. She likes her beauty rest. Max can go home at night and come back in the morning."

"So you think Rachel will be OK?" I asked.

I needed reassurance.

"Sure. I've got my Baretta nine millimeter with me, and I can get the Savage Pump Action with the short barrel from under my car seat now," Buddy said.

"Wait a minute, you guys. Calm down, the both of you. There's no danger right now. They want me to vote for the ordinance. They won't harm me before the vote."

Rachel's mood had brightened somewhat. She realized even before the two smart detectives that the bad guys wanted her to vote "right" and would leave her alone until the vote.

"I don't know about that. Look what happened to Judy," I said, still worried.

"Well, maybe they approached Judy, and she told them to go to hell," Buddy suggested.

"That sounds like Judy," Rachel said.

"I still want you out of the way until we figure out what's going on and find that son of a bitch. You said they might postpone the vote on the moratorium. Keep your reservation and get on the plane to Paris next week," I said to Rachel as I grabbed her for another hug.

"Franklin Reed called for you before the threatening phone call, Gene. He wants you to come to his office tomorrow at ten for a meeting with Fran and her dad," Rachel said.

"What's up?"

"A defense meeting, he said. He believes the DA's office is looking into going to the grand jury."

"This guy who called Rachel could be yet another suspect. He killed Judy Harris and left her body in our trunk. He said he's warned Rachel twice—now and when he killed Rachel's dog and in her Volvo. He could have also killed

Warren Roberts to quell his report. A warped mind might see a damaging study as sufficient reason to kill," I said.

"Sure. It's possible. It's far fetched that someone would kill for that, but he or she is nuts anyway if they killed Judy Harris 'cause she wouldn't vote right," Buddy said.

"And Sky Leonard could fit that description," I suggested.

"Yes, but we thought the man who killed Rachel's dog, Danny Boy, wore a size 16-EEE,' Buddy said, 'and now we have a man's voice on the phone. Maybe they're in cahoots."

"You're certain no one fitting that description has visited Sky?"

"No way. We've checked out every person who's met with her. She could have brought in some dude from out of town of course and contacted him only by phone. You recall that you didn't want to tap her phone," Buddy ribbed me.

"Well, at least we have someone else to suggest as a suspect at that meeting tomorrow," I said.

Buddy insisted that he spend the night with us since he would be watching Rachel in the morning anyway while I attended Franklin Reed's meeting. That way, he said, he wouldn't have to go home and then come back up the mountain. I believed he wanted to stand guard and make Rachel feel more comfortable with both of us there to protect her. I checked our special locks and left the spotlight on. Rachel made up the sofa bed in the front room for Buddy, and she and I retired to my bedroom. I noticed his shotgun protruded from under the sofa.

Nothing happened that night. Buddy, Rachel and I ate breakfast. No fresh-baked goods today—strictly eat and run. I ventured to town, arriving at Franklin Reed's office ten minutes before the meeting. Fran Roberts and her dad, Jack Phillips, walked in soon after I did. Fran looked terrible. New wrinkles creased her forehead, and I perceived red lines in her eyes when she removed her sunglasses. Franklin shepherded the three of us into his oak paneled conference room. Law books took up an entire wall of the room, floor to ceiling. I could still detect the odor of new carpet and fresh paint.

Franklin looked at me after we sat at the table and coffee had been poured—didn't smell as good as ours.

"Gene, I've asked you to this conference because I anticipate the DA's office taking their case to the grand jury pretty soon. John Lawrence is pushing them pretty hard. I thought we would all discuss the case in order to prepare. I assume you can speak for Buddy Bennett as well as yourself?"

"Yes. Buddy is handling surveillance today so he couldn't come. I can speak for both of us as we have regular meetings and since I'm the one you hired to coordinate the investigation."

"So you have another suspect?" Jack Phillips said as he leaned forward.

"Several, in fact. Just honed in on another one yesterday. More than one person might have wanted Warren out of the way. We are looking in different directions. But we don't have enough hard evidence yet to nail down the killer," I said.

"We're getting a little ahead of ourselves," Franklin said. "I want to describe our legal situation first, and then we can get to Gene's report. Detective John Lawrence is pressing the district attorney's office to seek an indictment of Fran based on the circumstantial evidence and his contention that no one else could have killed Warren. The DA has to show the grand jury that he has enough to warrant a trial."

Fran sank in her chair. Her dad rose from his.

"He can't be serious. He doesn't have any god damn evidence."

"The gun was registered to Warren. People saw them arguing in public. Fran had no alibi that night. And the DA will contend Fran was jealous of Warren for seeing another woman," Franklin said.

"That doesn't amount to shit!" Jack Phillips boomed.

"They also have a witness who saw a woman maybe Fran's size leaving the alley around the time of the murder," Franklin went on.

"I think they have a problem with that witness, Franklin. We know for a fact that the witness couldn't identify anybody. She was so far away all she saw was a feminine figure in the distance," I said.

"Positive?" Reed asked.

"Yes, for sure. I can't disclose my source because I promised I would keep it confidential, but I know the details of her interview with the police."

"They don't have a prayer of getting an indictment then, right, Franklin?" Phillips asked.

"The gun and the supposed motive alone are insufficient. The DA will also tell the grand jury that the Napa police have made an extensive investigation and that that no other possible suspects exist," Franklin replied.

"Bull shit!" I said. "John Lawrence assumed Fran killed her husband and hasn't considered any other possibility. He's either lazy or he has made up his mind or both."

"What do you have?" Franklin asked me.

"Warren's partner is a possibility. He wanted to expand, Warren didn't. I sense he resented Warren and believed he could get along without him. He stands to make a lot more money with Warren gone. He could have hired the woman seen leaving the alley to kill Warren. And then there's the moratorium business. It seems a long shot, but someone on either side of the issue could have killed Warren to suppress his report. This motive became a bit more probable when Judy Harris was killed. Judy didn't favor the moratorium. Commissioner Rachel Bernard feels the same way and she has been threatened. There might be a connection," I said.

"What about Warren's girlfriend? Who's she?" Fran finally entered the discussion.

"We haven't been able to connect her to the murder. But we haven't ruled her out, either. Warren met her through his work. He told her the two of you were getting a divorce," I answered.

"We had discussed divorce, but I had hoped we could get back together," Fran said.

I saw tears well up in her already red eyes. I felt pity for Fran. I remembered her as the innocent girl I had loved those many years ago. Now she faced living alone and maybe going to prison. Helping her was no longer just a job, it was a mission.

"I can't imagine the DA going to the grand jury without more than he's got if the witness is not viable. But if they ever get an indictment, Gene, we'll have to build our defense on the possibility that someone else could have killed Warren in addition to the weakness of the evidence. It's good that you've identified other possible suspects. We'll go for reasonable doubt. Better yet, find us the murderer," Franklin said.

"We intend to. We're watching several people, digging into their pasts and doing research. We have several good leads. I think we'll have a breakthrough pretty soon."

I put on a bold front.

Fran said, "I'm very grateful for your help, Gene. You know I couldn't have killed Warren."

"Finding out about their witness was good work, Ventura. Can we talk outside?" Jack Phillips asked.

And with that, we all got up and walked out of the conference room. What did Jack Phillips want with me? I was sure he wouldn't chew me out again, but with him you never knew. I followed him out the door of the law office to the sidewalk. He turned to face me.

"I want to talk to you about your grapes. I might have some interest in buying your entire crop. My marketing guys think we can sell a super premium Zinfandel, and your grapes might just work if we can buy them right."

"Come out to the farm, Mr. Phillips. I'll show you

around, and we can talk about it. I've had some good interest, but we haven't signed a deal yet," I fibbed.

"I'll come out to your place tomorrow about nine o'clock, and call me Jack."

He shook my hand and walked away to his car where Fran waited for him. I'll be damned! What a surprise! I wondered what that old coot was up to.

CHAPTER 34

I STAYED UP LATE THAT NIGHT AFTER THE MEETING, pondering Jack Phillips' interest in my grapes. I felt awkward doing business with him while investigating his son-in-law's murder. I wanted Rachel's input. I could just make some excuse, like I had already received a pending commitment from someone else. I was sitting in the kitchen drinking my third espresso when Rachel came in, wearing her robe and rubbing her eyes.

"I heard the coffee machine. Why are you up at this hour?"

"Sorry I woke you. I've invited Jack Phillips over in the morning to talk about buying my grapes. I wonder what he's up to?"

Rachel sat down across the table from me and said, "Maybe he just wants to buy the best Zinfandel grapes in the valley. Perhaps he found that all of the other top-notch Zin grapes have already been put under contract."

"But why now, while we're in the midst of trying to help get Fran off the hook? I'm pretty sure he never bought grapes from Pop."

"Maybe it's just coincidence. He needs grapes like yours at the same time that you happen to be working with Franklin

Reed to save Fran. I can see that you're suspicious because of the timing. Remember, this is the season when everyone contracts for his grapes. Winery people are a close-knit group, always gossiping and talking shop. Maybe Phillips heard that you hadn't sold your fall crop, and it fits his need."

"Besides, Chateau has always been a medium-priced label, a volume operation a cut above the bulk wineries but not near the quality of the wines with the high price tags. Chateau produces the popular varietals for the most part: Cabernets and Chardonnay, along with some Merlots and Sauvignon Blancs but no Zinfandels. The demand for premium Zins increases each year, and I suspect Phillips wants to get in on the action. I'm certain his customers have told him to do it," Rachel said.

"Perhaps. Then there's his personality. He has an ego the size of a tyrannosaurus. How do I work with a man like that?"

The caffeine had started making me jumpy.

"You'll deal with his winemakers, not him. They'll monitor the growing season and make the final decision about when to harvest, based on their criteria about levels of sugar, acid, and pH. You should see little of Phillips once you sign the contracts," Rachel said.

"Would I be better off selling to someone else?"

Rachel got up from the table, poured herself the remaining espresso from the pot, added some cream, and turned off the machine. She sat back down and continued.

"The relationship would be the same with any winery. It's not like selling a pair of shoes it's a partnership. Phillips has the ability to buy the entire crop; not many others can. You could sell to Chateau for years with a long-term contract."

"But couldn't we get a better price on the spot market?" I asked. "Demand is always high for best quality Napa grapes, and people prize Zinfandels grown on hillsides like ours."

"A long-term contract with a heavy hitter would provide steady cash flow, and you wouldn't have money
problems like you do now."

I got up from the table and started pacing.

"But if I get in bed with them, those Chateau people will
come over here all the time, telling us how to grow our grapes.
They'll decide about irrigation and pruning and trellises, even
about managing pests."

"You'll decide these things together in actuality. It won't
be so bad. They've got good people who know their stuff, but,
since they have little experience with Zinfandel grapes, they'll
need a lot of advice from you and Ernesto to get the best fruit
possible."

"I'll at least talk to him. What do you think about pricing?"
I asked.

"Some people go for an average of the price of similar grapes
in the four north coast counties. Others try to create a ratio
between the grape prices and the retail bottle prices. But location of the vineyard is critical. Zinfandel grapes from Napa and
Sonoma sold last year for more than twice as much as those
grown at Lodi-Woodbridge near Galt, south of Sacramento."

"So we ought to come out all right if we have good weather.
You know the market. Will you help me?" I asked.

"Sure, mon amour, I'll help you with everything, but please
sit down, you're making me nervous," Rachel said. "Just talk
to the man. See what he has to say."

We went to bed and set the alarm for eight o'clock.

I heard a horn honking after finishing dressing and eating
breakfast. We saw Jack Phillips parking his pearl gray Land
Rover. We stepped out to meet him.

He had dressed up to tromp around in the vineyard and
looked as if he had stepped out of an Abercrombie and Fitch
catalogue. No jeans, work shirt or windbreaker for this dude.

He reminded me of old safari photos with his matching tan outfit, his shooting jacket, and his Aussie-style hat.

"Hello, Mr. Phillips, come right in," I said as we moved toward the door.

"I told you to call me Jack. I like how you've converted this old stone winery into a house. I've never been here in all these years."

"The house is pretty much the way it's been since Pop bought the place just after the war. He and Mamma did all the remodeling; all I did was grow up here."

"It reminds me of the way Napa used to be in the old days when my father started Chateau Carneros. And who is this pretty lady?" Phillips asked.

"This is Rachel Bernard. Rachel, meet Jack Phillips. Rachel's helping me update the vineyard."

Jack nodded his head at Rachel and put out his hand. "Oh yes. I've heard of you. Didn't you make wine at Premier?"

"Oui, c'est moi," she said. "Have you eaten breakfast?"

"Yes, thank you. I'd like to see your vines right away."

I had decided to be direct with him.

"I'd like to ask you about any possible connection between my investigating Warren's murder and your sudden interest in buying my grapes."

"None. What connection could there be? My lawyer hired you because of your police background. Franklin Reed said you had time to run the investigation because you brought in Buddy to help—he's a good man—and I assumed you had help here at the farm. People said your family grew some of the best Zinfandel grapes around from your pop's old vines. I heard you hadn't signed a contract yet. That's why I'm here."

"But why me? Couldn't you buy grapes elsewhere?" I asked Phillips.

"I may still do that. But first I want to see what you have. The boutique guys are making big bucks selling a high-priced Zinfandel. No reason we can't make a better wine than theirs, so I've decided to come out with a wine under the Chateau Carneros Select label, and I want the right grapes. Simple as that."

Phillips, Rachel, and I went out to the vineyard, and I showed him sample plants from the various sections. He examined the vines with care and paid particular attention to the spacing between the plants and the rows. Phillips knew his business. We came back into the house after about three hours, and he tasted four bottles of our wine from different years. I had opened the wine earlier that morning to let it breathe.

"The bouquet is of blackberries, but the flavor is more like cassis. How do you know this wine was made only from your grapes? Did your dad make this wine himself?" Phillips asked.

He liked what he had tasted.

"No. Pop's deal with any winery specified that they bottle six cases of wine made only from our grapes just for us. I think that condition mattered as much to him as the contracted price. He loved to give people his own Zinfandel."

"I'll take these opened bottles with me for my winemaking staff to taste. I'd like to make this kind of wine. I assume you'll work with me on the price and let our people supervise the picking if we decide we want your grapes and I buy the whole lot," Phillips said.

"If you want to contract for our grapes, we'll sit down and see if we can work something out, but I have to consider the other buyers." (Pretty sly, huh?)

"Hrmph. You'll be better off working with Chateau Carneros than with anyone else in the valley. I've got resources no one else can offer."

"Let's talk about it," I suggested as I corked the four bottles of wine and placed them in a divided cardboard box for him to take.

Rachel and I prepared a quick lunch after Phillips left. We

reviewed his visit as she made a salad from fresh spinach, Maytag blue cheese, and sherry vinaigrette. I warmed a pot of minestrone from the 'frige and toasted Italian bread slices spread with roasted garlic and virgin olive oil.

"I thought that went well. I think he'll come back," she said.

"He liked the wine well enough. He'll be tough to deal with though, and I still have reservations about getting in bed with that old buzzard. He'll treat me like an employee."

"You'll have your attorney negotiate the contract. How he treats you will depend on how much he needs your grapes and how you respond to him. I'd try it for one season. Then we'll find someone else if it doesn't work out."

No secret that Rachel favored selling the grapes to Phillips.

"I appreciate your help and love having you here, too," I said.

I came up behind her and put my arms around her waist. She turned around and gave me a great hug. Rachel's hug felt like the first sunny day in April, warming me from the top of my head down to my toes. I forgot what we were talking about.

CHAPTER 35

I CAUGHT THE PHONE ON THE THIRD RING.

"Hello."

"Gene, th-this is Casey Hammon. S-Someone tried to kill m-me," he stuttered.

"What happened? Are you O.K.?"

"I flew into S-sacramento from New York, picked up my car, and was d-driving to the paper. I came around a curve, and s-someone fired at me, probably a rifle. The b-bullet shattered the windshield and lodged in the front s-seat only about s-six inches from my head."

"Did you call the police?"

"Yes. They pulled the s-slug out and said they would investigate. I asked if they could protect me. They s-said they couldn't 'chaperone' everyone who gets shot at. Gene, I'm t-terrified."

"You should be. Most police departments are understaffed. Why do you think they shot at you?"

"It must b-be the eco-terrorism story. I f-found some incriminating st-stuff in New York." He repeated, "I'm f-frightened, Gene. Can you help me?"

"How?" I asked.

"D-Do you know where I can hide?"

I scratched my head. I'd just met this guy.

"Why me?"

"You're the only h-hard p-person I know. I d-don't know anyone else to t-turn to or who I might hire to safeguard me."

I lowered my voice and tried to calm him.

"I'll help you now. We'll talk about money later. I think you'd be safe at my farm. Where are you?"

"I'm here at the newspaper office in S-sacramento."

"Do they have a security guard?"

"Y-yes."

"Other people around?"

"Yes. I'm at my desk in an open area with about twenty others."

"Good. Stay there. Don't leave the building. Don't go out to eat or anything else. Don't be alone—stay around other people—remember, bad guys don't like witnesses. Does your building have a back door?"

"Y-yes, for deliveries."

"After dark, around seven o'clock, my partner Buddy Bennett will call and tell you he's at your rear door. Don't leave your office until you hear from him. What's your phone number?"

"C-Can't you c-come, Gene?"

"You'll be fine. Buddy's an ex-sheriff and he's well armed. The shooter would recognize my truck if he's who I think he is."

"C-Can't you b-borrow a c-car?"

He was trying my patience. "Listen, Casey. Stop whining and do what I tell you if you want my help. Now, what's your phone number?"

"It's 916-321-1109, extension 401. I'm sorry. I'll do what you say."

Casey stopped stuttering. He began to regain his focus.

"You're not going to believe what I uncovered back East, either."

"Goodbye, Casey. Remember, don't leave your office until you hear from Buddy."

I wanted to stay with Rachel. Buddy agreed to drive to Sacramento. He had had business at the capitol through the years and knew the way to the Sacramento Bee office.

Rachel and I attempted to remain calm. I hoped Buddy and Casey would get back here in one piece. We kept watching the clock as we waited. Time creeps by when you're worried about someone who you care about. We needed to keep busy and decided to make a pizza dinner. I knew they'd arrive hungry. I blended the semolina flour with fragrant olive oil and spring water and began kneading.

Buddy and Casey showed up about eight forty-five. They thought no one had followed them. Casey looked like something the cat had dragged in. Mild-mannered professors and reporters aren't used to being shot at, and Casey was no Clark Kent. He shivered. His eyes teared. He seemed to have shrunk in size, his shoulders slumped forward, his chin lowered toward his chest.

I tried to tease him, "Come on, Casey. People shoot at Buddy and me all the time. It's not so bad."

He looked up and rolled his eyes at me.

We adjourned to the kitchen, and I poured Casey and Buddy a full three fingers of the RMS Brandy. Casey managed to bring his glass to his lips only by holding the glass steady with both hands. I, on the other hand, had no trouble taking a small taste from a shot glass. The flavor of aged brandy warmed my gullet.

"Thanks for helping me. I'll try to stay out of the way and not bother anyone," Casey said to us.

"It's all right. Buddy, Ernesto and I are guarding Rachel here at the farm, and it's about as easy to watch two people as one. Don't go outside the house without one of us," I said.

"I've changed the bed linens in the guest room. You'll be comfortable there," Rachel said to Casey.

"Now, tell us why someone would want to kill you," I asked Casey.

Buddy and Casey sat at the pine kitchen table while Rachel and I went ahead with dinner.

Casey's eyes lit up, and the shooting seemed forgotten for the moment. "I got lucky in New York. I found out where the money comes from to fund some of the eco-terrorist groups like SANE. They must have found out about my nosing around. They thought that by killing me they could keep the truth from coming out. I suspect the banker who got caught as a result of my investigating found out that I was the one who blew the whistle. He must have told his contacts."

"Maybe they were just trying to scare you. So where did the money come from?" I asked.

I shaped the pizza dough into rounds and put it in well-oiled pans. Using lots of oil "fries" the bottoms of the crusts, making them brown and crisp.

"I'll tell you. Just please keep this to yourselves until my story breaks."

"Scout's honor. So out with it." Buddy had become impatient after babysitting Casey for four hours.

"First, I went to the Maine Bureau of Banking office in Augusta and asked permission to look at SANE's banking records. They were also investigating SANE by coincidence. We agreed to exchange any pertinent information. A random audit of electronic transfers showed that all of SANE's various deposits over a six-month period came from only from one bank."

Rachel tore six or seven kinds of greens for the salad.

"Is that unusual?" she asked.

"SANE and LIFE are non-profit corporations. Charitable donations normally come from a great many sources. Only one single source for such donations is an anomaly and raised a red flag. State banking agencies now check large electronic deposits at random because of the increasing number of incidents of money laundering. I already knew SANE's bank in Portland followed the required procedures, reporting deposits over ten thousand dollars to the IRS."

"Did they tell you which bank all the deposits came from?" I asked.

"After some cajoling and indicating that my story didn't require his name, I convinced the head of the bureau's compliance division to tell me the name of the bank. He said 'Empire Federal Savings Bank in New York City'."

Casey sat forward, putting both elbows on the table, showing excitement.

"I drove back to New York and met with the security officer, Kevin Goodrich, at Empire Federal. I showed him my press card and explained that the State of Maine was checking on why all deposits to the SANE account came by electronic transfer from only from one bank—his." Casey continued, "It made Maine's Bureau of Banking suspicious since, like most banks, they have been alerted to look for anything that smacks of money laundering."

I sautéed shallots, purple onions, and three kinds of mushrooms, and spinach in garlic-flavored virgin olive oil to put on the pizza while I listened. I had to raise my voice a little over the noise of the sizzling vegetables.

"Did Goodrich deny Empire's involvement and try to cover his ass?" I asked.

"No, he looked surprised, and I could see his increasing concern. Several accounts at Empire all transfer funds regularly to SANE's one account in Portland, Maine. I asked Goodrich to give me the account names and numbers."

He said he didn't have the legal authority to give out the

information that I asked for. He turned away from me and turned on his computer and punched a few keys. Then he surprised me by excusing himself and saying he had to go down the hall and would return in ten minutes."

"So he left the computer screen on for you and could deny ever giving you the data?" I said.

"That's right. I had copied the screen before he returned. The accounts all had environment-oriented names, like 'Animal Protection Society' and 'Rhode Island Endangered Water Fowl Agency' and 'Stop Logging in the Hudson River Watershed'. Another was 'Oceanic Discovery Corporation'. Goodrich returned to his office looking worried. He had checked with another bank officer and learned that all of these accounts received substantial wire deposits from like-named accounts in some small banks he'd never heard of in Liberia and the Seychelles Islands."

"Another red flag?" Buddy asked.

"You bet. Both countries are infamous tax havens where 'off-the-shelf' banks are easy to purchase from the government."

"Whoa. What's an 'off-the-shelf' bank?" Rachel asked.

Casey replied, "You pay and then you own a bank, just like buying something in a store. The only qualification is that you must use a name that no one else uses."

"I asked Goodrich if the computer could tell if the deposits that came from the Seychelles Islands and Liberia were reported on the IRS Form 4789 as required by law for deposits over $10,000. The records showed all accounts were opened three years ago and that Empire Federal had never reported any of those deposits to the IRS. Goodrich appeared shocked. He realized one of his bank officers had hidden deposits from the IRS."

"Smells like a bribe," Rachel said.

Speaking of smelling, I caught a whiff of my sublime sautéed veggies.

CHAPTER 36

CASEY RESUMED HIS STORY, telling us, "Goodrich was appalled. He knew about the black eye the Bank of New York had received when one of their officers participated in a money-laundering scheme with Russian criminals. He made a phone call and found that only three people in his bank were in a position to keep the deposits secret. He would run a check on all three and get back to me. I promised as a condition to keep the bank's involvement secret until they finished their investigation and did some damage control."

"Did you do that?" I asked.

"Sure. I only had allegations at that point. I checked into the New York Hyatt and waited for his call. I stayed close to the phone for three days. Then Goodrich called and asked me to come to the bank. He met me with the bank's VP/Public Relations in a private office. They offered me a deal. They would give me the guy's name and his scam if I would write that I gad gotten full cooperation from the bank. The PR guy wanted a statement in the story that Empire Federal worked fast to find the culprit and to turn him over to the FBI. I agreed to include a quote from their chairman or president or whoever in the story."

Rachel looked over from the stove where she was sautéing Granny Smith apples and flaming them with brandy for the apple crisp.

"How did the bank catch him in just three days?" she asked.

"They jumped on it once I pointed out the problem. I suspect teams of bankers worked through the night checking out the three bank officers. The wife of one of their assistant VP's, Eric Jensen, bought a summerhouse last year in the Hamptons. They don't make enough money to afford that, even with their combined salaries. Jensen said when he was questioned that his wife inherited the money from an aunt in Sweden. The intimidating Goodrich then asked Jensen for the aunt's name and the name of the town in Sweden so he could check the death certificate and the will."

I covered the pizza dough with the softened vegetables, thick slices of smoked mozzarella, ribbons of basil pesto sauce, and covered the pizzas with shaved Parmesan cheese. Three pairs of hungry eyes followed every movement as I put them in the hot oven.

"Was Jensen smart enough to have prepared copies of the will or estate papers?" Buddy asked.

"Nope. He never thought he'd get caught, much less interrogated. Goodrich squeezed, and it didn't take long for Jensen, an amateur, to cave. Goodrich said Jensen stammered and stumbled for a while and then admitted he took bribes to open the sham accounts and to keep deposits from Liberia and the Seychelles a secret from the IRS. He received one point commission on all deposits for his help."

"How much money did that involve?" I asked.

"A lot. Four to five million in deposits each month in the various accounts, and the bribes went into Jensen's numbered Swiss account. Jensen told the FBI the whole story in hopes of getting a break and offered to surrender his ill-gotten gains. He told me the same tale, of how an English-speaking, dark, foreign man came to his house one Saturday. He offered Jensen big bucks just for failing to report electronic deposits that came into the special accounts from the Second Bank of Liberia and Victoria Seychelles Savings Bank. Jensen also exchanged the foreign currency for dollars and transferred money from those accounts to SANE's account at the bank in Portland, Maine.

The aroma of baking pizza filled the air. Noses twitched as we all breathed in the redolent fragrances of melting Parmesan and sweet basil. I recalled the grand baked pasta dishes and rolls and pastries Mamma baked for us in this very kitchen.

"Had Jensen ever met the man before?" Buddy asked.

"No, but the stranger sure knew Jensen. He knew that Jensen needed money and owed large credit card and medical bills. The foreigner assured Jensen that no one would get hurt and that Jensen could become a hero to his wife with his new riches. Jensen never knew the man's name, even though he met him each month to get instructions."

"Whose money did they launder?" I asked.

"Jensen says he was never told but sometime later he found out by following his contact to the Iranian Office at the U.N. He said he never would have cooperated if he had known the money came from Iran. He knew the Iranians played for keeps. Jensen became frightened and put the laundering scheme on paper. He stashed it in his safety deposit box at the bank, to be opened only upon his death. He's been indicted in Federal Court. He says his wife did not participate in the scam. She just thought the windfall came from a smart investment at the bank."

Rachel came over and sat down with us. The old chair legs made a scratching sound against the floor.

"I don't understand. Why Iran, and how did they get away with it?" she asked.

"I did further probing," Casey said, "An average of over 500,000 transactions are transferred electronically (EFT) world-wide each day. The total is over four trillion dollars; only a tiny part is illegal. No paper trail. I suspect Iran launders to S.A.N.E. and others to create mayhem and disharmony in North America. I'm certain the people at S.A.N.E. know where the donations come from. They have to know, " Casey said, pausing in his tale." Isn't the pizza ready yet?" he asked.

"Just about. Does the tremendous volume make the money launderers harder to catch?" I asked.

"Authorities almost never apprehend them unless a crooked banker gets caught spending a lot more money than he makes, like Jensen," Casey went on. "The U.S. laws protect foreign financial manipulators even then. Only seven crimes can trigger a foreign money laundering investigation: bombing, robbery, murder, drug sales, bank fraud, kidnapping, and extortion. Other crimes like stock fraud, manipulation of funds, and corporate embezzlement don't meet the laundering smell test."

"Pizza time," I called.

I brought the two large pizzas to the table and cut them into wedges. Rachel served her salad dressed with balsamic vinaigrette and fresh thyme. Buddy opened two bottles of Beringer Founders' Estate Zinfandel, an excellent medium weight Zin that matched the basil flavor of the pizzas. Rachel reset the oven and started baking the apple crisp.

"Where the hell are the Seychelles Islands?" Buddy asked with a thread of melted mozzarella on his chin.

"Off the coast of Madagascar in the Indian Ocean. The Seychelles was a British colony until 1976. Now launderers love the place because of the loose banking laws and because it's a great place to do business."

"What do you mean?" Buddy asked.

We heard an audible crunch as Casey bit into the pizza.

"The Seychelles Islands are famous for their natural beauty—waterfalls descending from rugged mountains, inviting white beaches, jungles thick with mango and banana trees. Great wildlife—giant tortoises walking around everywhere. Temperate climate all year round. One can pamper oneself at the Alphonse Island Resort for six hundred dollars a night while finding a way to get illegal money into the U.S."

"How does the scam work?" I asked in between bites.

"I called the man at the Maine Bureau of Banking, and he told me the set up. You hire a lawyer in Victoria, Seychelles, or one of the other tax havens to set up a shell corporation with a local attorney as the director. He pays the government and acquires a bogus 'off-the-shelf' bank in that country without difficulty. He takes your foreign currency, like Iranian rials, and converts it to Seychelles rupees. The local lawyer then wires the rupees to fraudulent accounts in the U.S. where someone like Jensen converts the rupees to dollars. Then they wire the laundered dollars to designated accounts such as SANE's account in Maine."

"So it's difficult to the trace the money to its original source since no banking records exist," I commented.

"No wonder no one knew where Sky Leonard and SANE got their money," Rachel said.

"Now I can see why they shot at you. They need you silenced," Buddy said.

"Right."

The bell on the timer rang. Rachel brought the bubbling apple crisp from the oven along with a bowl of cream whipped with Cointreau. I made four cups of cappuccino. We ate well that night.

The long day finally caught up with Casey. He finished his coffee and went straight to bed. I worked out a schedule with Buddy to make certain either he or I or Ernesto with his big 12-gauge was always at the house with Rachel and Casey. I didn't expect the killer to storm my home but, then, I didn't expect him to kill Judy Harris, either.

CHAPTER 37

"WE GOT A BREAK AT LAST, GENE."

I heard new excitement in Buddy's voice. I held the phone to my ear with my left hand and continued to stir savory goat cheese scrambled eggs with the right.

"Max, my old deputy, watched Sky's house last night and saw an extra big fellow—over six-and-a-half feet tall—sneak in the back door of the darkened house after midnight. The guy slinked out before dawn. Max said he looked back over his shoulder several times. Sky's friend got in a big black Ford Expedition and took off. Maybe he's the guy who left the big footprint in Rachel's backyard, but it was too dark to see if his feet were big enough to be 16-EEE's."

Buddy went on, "Anyway, Max followed the guy without being spotted. He drove over the Bay Bridge to an address off Grand Avenue in Oakland. Max got the house number and he did something smart after the big man parked his SUV in front of the house. Max broke into the Expedition with a jimmy and, wearing rubber gloves, took a comb and an empty prescription bottle from the front seat. He also made a list of the stuff in the SUV. Max assured me no one could ever tell someone had broken in. We'll check his DNA from the comb to see if it matches the blood found at Rachel's and get his fingerprints off the bottle for the FBI's Automated Fingerprint Identification System."

I took my eggs and rye toast to the table, bringing the telephone with me.

"Hot damn! That's great. Max deserves a bonus. We'll get him enough Scotch whiskey to last him a year. I know this big guy must be the one. Do we know anything about him?" I asked.

"Not yet. Max found no auto registration or insurance papers in the Ford, not even a gas receipt with the guy's name on it. We'll know soon if he's ever been arrested," Buddy said.

"I'm not ready to bring the Napa police in just yet. I'll assume for now that he's involved. Seems like Sky lied again when she told me she didn't know any man that size. I want to know more about this guy and see if he fits into Warren Roberts' murder. Can you have someone else run a faster fingerprint check on the Q.T.?"

"Sure. One of my old deputies still works with the sheriff's department and could do it."

"I'll also check the ownership of his house in Oakland and his license plate. Give me the address and license plate number," I said.

"1711 Valdez Street, license number California JHI45T. The empty prescription bottle had contained Prednisone, a steroid. A bunch of stuff filled the back of the Expedition: a large tool kit, spare fan belts and hoses, some weights like dumb bells, and a new black body bag—you know, the kind they use in boxing gyms." We said good-bye.

I turned my head and looked toward the back of the house where Rachel still slept. Should I tell her we believed we found the man who killed Danny Boy and who threatened her, or should I wait until we confirmed the fact? I let her sleep and called the county tax office.

Rachel came into the kitchen all sleepy-eyed as I waited on

the telephone for the clerk to tell me who owned 1711 Valdez Street. She put her arms around me, nuzzling the back of my neck. I shivered with delight.

"Who was that on the phone?" she asked as she reached over and made a sandwich with the rest of my eggs.

I told her of Buddy's phone call.

"Who is that batard?" she asked with her eyes wide open. "Whoever he is, he killed my baby. Can you imagine? The fiend nailed that note to him!"

"We don't know yet. The county just told me the California Boxing Association; whatever that is, owns his house. Buddy is having the fingerprints checked, and I'll get a name from the license plate."

She sat down next to me.

"Have you called Mike Edwards to pick up the culprit? I hope they sic that bully detective John Lawrence on him."

"Oakland's not in Mike's jurisdiction, and I want to keep this quiet for awhile. I want to know who he is and what he's done. I want to make certain the police have strong enough evidence to convict him, if indeed he killed Warren Roberts"

"How are you going to do that?" she asked.

"I'm not sure."

"How about fixing me some more of those yummy eggs while you're thinking about it?"

Buddy showed up late that afternoon. He opened his brief-case and took out a report.

"We've found out today that his name is Daniel Patrick "Paddy" Flynn, and he's one rotten egg. He's forty-six years old, born in Bakersfield," Buddy said.

"What's on his sheet?" I asked.

"Plenty. It's longer than a certain body part." Rachel giggled; Buddy blushed just a bit.

Buddy went on. "He went to juvenile at sixteen for beating

up his teacher, served time for assault with a deadly weapon, last sentence was for a federal weapons violation. He's been suspected in four murders, the last one while he was in Leavenworth. Seems someone knifed a rival of the Arian gang with a shiv. None of the murder charges stuck. FBI notes in the file indicate he's a muscle for hire."

"What else do you know about him?" Rachel asked Buddy.

"Well, he was a professional boxer."

My ears perked up.

"Not Paddy Flynn, 'The Irish Hammer'! I remember him. Must have been in the late seventies, early eighties. He fought around the Bay Area and went on to be a minor heavyweight contender back East. I saw him fight on TV once. He got beat by a fighter named 'Animal Lopez'. I recall Flynn had a hard right but wasn't swift. Agile fighters gave him fits. They wouldn't stand still and let Flynn hit them."

"That would explain the boxing stuff in his Ford. Must be the same man," Buddy said.

"Yeah. Both the SUV and the house are registered to the California Boxing Association, too."

"Can't they arrest him for killing Danny Boy if his DNA matches the blood found in my backyard? Call the Oakland police," Rachel said.

"I think we should do that, Gene. Let's call Mike Edwards and tell him what we know. Remember, we promised. He'll work with Oakland PD. They can pick him up," Buddy said.

"Charging him with killing a dog's not enough. He'd get a slap on the wrist. I don't want this one to fall through the cracks. I want to know what else he did. I've decided to look around 1711 Valdez Street."

"That's stupid; he's a killer!" Rachel shouted.

"I don't plan to have tea with him, just look around and see what I can learn. I'll make certain no one's at home. Neither

Flynn nor anyone else will ever know I've been there. If evidence of his killing Warren Roberts is there, I want to make certain the police find it when they search the place."

"This doesn't sound good to me," Buddy said.

"Yeah, I have a horrible feeling about it, too," Rachel echoed. She touched her throat and had a worried expression on her face.

"I've made up my mind. I have to see what's in that house."

"I better go with you, since you're set on going." Buddy said.

"No. It's easier for one person to weasel in than two. I'll be OK. I'll take my .357."

"I don't like it. It's too dangerous. Flynn sounds like a psychopath," Rachel said.

"At least stay in contact with me while you're over there. I'll wait at the Oakland police station on the phone. In case something goes wrong, I can round up a posse and get there in minutes," Buddy said.

"You two sound like old women, but OK, I'll take my cell phone and leave it on while I'm at Flynn's if you two will stop picking on me. I'll talk to you every step of the way."

"I'm afraid you want to meet Flynn to get back at him for what he did to me," Rachel said. "Don't do it on my account. I'll be happy just to see that bastard behind bars. You don't have to prove anything."

CHAPTER 38

"HOW DO WE DO THIS CELL PHONE bit?" I asked. I had come over to Buddy's house to finalize arrangements before driving to Oakland.

"Just as if you had a police radio. Keep your cell phone on and talk to me in a low voice. How do you propose to check out Flynn's house?" Buddy asked.

"I'll wait 'til dark and park the truck around the corner on Grand Avenue. I'll find a dark place in the shadows across the street and wait until Flynn leaves. If he stays home, I'll go back tomorrow night and try again."

"I've never seen you so pumped up." Then Buddy grinned. "I like the outfit. The black watch cap's a nice touch. You look like a cat burglar except for the cannon bulging under your jacket. I brought an old set of tools I once took off a burglar. Take it with you."

"I feel funny about breaking into someone's house. I've never done this before without a warrant. But damn it, this could be the key to all that's happened. I don't want to blow any court case against Flynn by tainting the evidence. I just want to know what's there. Then we can call Mike and tell him we spotted Paddy Flynn at Sky's and that we suspect he's the big 16-EEE guy who killed Rachel's dog. Mike can pick him up at his house. If the police find evidence of any other crime that just happens to be out in the open, so be it."

I got out of the truck and took my position near Flynn's house. I placed my cell phone in its holster, connecting the headset to free my hands. I put on a pair of latex gloves and took my night vision scope from my jacket pocket.

Now I was ready.

I whispered, "OK, Buddy, in position. Can see his house and SUV. Fine mist covering the moon and no streetlight, but can see well with the scope. Can you hear me?"

"Loud and clear."

"Hope Flynn doesn't decide to stay home all night. The cold wind from the bay is stinging my face."

"Bad night to be a burglar. Give it an hour or two, and then pack it in."

"Know you don't like this, but I feel in my gut that this case is about to break. Somehow Flynn's involved. He's a pro. If he smells the cops are on to him, he'll clear out faster than a Marichal fastball. I don't want that to happen. Hey, front door just opened. Two people coming out—Flynn and someone a lot smaller. Young man in a light-colored sweat suit—everything looks green through this damn scope."

"What now?" Buddy asked.

"Flynn getting in his Ford, other fellow starting to jog. Running past me. Flynn's driving off. I'll wait ten minutes, make certain he doesn't come back. I'll circle the house, check for an alarm, and look for the easiest way in. Maybe I'll find a window opened a crack. Otherwise, I'll use burglar tools. Wait a minute—here comes somebody—it's the young man in the sweats."

He approached me slowly.

"Hey, Mister, why are you watching Hammer's house?"

I didn't have a good answer to that question but I tried.

"Whose house? I'm with neighborhood security. Some break-ins have occurred so I'm watching this block."

He moved closer. "That sounds like bullshit to me. I'll just keep you here until Hammer comes back, and you can tell him that story."

He started to grab me, and I pushed him back. He took a boxer's stance with his left fist up high and the right close to his chest. He looked about seventeen or eighteen; still had a zit on his cheek. He rose up on his toes and started to dance toward me as if in the ring.

He said, "You better not mess with me. I'm a middleweight. Hammer's training me. I can kill you with my fist. And I'm on the card next Friday in Bakersfield," he bragged.

"You don't look like much to me."

I hoped I sounded braver than I felt.

That did it. He threw a straight right at my head. I ducked and closed in on him, wrapping my arms around his chest. I stomped hard on his foot with my heavy, steel-toed, Red Wing work shoe. He wore only canvas sneakers. He screamed in pain and lowered his fists.

"That's not fair," he whined.

I clipped him on the point of his chin with an uppercut swing that came all the way from my knees. He crumpled to the ground. He needed to learn that there are no Marquis of Queensbury rules on the street. I pulled his unconscious body back into the shadows and cuffed his wrists and ankles just to make sure.

Then my right hand began to throb. I knew I had bruised my knuckles good. I couldn't recollect the last time I had hit anyone. I put the headset back on.

"You OK?" Buddy asked on the cell phone.

He sounded anxious.

"Yeah, It was the kid who walked out with Flynn. Must have seen me and turned back to check me out. Not armed. Hit him hard. I'll be long gone before he wakes up."

"Close call. Heard what he said about being a boxer. Didn't tell me you could fight," Buddy said.

"To tell the truth, I cheated. Tell you about it later. Looks like Flynn's not coming back. I'm going in."

"Just hurry. Get in, get out, and get gone before Flynn comes home. I'm growing more nervous. Keep telling me what you're doing."

I straightened my wobbly knees, crossed the street, and walked to Flynn's house.

"Just found the alarm behind a pole in back of the house. Clipping the wires. Unusual metal building attached to back of house. Going around to the side now. Locked door on the side of the garage. Good, hidden from the street. Have to use your tools. OK, I'm 'in like Flynn'."

Buddy groaned.

"Tools work. You could always go into the burglar biz, start a second career in your retirement."

I still spoke just above a whisper.

"Stop with the jokes. Find what you need and leave."

I opened the door without making a sound and checked to make certain I hadn't left any marks on the lock and door jam. I closed the door behind me.

"Wow! You should see this place! Flynn's turned his garage into a series of workshops. He has an auto mechanics service area complete with hydraulic lift at the front. Shelves with auto parts and tools halfway up the wall. I smell gasoline, motor oil, and sweat."

"Wonder why he needs all that?" Buddy asked.

"Don't know, but there's a big steel wedge leaning against the wall under the shelves. Damn. It has holes for bolts. Could rig it to his front bumper as a battering ram. It's too dark, but I'd love to see if there are any blue paint chips that match Rachel's Volvo. Let's see what else is here. I hear static when I change directions. There are chairs in front of a big screen TV/ VCR in a back corner with hundreds of videotapes on a rack, all labeled for old boxing matches."

"Everyone needs a hobby. Anything else in the garage?"

"Walking to the other corner now. Whoops, the 'low battery' light is flashing on the cell phone. I should have recharged the battery. I may fade out at any time. Holy shit! He's got an arsenal in here. Gun racks with rifles and pistols and shotguns and a collection of scopes and barrels and stocks, two .45 automatics. Which one did he use to kill Judy? Bunch of loading equipment on a table so he can load bullets and shells. Machine next to the table, a milling machine. Next is a boresighter and chambering reamer. He's a gunsmith, too. Garage is a redneck's Shangri-la. Uh oh! I hear the connecting door from the house to the garage. God, I hope you can still hear me."

I reached in my jacket to pull out my gun, but not fast enough. Paddy Flynn turned on the lights and stood in the doorway with a large, black revolver pointed at my midsection.

CHAPTER 39

"LEAVE IT IN YOUR JACKET. You got the alarm but you missed the separate motion detector in the garage. It transmits a signal to my beeper. I found young Rocky out like a light across the street in the bushes. I guess he's not ready for the big time after all. Tsk, tsk. Doesn't yourself know breaking and entering is agin' the law? Two to five for the first offense, isn't it?" Paddy Flynn asked.

"Well, call the police. I surrender," I said.

"I think not. I'll take your gun, laddie, and you empty your pockets. Just keys and a dead cell phone. What's this? A Russian night scope. Well, it's me scope now. No ID—that's smart—but, of course, I know well who ye be." He spoke with a brogue.

"Napa police know I came here. They'll come down on you if you kill me."

"Nice try. I don't think so. They'd be here now if you'd told them about me. Yourself just decided to do some freelance work. You didn't really think you'd get the drop on me, didja'? Go inside."

He motioned to the door with his pistol. The giant walked behind me and steered me into his house.

He continued, "Kill you? You deserve killing. You've been

236

a burr in me shoe, as me old da' used to say. I think we'll have a wee bit of fun first."

He towered over me by at least six inches. A large head befitting his size sat atop a powerful neck. He told me to walk to the back of the house and followed me through the door and down two steps to the metal addition.

I saw that he had outfitted the entire single room as a boxing gym, complete with a full-size ring, punching bags, free weights, and exercise machines—a decor by Everlast. The bright fluorescent lights made my eyes water.

"Stillman's Gym's got nothing on you," I said.

"I trained at Stillman's when meself was in New York before me fight with Leroy Boone at the Garden. Didja' know they ranked me number six in the world?"

I figured if I kept him talking, I might buy some time; maybe figure out how to get away.

"Did you ever fight for the title?" I asked, feigning interest.

"Came close, real close. Me manager had lined up a bout with Ron Lyle after the Lopez fight. Winner would fight the champ, Larry Holmes. But the judges in the Lopez fight robbed meself. If we had time, I'd show you the tape."

"Can we see it now?"

"Oh no, m'boy. Not now. We have to finish our game."

"How many fights did you have?" Like I gave a damn.

"Well, meself started in the Golden Gloves. . . . . but enough blarney. I'm going to tie you up so yourself doesn't get into trouble. I'll be back before you can miss me," Flynn said.

He bound me arms to me sides and me feet together at the ankles with duct tape. (Damn, I'm starting to think like he talks.) He sat me in a folding chair, tied me to it with a rope around my waist, and put another piece of tape over my mouth.

I had time to wonder what kind of torture he had in store for me. I knew his "game" might be fun for him but painful for me in the extreme. If only the damn phone hadn't died out and Buddy had heard him surprise me! I tried to remain calm so I could think straight, but a block of ice began to form in the pit of my stomach.

He came back to the gym wearing Kelly green boxing trunks with socks and black leather shoes. Was he going to make me fight him in the ring? He walked up to me and yanked the tape off my mouth.

"You're going to help meself work out tonight," he said.

Flynn's body looked like he could still fight in the ring. He must have weighed two-sixty or two-seventy but he had no fat anywhere. Well-defined muscles bulged in his arms and legs. I noticed a fresh pink scar on his left forearm. (Good for Danny Boy!) His shoulders and chest stretched from here to Sunday. His shaved head resembled a pumpkin, and tattoos covered both forearms. He had tattoos of teardrops between his thumb and forefinger, a gang sign.

"You wouldn't last five minutes in the ring with me. Wouldn't be a fair fight. I have me a another plan," Flynn said with a grin. "This'll be fun."

He half-carried, half-hopped me over to a corner of the gym where a black Everlast body bag hung from the ceiling by a chain of three-inch links. Flynn unhooked the body bag from the 8-clip at the end of the chain, set the bag aside, and raised the chain with a hand crank. Starting just above elbows, he began wrapping me with duct tape all the way down to my ankles.

I got it. I got to be the punching bag! Bile came up, and I started to retch.

That seemed to piss him off. He had an abrupt mood change. His steroids must have kicked in. Hate filled his eyes. With unnecessary roughness, he passed the chain under my armpits and placed me in position, locking the chain to the 8-clip behind me. He turned the hand crank again, tightening the chain that ran from my chest up and through a pulley over my head and back to the crank. This raised my feet about eighteen inches off the floor.

"Is this necessary, Flynn? Why not just shoot me and get done with it?" I asked.

"Hitting the punching bag bores meself. And you can call meself Hammer. Besides, I'm wantin' you to die slow, breakin' your bones one by one. I want it to hurt."

He gave me a gentle push with his fingertips and watched me swing back and forth. He seemed satisfied and walked away.

They say your life flashes before you when you're about to die. They're wrong. I just felt sad and regretted that I had come here alone—stupid me. I should have listened to Buddy and Rachel. Rachel—God, I'm going to miss her.

Flynn came back. He had taped his hands and was putting on fourteen-ounce, lace less, leather, Everlast boxing gloves. He started me swinging again and gave my chest a light tap.

Thump.

"I saw the scar on your arm. What happened? Did an Irish setter bite you?" I asked.

He moved away on his toes and jabbed, again a light tap.

Thump.

"Sure, and I'll tell you, seeing as how yourself ain't goin' nowhere. Goddamn dog made me bleed."

Thwack. Thwack. More light left jabs to the midsection.

"And Sky Leonard paid you to scare Rachel?" I asked.

"Paid me?" Now he was dancing. "No way. She just said for me to scare her, so I did."

Thock. This jab was a little harder, now to my right side.

"And she told you to poke a hole in my brake fluid tank before I drove down the mountain?"

Now I started to spin with the force of each blow.

He closed in and sent two hard left jabs to my left shoulder. Thock. Thock.

Flashes of light exploded behind my eyes as the blows landed on my bad left shoulder. But I wouldn't give him the satisfaction of crying out.

Flynn said, "She didn't like you when you came to see her. Said yourself was smart and could cause her trouble. Wish she could see you now, you don't look so keen."

Thock. Another left jab glanced off my ribs. I gasped.

"And you did Judy Harris?"

Thock. Thud. A combination this time, left jab and right cross waist high. Again, I kept the vomit from coming all the way up.

"Damn bitch wouldn't take the bribe money like that supervisor Gabe Houston did. He decided to take it when I nabbed his kid after school one day. That gave Sky one vote. Judy Harris on the other hand, threw a fit. She called Sky, told her she was going to call the FBI. I didn't want me pretty colleen to worry, so I thought I would help out. 'Twas easy. Grabbed Harris when she came home from work and took her out to the Napa marshes."

"And Sky told you .....to put Judy's body in Rachel's trunk.....and ram us on the highway?"

Thwack. Another short right to my chest. The pain knifed through my body. I wanted to scream.

Thock. Thock. Thud. Two hard left jabs to my chest and a short right just under my left ribs. My bruised chest heaved in pain.

"That was me idea. Figured it'd get your girlfriend to vote right."

Flynn stayed in prime condition. Beads of sweat at last had formed on his brow.

"You're a sweetheart of a guy..... How much did Sky pay you?"

"No way. Sky's me lady."

I started to tell him Puck was screwing Sky, but why make him even madder.

He breathed harder.

"She lets me spend the night with her once a month. ''Tis the best piece I've ever had. She promised meself she'd go away with me to Vegas if I helped her with the friggin' moratorium. She gave me some expense money for what she called 'lobbyin'.''"

The constant spinning made me dizzy. Thud. Another hard punch to my right side. I heard a rib crack. Now I yelled. That seemed to make him happy.

He backed off and laughed. "Havin' me a good workout!"

"And shot.....at poor Casey Hammon.....in Sacramento?" I asked with difficulty.

"Just wanted to spook him so he would think twice about writin' about Sky's pals back east, makin' trouble for them."

The pain was overtaking me. I was feeling faint. Flynn tapped my cheeks to keep me awake. He calmed down. Beating me was pure pleasure, like sexual foreplay. This psychopath was toying with me.

I was at the point of blacking out, my eyes half-closed and my head whirling. I could only ask with one word at a time.

So.....you.....killed.....Warren.....Roberts?"

"Who the fuck is Warren Roberts?

CHAPTER 40

I HURT TOO MUCH TO BE DEAD. My gut ached. I heard Rachel and Buddy whispering.

I came to and blinked as I opened my eyes. Looking down, I saw my chest bound with tape. An IV attached to my arm snaked down from a bottle of clear liquid on a pole stand next to my bed.

"I think he's awake," Rachel said.

"Where am I?"

She leaned over and kissed my cheek.

"You're at Queen of the Valley Hospital in Napa."

"How do you feel?" Buddy asked.

"Like I was run over by an 18-wheeler!"

"Not surprising," Buddy said. "You've got three broken ribs, a contused chest, and your liver's bruised."

"How did I get here?" I asked, bewildered.

"Buddy brought you," Rachel said.

"What happened at Flynn's?"

"I grabbed three detectives, and we raced over there. We heard racket from the garage and broke down the door. We found you unconscious and swinging from a chain. Flynn was trying to wake you up. He seemed pissed that you were out. Anyway, I cuffed him and got you down. The Oakland guys took him in and charged him with attempted murder and assault with a deadly weapon— his fists."

"I owe you big time, Buddy. Flynn planned to beat me to death. How did you figure out I was in trouble?"

"I panicked when your cell phone went dead."

"Buddy brought you here three nights ago," Rachel said.

Amazed, I asked, "Three whole days?"

I looked over at Buddy. "You know that beast killed Judy?"

"Yes, we matched the .45 in his gun collection to the bullet. The lab's confirmed it." Buddy said.

"He also killed Danny Boy and screwed with my brakes and threatened Rachel. He even took a shot at Casey Hammon in Sacramento," I said.

A nurse came in to give me a shot for pain in my right hip. I could smell the rubbing alcohol from the cotton ball she used to swab the target. It felt like the bite of a giant mosquito. She said it would take a few minutes to work.

"We know what he did, Gene. I know the Oakland police chief from the old days, and he let me have a session with Flynn. Flynn signed a statement."

"We still need to find Warren Roberts' killer and clear Fran— Flynn didn't do it," I said.

"He told us that."

"He didn't even know who I was talking about when I mentioned Warren's name. I believed him. He seemed to enjoy telling me about that other stuff though, thinking that dead men—that's me—don't talk."

Rachel cringed and said. "The doctor found it amazing you didn't suffer any permanent damage."

"Wonderful," I said with sarcasm in my voice. "But it doesn't make it hurt any less. Boy, I should have listened to you guys when you told me not to go over there alone. I thought I could go in and out without getting caught."

"At least the son of a bitch is in jail," Rachel said.

My stomach hurt less. The shot was working its medicinal magic.

The door to the hospital room opened, and Mike and Sally Edwards walked in.

"Mike and Sally have visited you every day since you got here. Sally brought the lovely flowers in the vase over there," Rachel said.

Mike patted my shoulder—I winced— and Sally kissed my forehead.

She said, "You look much better today. Our kids were worried about their Uncle Gene."

"Tell them I'll be OK."

"You made one hell of a punching bag, Gene. Lucky he didn't kill you," Mike said.

"He could have. Didn't hit me once in the head. Just toyed with me at first. But thank God, that gave Buddy time to get there. Where is Flynn now, Mike?"

"We picked him up after they arraigned him in Oakland for assaulting you and brought him to Napa and charged him with murdering Judy Harris."

"Did he give up Sky Leonard?" Buddy asked.

"No, he said she never told him to kill Judy Harris or to threaten Rachel. Said he did those two things, your brakes, and took a shot to scare Casey Hammon all on his own."

"What about the money Sky gave him?" I asked.

"Flynn said Sky told him to use it to help get the moratorium ordinance passed but never specified how."

"She's guilty as Zin!" I said. "He's covering up for her."

"Doesn't he know she was just using him? She didn't give a damn about an oaf like him, just about what he could do for her," Rachel said, offering a woman's perspective.

Mike said, "Flynn's infatuated or maybe pussy-whipped.

He's also an odd duck. He doesn't mind prison, says he'll run the boxing team for the warden. He asked me if I thought he could take his VCR and all his fight tapes with him. He'll plead guilty and escape possible execution."

"Shit!" I said, striking the mattress.

"Mike said, "Flynn implicated Sky in his confession. The U.S. Attorney in San Francisco thinks he can indict her under the Hobbs Act. This federal statute prohibits the use of violence to interfere with interstate commerce. They plan to use this statute with eco-terrorists, if and when they ever catch one. Speaking of which, we've got enough on Sky—impeding the making and interstate marketing of wine, knowingly receiving laundered money, and breaking federal and international banking laws—that we've already picked her up. Flight risk, you know. She's enjoying the hospitality suite of the Napa County jail as we speak."

I pressed the button beside my bed and called for the nurse.

"Can we get you anything?" Sally asked.

"Thanks. I appreciate the flowers and your visit, but I want to go home to the farm to recuperate," I said.

"Don't rush it. You're still hurt," Rachel said with a smile. "Besides, who said I would nurse you when you got home?"

The nurse came in. I asked her, "Can you give me some pain pills and let me go home now?"

"Not tonight," she said. "Doctor Nassam wants to keep you here for another day or two for observation. You took quite a beating."

The nurse, shooing Buddy and Mike and Sally out of the room, said, "Visiting hours ended long ago. Only Ms. Bernard can stay."

"Tell Dr. Nassam I'll stay tonight, but I want to go home tomorrow," I told her.

"We'll see what he says during rounds tomorrow," the nurse

said in that tone nurses always use to show that they're in charge. "I'll give the doctor your message."

The nurse left. Rachel and I found ourselves alone. Rachel got up from her chair and sat on the bed next to me and put her arms around my neck with great care.

"Boy, was I scared. Buddy called me, and I met him here when they brought you in. We thought you were in a coma."

"I'd have been in a permanent one if it hadn't been for Buddy coming to my rescue. Flynn planned to kill me as the climax of his workout. If I'd known he'd stop hitting me when I passed out, I would've done it much sooner. Flynn's nuts, but, in his boxer's mind, hitting someone who's unconscious just isn't acceptable," I said.

"Even though he'd tied you up and you couldn't fight back?"

"Even then. He wouldn't hit me unless I was awake. It's not logical or rational, but that's a boxer's training."

"Thank God, Buddy came to the rescue just in time," Rachel said.

"Old Russian proverb: 'Pray to God, but keep rowing."

"Say again?"

"In other words, God helps those who help themselves."

I extended both arms and stretched my sore muscles.

"I feel much better now."

"You're just feeling the effects of the shot."

"Yeah, I'm getting drowsy, too. Let's call it a day."

CHAPTER 41

A NURSE AWAKENED ME AT THE UNHEARD of hour of six a.m. She asked me how I felt, and I mumbled, "Sleepy."

She took my temperature and blood pressure and gave me the morning shot for pain. I tolerated the routine, turned over, and went back to sleep.

Breakfast came at 8:30, a much more reasonable hour. I could hear Rachel brushing her teeth in the bathroom. The food tasted bland, but I ate every crumb. I guessed I hadn't had a solid meal in almost four days.

"What day is it, Rachel?"

"Saturday."

"Good day for us to go home."

"Do you want me to get you a newspaper?"

"No. I think I'd like to catch some TV. Come sit on the bed with me."

"You must feel better," Rachel said.

"It's about time, after sleeping 72 hours."

I turned on the television with the remote next to my bed. I found an old movie channel, and the credits rolled for Billy Wilder's masterpiece "Some Like It Hot" starring Jack Lemon, Tony Curtis, and Marilyn Monroe. Near the beginning of the film, Lemon and

Curtis disguise themselves in women's clothing to escape from the gangsters chasing them and hide in a traveling all-girl band.

I almost jumped out of the hospital bed. I leaned forward and grabbed Rachel's hand.

"That's it! Something's been gnawing at me ever since I saw the police videotape of the mysterious woman coming out of the alley. Help me get dressed. I need to go see something."

"Hold on a second. You can't go anywhere and you damn sure can't drive."

"OK, then you drive. How did you get here?"
"I rented a Toyota."

"Good. Now, either get my clothes, or I will."

"This is crazy, Gene."

"I know how that asshole did it and I've got to prove it. I'm going with you or without you."

"Don't get excited. I'll help you but I'd be happier if I knew what we're doing."

I got out of bed. My legs wobbled a bit. Rachel helped me to the bathroom. Although it hurt some, I managed to get dressed. I stood pretty steady. I took a minute to check the address in the phone book.

"Look down the hall and see if the coast is clear. I don't have time to argue with nurses now."

Rachel peered out the door of the hospital room. All was quiet. We sneaked to the stairway at the other end of the hall from the nurses' station. I hobbled down the stairs, and we went out the rear door of the hospital. We walked to the parking garage and got into the Toyota.

"Where do we go?" Rachel asked.

"Take Jefferson south through downtown, turn left on 3rd Street and right on Seminary. I'll tell you where to stop."

We heard a slight rumbling sound in the distance.

"What's that?" I asked.

"We're in an earthquake alert. Geologists report some tremors on the seismograph. Foreshocks can precede a quake, but the radio said there's nothing to worry about."

"I hope not. Napa's last quake was in 1990. Maybe you remember it. Pop said the damage reached almost $100 million; took two years to recover. There's a fault extending all the way from Old Sonoma Road to St. Helena, and it acts up every few years."

I told Rachel to pull up in front of a two-story apartment building on Seminary. I looked for the green Buick but didn't see it. I called 421-6942 using her cell phone. No one answered.

"Good," I said. "No car, no answer. No one's home."

Rachel still had the little pistol I had given her in her purse, and I found a flashlight in the glove compartment. I took them and put them in my pocket. I had learned my lesson in Oakland.

"Where are we going?" Rachel asked.

"Not 'we'—just me. Lock the car doors and wait for me. Call Mike Edwards if I'm not back in 15 minutes. But don't call him before that or get out of the car."

"Be careful, mon cheri."

My poor body was stiff as I climbed the stairs on the outside of the building and down the exterior walkway to #215. Cheap lock; it opened with a credit card. I put on a pair of rubber gloves I'd swiped from the hospital. I hoped this would turn out better than the last time I broke in.

I entered the apartment, took out the flashlight, and went into the only bedroom. I prayed he'd kept them. I found two closet doors on the wall opposite the king-size bed. I opened the first closet, shined my light in, and did a double take.

"Hot damn!" I muttered to myself. The closet contained short-sleeve dress shirts and several pair of brown polyester pants. And it was impossible for there be two "Pollack" ties like that in all of Napa County. Why's his stuff here?

I found what I came for in the second closet on the top shelf behind two folded blankets. I spied an old, tan, Samsonite, hard-sided suitcase, circa 1960. I took the suitcase down and opened it, careful not to disturb the contents. Voila! I found a long navy dress, a pair of blue dress pumps, and tucked up inside the dress a brown woman's wig with bangs. I put everything back and replaced the suitcase and the blankets in the exact same spots. I turned off the flashlight and left through the door I had come in, careful to push the lock button on the doorknob. I went back down the walkway and started down the steps.

"What the hell is he doing here?" Victor O'Connell said from the bottom of the stairs.

"Let's kill him!" John Lawrence shouted, standing behind O'Connell.

I ducked down and pulled the .38 out of my pocket.

"No, that's stupid. Let's get out of here and drive north. We can get to Canada by tomorrow night."

Lawrence and O'Connell ran toward O'Connell's green Buick parked in the next block. I held on to the rail and came down the stairs as fast as my bruised body would allow. The ground began to shake as I reached the bottom step. What began as a low rumble became louder and deeper. I fought to keep my balance as the trembling became more violent. I had experienced tremors in San Francisco before, but nothing like this.

This was the real McCoy!

O'Connell and Lawrence were thrown to the ground, then got up, and managed to reach their car. I just made it to Rachel's Toyota without falling down.

"What's going on?" she asked.

"I found the dress and wig O'Connell used when he killed Warren Roberts. O'Connell and Lawrence saw me leaving their apartment and they plan to escape to Canada."

"Now I know why we ran out of the hospital. What do

you want me to do?" she asked with excitement in her voice.

"We have to follow them until we can get the Napa police to stop them on Highway 29. Can you handle a car chase?"

"I wish the ground would stop moving, but sure, I'll do it," Rachel said, gripping the steering wheel.

The green Buick raced through Napa for the Napa-Vallejo Highway (29), with O'Connell driving. They took a left on Oak Street, turned right on Seymour, and wheeled around the corner, tires screeching, turning left on 1st Street toward the highway. Meanwhile, I reached Mike Edwards after four tries on the cell phone.

"Hey, Mike, I can prove Victor O'Connell killed Warren Roberts. He and John Lawrence saw me at O'Connell's apartment and they're trying to flee on Highway 29 North. Rachel and I are behind them. Can you send a car to head them off? A 1995 green Buick sedan, California license RTS47G."

"How did you . . . . . ?"

"I'll tell you everything later; just stop these guys!" I shouted.

"All hell's breaking loose with this damn earthquake! Radio says it's 6.2 on the Richter Scale. Everyone's gone. Phone's ringing off the wall, but I'll try to get someone. Stay with them, Gene, but don't—I repeat, do not, confront them," Edwards said.

Dogs and cats—more than I could count—scurried everywhere, disturbed by the clamor.

The scary reverberating sound grew much, much louder. We saw a three-story, old, wooden, Victorian house off to our right swaying back and forth on its foundation, the roof hanging halfway to the ground. This one came a whopper.

"They've turned north on Highway 29," Rachel said as she stayed on their tail, two car lengths behind them.

O'Connell accelerated to 65, and the Buick got smaller. A cloud of smoke the color of brown sludge drifted across the highway from our right as we neared Lincoln Avenue.

"Look at the wisp of smoke coming from the temporary building behind Davis Community School," I said. "Electric wires have fallen on top of the roof producing a huge shower of sparks."

Brilliant orange flames erupted at that moment.

"I'm grateful no kids were there."

The main school building shook, and windows popped out and fell to the ground, creating a border of shards around the building's foundation.

"Watch out! Lawrence is leaning out of the car window on the passenger side aiming his automatic at us," I shouted.

Lawrence's first shot missed wide to our right. He looked back at us with half of his torso hanging out of the speeding Buick. The second shot knocked off the outside mirror on my side—way too close for comfort. I could see the hate in his eyes.

"Try changing lanes."

"The traffic's bumper-to-bumper headed south," Rachel said.

Drivers honked their horns and yelled at one another. Pandemonium reigned.

"Yeah. Everyone's evacuating, going south on 29 to escape the quake, traveling toward Vallejo and on to San Francisco. The epicenter must lie north of here."

We neared Trancas. Mrs. McDonald's restaurant looked undamaged. We saw a fire engine red Mazda Miata on the access road going the other way. He was approaching the gas station catty-cornered from the restaurant. A fire hydrant was gushing water and filling the street; the traffic light didn't work, either. The driver lost control, did a 360, and slid into the gas pumps, releasing a flood of gasoline. This caused an explosion of such magnitude that the sheer force blew three pedestrians onto adjacent property. Pieces of plastic and glass, splinters of wood, and chunks of cement rained down around us. The flaming Miata shot at least fifty feet in the air. We heard the driver's piercing scream.

News helicopters from San Francisco hovered over the devastation like dragonflies.

Rachel had to get up to 75 to catch up with the green Buick. We passed Trancas Street. Redwood Middle School seemed OK, but three school buses lay thrown on their sides, looking like resting yellow behemoths.

John Lawrence fired at us twice more. We heard a zing as the bullet grazed the roof of the Toyota. Pretty good shooting from a car moving at that speed.

Rachel screamed, "A foot lower and we'd be dead!"

Rachel had difficulty keeping the car on our side of the road as the highway shifted under us near the intersection with Trower Avenue. Flames shot out the upstairs windows of the fire station on the northeast corner. The firemen stood out front aiming their hoses at their own building. The fire alarm continued its constant blare.

We observed the strangest sight off to our left as we passed Salvador Avenue. The upheaval of the earth had damaged the railroad track that runs parallel to the highway. The track that carries the famous Wine Train had buckled under the pressure, moving steel rods like they were toothpicks.

The Buick reached 90 miles per hour. Rachel stayed right with them. Two minutes later, we could see multiple bands of bright yellow crime scene tape stretched across the northbound side of Highway 29. A frantic patrolman waved a pair of bright red flags.

"Road closed! Road closed!" he yelled.

O'Connell hit the brakes and skidded through the barrier.

The epicenter of the earthquake crossed the highway cutting it in two at the south edge of Yountville. The shearing movement along the fault had broken the highway. It had created a deep crevice in the earth 40 feet wide and a mile on either side of the highway.

The green Buick finally came to a stop. The front half of the sedan, including the front wheels and doors, hung over the gap in the earth. The patrolman dropped his flags and ran to the spot.

Rachel came to a stop about 50 yards behind the Buick, and we jumped out.

We approached the dangling vehicle. We could see the skid marks and smell the scorched rubber.

The Buick shifted forward, nose canting down.

"Don't move! Stay still!" the patrolman hollered at the two men. "I've radioed for a wrecker with a winch. They'll attach it to the rear bumper and pull you out. The wrecker's with a police escort only three miles behind us."

The Buick teetered.

"Help us!" screamed Lawrence.

"Any movement could shift the car and send you over. Be still! Don't move!" the patrolman said again.

A roar came from the giant crack in the ground and a large puff of hot dust smelling of sulphur rose from the depths.

We heard the siren of the police car in the distance.

"Take it easy. Help is almost here," I yelled.

All of a sudden, Lawrence undid his seatbelt and began to climb over the front seat toward the back.

That tipped the scale. The heavy Buick tipped forward and fell headfirst into the bowels of the earth.

Terrified screams shattered an eerie moment of silence amidst the chaos and noise of the earthquake.

Through her tears, Rachel said, "Just like in the Old Testament when the earth opened and swallowed Korah and his followers:

.....the ground under them burst asunder, and the earth opened its mouth and

swallowed them up.....

Book of Numbers, Chapter 16:31

CHAPTER 42

THE BLACK-AND-WHITE PULLED UP NEXT TO Rachel's car, escorting the now superfluous wrecker. Mike Edwards opened the door on the driver's side; Buddy emerged from the other side.

Dust still billowed from the crevice. They approached us.

"The green Buick went over the side with Victor O'Connell?" Mike asked.

"Yes. With John Lawrence, too," I replied.

"How did you know O'Connell killed Warren Roberts?" Mike asked.

"Buddy found out and told me about the life insurance policy before I went to Flynn's house. Warren and O'Connell signed a Buy/Sell Agreement before they left Chicago. In case either partner died, an insurance policy would pay the survivor $500,000. O'Connell had until December 31st of this year to file the claim, months after interest in Warren's murder would have died down," I said.

"But you told me O'Connell said they had no life insurance," Rachel said.

"Another lie. Killing Warren would accomplish two objectives. Victor would own the company outright with money to expand and he would have a chance to retaliate against Fran for dumping him more than twenty years ago. I imagine he borrowed the gun from Warren for target practice and bought a wig as close to Fran's hair color and style as he could find. He knew they'd consider the wife first as a suspect."

I went on. "Buddy and I were convinced Victor was involved in Warren's murder but we didn't know if Flynn fit in, too. And we had trouble with the woman seen coming out of the alley at the time of the murder. Remember, Mike, the old movie, 'Some Like It Hot", where the men dressed up as women? Seeing that jogged my mind. I should have thought of the disguise angle before. O'Connell hoped someone would see him that evening in his getup. I found the wig and the dress and high-heeled shoes in a closet at the apartment."

"So you went over to Vic's apartment yourself to find O'Connell's dress. You know, you could have tainted the evidence," Mike chastised me.

"No one would ever have known if O'Connell and Lawrence hadn't shown up. I left no traces."

"What about Lawrence?" Mike asked.

"It blew me over when I found his clothes in O'Connell's closet. We two great detectives never even suspected that they knew each other."

"I guess we could assume they roomed together to save on rent," Rachel suggested.

"Right, in an apartment with only one bed," I said.

A spasm shot through my stomach. I grimaced. The shot had worn off.

"We better get you back to the hospital," Rachel said.

"You'll need to come into the station and make a statement when you feel decent," Mike said.

I put my better arm around Rachel's shoulders.

"Hope it can wait 'til I get back from France."

"France?"

"Yes. When I was hanging like a side of beef and getting beaten to death, I realized what's most important. I'm going to France with Rachel. Her parents should meet their daughter's fiancé.

VEAL CACCIATORE CALABRIA/PARMESAN POLENTA

3 pounds veal shoulder or leg, sliced
2 tablespoons white flour
3 tablespoons olive oil
1 teaspoon salt
½ teaspoon ground black pepper
1 medium onion, chopped
2 garlic cloves, whole
2 cups chopped celery
2 cups chopped carrots
1 cup chopped green pepper
1 cup Zinfandel or other red wine
2 teaspoons fresh oregano, chopped
2 teaspoons fresh rosemary, chopped
3 teaspoons fresh thyme, chopped
2 bay leaves
1 28-ounce can Italian tomatoes, crushed
Peel from one lemon
½ cup fresh Italian parsley

Place flour seasoned with salt and pepper in a paper bag with the veal. Shake the bag so all slices are evenly coated. In a deep skillet, brown veal over medium high heat in 2 tablespoons of olive oil. Remove veal and save. Add remaining olive oil to skillet and add onion, garlic, celery, carrots, and green pepper. Sautee vegetables for 5 minutes until soft. Add the red wine to the skillet and raise heat to high, boiling the mixture for 5 minutes to reduce the volume. Add tomatoes, herbs, lemon peel, and parsley to the skillet and when sauce reaches boiling point, reduce heat to simmer and return the veal to the skillet and cover the skillet. Simmer for 20 minutes until veal is tender. Remove the cover and raise the heat, reducing the sauce to desired thickness, about 5 minutes. Remove garlic, lemon peel and bay leaves, and serve with Parmesan Polenta. This southern Italian favorite should be served with Zinfandel or any other bold red wine.

PARMESAN POLENTA

3 cups stock, chicken or vegetable
3 cups milk
2 cups yellow corn meal, stone ground preferred
4 tablespoons unsalted butter
½ cup grated Parmesan cheese
½ teaspoon ground black pepper

Bring stock and milk to a boil in a saucepan. SLOWLY add cornmeal in a stream, stirring all the while with a whisk. Reduce heat to simmer and continue to stir for about 12 minutes until the polenta pulls away from the sides of the saucepan. Remove from heat and stir in butter, cheese and pepper. Serve warm.

FRENCH BRANDIED APPLE CRISP

6 tart apples, like Granny Smith
½ cup granulated sugar
½ teaspoon ground cloves
1 teaspoon cinnamon
1 tablespoon lemon juice
1 teaspoon unsalted butter
½ cup brandy

Topping:
¾ cup sifted white flour
¼ teaspoon salt
6 tablespoons soften unsalted butter
½ cup chopped pecans or walnuts
½ cup granulated sugar

Preheat oven to 350 degrees.

Peel, core, and slice apples into a bowl. Mix with sugar, spices, and lemon juice. Melt butter over medium heat and sauté apple mixture for 5 minutes and add the brandy. Flame the brandy when it is warm. Place apple mixture in a 1 _ quart baking pan and make the topping. Blend flour, sugar, salt, and butter together until it becomes a crumble, mix in the chopped nuts and cover the apple mixture with the crumbs. Bake 40 minutes or until apples are tender and crust has browned. Serve with vanilla ice cream.

LAYERED VEGETABLE FRITATTA

1 tablespoon butter
2 tablespoons olive oil
6 large eggs
½ cup cream or milk
1 medium onion, chopped
3 cups cubed vegetables; choose from mushrooms, bell
   peppers
eggplant, broccoli, artichoke hearts, yellow squash, or
   zuccini
1 cup shredded mozzarella cheese
½ cup shredded Parmesan cheese
½ teaspoon salt
½ teaspoon ground black pepper

Melt butter in an ovenproof skillet(cast iron is best) over medium low heat. Beat eggs with cream and pour egg mixture into the skillet. Heat a second large skillet, adding 1 tablespoon of the olive oil and the chopped onions. Cook the onions for 5 minutes and add the remaining olive oil and the cubed vegetables. Cook the vegetables 10 minutes until they are soft. Heat broiler to high. Cover the eggs, which have now been partially cooked on the bottom with the cooked vegetables. Sprinkle the cheeses over the vegetables and place skillet under the broiler for 3 minutes or until the cheeses melt, bubble and begin to brown. Cut into wedges and serve warm or at room temperature. This Italian version of an omelet is an excellent weekend brunch entrée.

ABOUT THE AUTHOR

Author Chuck Toubin has been a successful journalist, editor and businessman. Wine is a life-long passion for him, and he has been traveling to wineries in Northern California and other grape-growing areas in America and Europe for forty years. He also teaches wine courses to restaurant management classes. Chuck and Mary Toubin live in Austin, Texas, and have four grown children and one grandson.

SEND GUILTY AS ZIN TO A FRIEND

Send $12.95($14.95 in Canada) plus $2.95 shipping (plus 8.25% sales tax for Texas residents) to:

PUBLISHING VISIONS
3107 White Rock Drive
Austin, Texas 78757

Please send _____ copies of Guilty of Zin to:

_____
Name

_____
Address

_____
City, State, and Zip Code

_____
Name on Card

_____
Visa or Master Card Number

_____
Expiration Date

_____
Signature

Total: _____